The Casebook of Sheriff Pete Benson

BY

JOHN S. FITZPATRICK

RIVERBEND
PUBLISHING

THE CASEBOOK OF SHERIFF PETE BENSON

Copyright © 2010 by John S. Fitzpatrick

Cover art by Joseph Yaeger

Published by Riverbend Publishing, Helena, Montana

ISBN 978-1-60639-026-9

RIVERBEND PUBLISHING
P.O. Box 5833
Helena, MT 59604
1-866-787-2363
www.riverbendpublishing.com

DEDICATION

For the people central to my life
Connie
Steve, Julia, and Laura
Mike, Katie, and Jack
Natalie

ACKNOWLEDGEMENTS

A work of this type necessarily involves contributions from many people. First and foremost, I wish to thank my two long-time associates, Kay Haight for her outstanding secretarial assistance, critical insight and positive encouragement, and Barbara Effing for her copy editing. Phil and Jean Green, Alice McCabe, Alan Joscelyn, and Connie Fitzpatrick read early versions of the manuscript and offered a number of valuable suggestions for improvement. Chris Cauble and Janet Spencer at Riverbend Publishing did likewise, and I am very grateful to all of my reviewers for their assistance. Thanks also to Rodger Foster and Jerry Hallford at Morrison-Maierle, Inc., Helena, Montana, for assistance with the maps.

— *John S. Fitzpatrick*

CONTENTS

MAPS

CHAPTER ONE

The Name is Benson

The name is Benson, Pete Benson. I'm the Sheriff of Rhyolite County, Montana. These are my stories.

I came here nearly twelve years ago from Seattle, where I had been a detective with the Seattle Police Department. Initially, I resisted the idea of moving to Rodgersburg, my wife Connie's hometown. I grew up nearby in Butte. When Connie and I started talking about coming back to Montana, I was more interested in going to one of the state's larger cities and getting a job in a police department where my big-city experience would be valued. Connie convinced me the small town would be better for the kids, and she was right on that score about 250 percent.

Moving to Rodgersburg also alleviated, but did not eliminate, the tension in my marriage over my job. Police work is like a mistress. Both demand time, lots of time, and that time is taken away from the marriage and family. For a cop, the shifts are irregular, the workday long, and something is always happening that scrambles family plans.

I still remember that scene in our living room late one evening when Connie said to me, "Love, there is no shortage of bad guys in this world. There will be plenty of arrests in your future, but Tom is only going to be eight once, and Phil is only going to ask you to help him learn to ride his bike for a few days. Figure it out, Pete. What's more important?"

I applied for the job in Rodgersburg the following day, got hired as a deputy, and was elected sheriff fourteen months later. Being sheriff has turned out to be more rewarding than I expected, and better, too. Truth is, I didn't miss working major crimes once I got away from Seattle. In Rhyolite County the job is more peace officer than cop, helping people rather than pursuing them, and I like that.

Rhyolite is a large county geographically at 4,790 square miles, but its population is small, only 6,218 residents at the last census. There are more cows and elk than people. Usually it's a quiet place, but being sandwiched between larger, more urbanized counties—Missoula and Silver Bow— brings us a measure of spillover crime. The county takes its name from the volcanic rock which pushed up through a thick layer of limestone about 60 million years ago to form the mountains here. Once this was mining country. Today cattle raising and logging pay the bills. Recently the area has become a mecca for second homes and cabins as the city folk buy up one- to twenty-acre parcels of rural landscape.

The county is shaped like an elongated teardrop—irregularly round at the bottom, narrowing into a rectangular shaft at the top. It can be divided into four discrete sections. There's the lower valley, the center of which is Winslow, a town of about 500 people. The middle part of the county is known by one and all as "the valley," although the state's atlas describes it by its formal name, Madison Creek Valley. It starts in the canyon near Ajax and reaches west past Rodgersburg, the county seat, a good twenty miles. The south side of the valley is braced by the massive wall of the Rhyolite Range, which counts 12 snow-capped peaks over 10,000 feet. To the north about four miles away, across Madison Creek, lies the Blue Mountain Range. The valley is fertile, but at 5,700 feet the growing season is short and the only field crops are alfalfa, hay, and a small amount of grain. The ranches are large and widely spaced. The Rhyolite and Blue Mountains converge near Ajax, separated only by a narrow canyon locally known as the "Gap." The "Gap" is also the demarcation point between the two valleys.

The far western end of the county consists of mountains and forest. There are a few small ranches around its periphery. To the extent it has an economy, it's outfitting—guides taking out-of-state hunters and fishermen into the wilds for a fee.

Boulder Lake, more than 6,000 acres of crystal clear water, is the focal point of southern Rhyolite County. Once fed by the runoff from glaciers, the lake is framed by mountains on three sides. The views are impressive and generally enjoyed by people from elsewhere who can afford the land for recreational homes. Virtually all of the county's population growth is taking place at the lake and near Bonanza Basin, the ski hill just east of Rodgersburg.

The economy here is changing as it is in much of the western United States. The historic resource-extractive economy built on ranching, mining, and logging is giving way to one based on tourism. Unfortunately, jobs in the tourist industry don't pay nearly as well as those which they replaced, and people struggle to earn a decent living.

My friend Fred Early once observed that Rhyolite County was turning into a Caribbean nation, not because the climate was becoming tropical, but because the local folks were earning their pay by changing linens in hotels, mixing drinks, nannying children, and playing handyman at some rich dude's second castle. Truth is, if a vote could be taken today, the locals would overwhelmingly choose to send the outsiders packing in exchange for reopening the mines.

Rodgersburg was originally a mining town, but the last operating mine, the Galena Queen, shut down in 1983. Agriculture and governmental services are now the economic mainstays of this part of the county.

Roughly half of the county's population lives in Rodgersburg. The town sits on the south side of the Madison Creek Valley on a low bluff, part of a cluster of foothills that merge into Quartz Peak.

The heart of Rodgersburg is Tower Park. The name derives from a 160-foot limestone promontory at the southern end of the park where Tower Creek emerges from the mountains. When Rodgersburg was first laid out in the early 1880s the business district fronted both sides of the stream, but the great flood of 1897 washed away the center of town in a matter of hours. The town fathers then did something unique for the time, perhaps even special by today's standards. Instead of rebuilding the city where it was, they pushed the business district back about a half block on both sides of the stream, upslope and out of the floodplain, and dedicated the center of Rodgersburg as a park. Then they planted the park and boulevards throughout the residential area with all of their favorite trees from back home in the Midwest. Tower Creek slowly winds its way through groves of ash, maple, aspen, fir, and alder, a ribbon of blue bisecting both the park and the town.

Today the park has several types of recreational facilities ranging from basketball and tennis courts to playgrounds

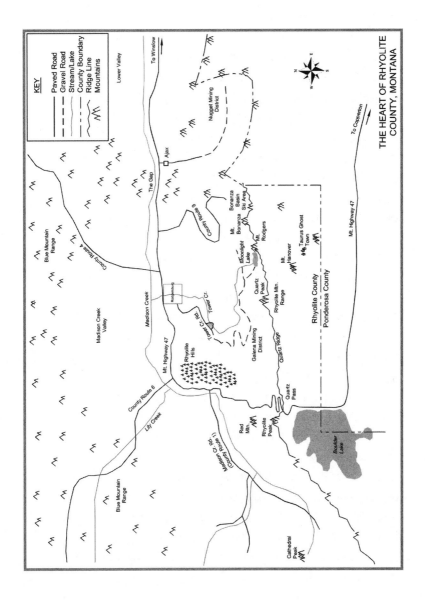

THE HEART OF RHYOLITE
COUNTY, MONTANA

and picnic areas. It's the hub of Rodgersburg's social life from May to September.

Before we get to the cases, a couple of disclaimers, if you will. I asked Benny Sells, a childhood friend from Butte, to read and critique an early version of this manuscript. Benny is a defense attorney by trade and has spent the last quarter century reading plaintiffs' briefs. He assured me that qualified him as an expert in fiction but not necessarily in the field of mystery. Benny suggested that I edit the manuscript to revise my role. He said I was "too boring" and that I needed to have some quirk, idiosyncrasy, failing, or flaw that would make me a more memorable individual.

That's a tough standard to meet. I am who I am and my personal ethics prevent me from presenting a bogus personality simply to get published. I recognize that other law enforcement personnel, particularly private investigators who have put their works to pen seem to have novel lifestyles. Florida private investigator Travis McGee[1] lived on his house boat, the *Busted Flush*, and always got the girl and the desperado. Even if I was free to get the girl, and I am not, having been happily married to Connie for close to twenty-five years, houseboats are pretty rare in the Montana mountains. We have "ice houses" to fish from on frozen lakes but that's about it.

Nero Wolfe,[2] a man whose intellect is exceeded only by his girth, divides his day between raising prize-winning orchids, eating gourmet meals fixed in his own kitchen by Chef Fritz Brenner, and solving crimes by applying his deductive capacity to the information compiled by his faithful associate, Archie Goodwin, while never leaving his home. I wish I could do that but, truth be told, my success as a

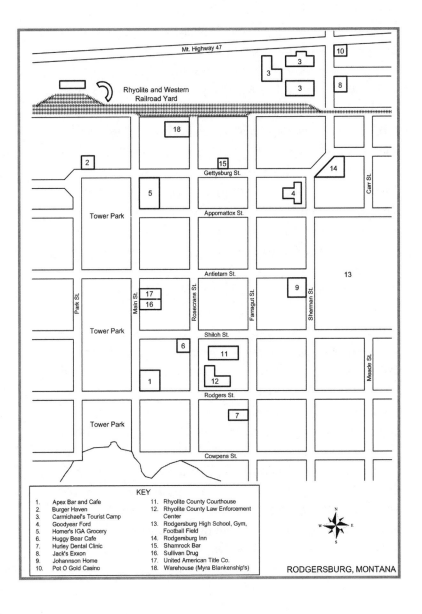

Mt. Highway 47

Rhyolite and Western
Railroad Yard

Tower Park

Gettysburg St.

Appomattox St.

Antietam St.

Tower Park

Shiloh St.

Rodgers St.

Tower Park

Cowpens St.

Park St.

Main St.

Rosecrans St.

Farragut St.

Sherman St.

Carr St.

Meade St.

KEY

1. Apex Bar and Cafe
2. Burger Haven
3. Carmichael's Tourist Camp
4. Goodyear Ford
5. Homer's IGA Grocery
6. Huggy Bear Cafe
7. Hurley Dental Clinic
8. Jack's Exxon
9. Johannson Home
10. Pot O Gold Casino

11. Rhyolite County Courthouse
12. Rhyolite County Law Enforcement
    Center
13. Rodgersburg High School, Gym,
    Football Field
14. Rodgersburg Inn
15. Shamrock Bar
16. Sullivan Drug
17. United American Title Co.
18. Warehouse (Myra Blankenship's)

RODGERSBURG, MONTANA

law enforcement officer comes from more plebian ways—collecting evidence, interviewing suspects, and making the case the old fashioned way—with hard work and a little bit of luck. And Connie raises rhubarb, zucchini, lilacs, and marigolds—cold-hardy plants—not orchids. Closer to home I've had the privilege of knowing two working gumshoes, C.W. Sughrue and Milo Milodragovich.[3] Both call Meriweather, Montana, home. Sughrue I've met, and Milo I know well, and I've never bought into their public mantras as hard drinking, drug abusing, two-fisted investigators. If anybody consumed the drink and drugs which they claim in their books, they'd be on life support in some hospital, not corralling some villain.

So, here it is. I'm basically a regular guy—married, two kids, three-bedroom house, two-car garage and a 30-year mortgage. I enjoy a beer or two but the local gin mills aren't a favorite haunt.

I am a prodigious reader—everything from military history and astronomy to comparative religion and forensics, but my writing skills are only average. That's why I teamed up with John Fitzpatrick to put this book together. He did a masterful job editing Dr. John H. Watson's narratives of Sherlock Holmes' visits to Montana, which was published under the title of *Sherlock Holmes: The Montana Chronicles*.[4] Fitz is a lobbyist by profession. I met him several years ago when I went to Helena to testify before a legislative committee hearing a bill being promoted by the Sheriffs and Peace Officers Association. I was pleased that he was willing to help me with the wordsmithing for this book. Now, sit back and enjoy an inside look at cases handled by a county sheriff in small town Montana.

CHAPTER TWO

Long Lost Treasure

In Rodgersburg, Montana, three o'clock in the afternoon Monday through Friday is coffee time. There are several coffee groups around town, and whenever my schedule permits it, which I admit is most of the time, I frequent the bunch that pontificates at the Apex Bar and Café, the nerve center of Rhyolite County's low tech information network—the gossip mill.

I was planted at my desk reading a book when Kay Best, the department's office manager and chief dispatcher, poked her nose through the door of my office and reminded me.

"It's 2:30, Pete."

"Thanks. I lost track of the time."

"Going to the Apex?"

"Where else?"

"Where else, indeed. You men and your routines. Trouble is, the minute a woman starts counting on you to be predictable, you're not."

"Can I get you anything to bring back?"

"No, I have to go over to the hospital to get Doc's signature on these commitment papers, but thanks."

Kay disappeared from my office doorway and I could hear her cowboy boots clicking across the tile floor of the anteroom toward the front door. She's a cowgirl at heart.

I hired Kay a couple of months after being sworn into office. She started out working part-time automating the department's filing system and transferring key records into an electronic format. I was impressed by her organizational skills and efficiency and asked her to take over the office manager's job a few months later. When my senior dispatcher retired, I had Kay take over that job as well. She's my right hand.

When it comes to insight into human behavior, Kay's a natural criminal investigator and head and shoulders above the rest of the staff, including me. In addition, between her and her husband's family, I swear she's related to one-third of the county. Kay can acquire information with a phone call that others couldn't get passing out hundred dollar bills. When she isn't running the day-to-day operations of the department for me, she's home helping manage the family ranch and looking after four kids.

Grateful for Kay's reminder of the impending coffee hour, I quickly returned to my book, planning to finish the chapter before heading down to coffee.

A few minutes later I heard, "Hi, dear. What has so completely caught your attention that your darling wife can stand here for five minutes and you not notice her?"

I looked up to see the smiling face of the Nordic milkmaid I am lucky to call my wife, Connie. Then I checked my watch. "Not five minutes, maybe two. Kay was just in here to remind me of coffee." I pulled my feet off the desk and closed the book. "Why aren't you still at work?" I asked.

"Charlie and Bill from the Fire Department are over at the school this afternoon for fire safety day. Bill has a little Dalmatian puppy with him and the kids just love it. Mary

Cahill and I are going to take a quick run over to Butte. There's a sale."

By this time Connie had taken a seat in the chair next to my desk and smoothed down her skirt. She had gotten her hair cut and permed last week and I still wasn't used to the look. She's worn her hair in either a shoulder length pageboy or a flip for as long as I could remember. The new "do" looked good, something I'd call the Goldie Hawn or Elke Summer look in fond remembrance of women's hair styles from my youth.

"So what are you reading?" she continued.

"The *Meditations* of Marcus Aurelius, a Roman philosopher," I answered and picked up the book to show her.

"On company time?" She asked with more than just a hint of incredulity in her voice.

"Certainly, it's after skiing season, before fishing season, there's not a tourist in town and basically there's nothing to do."

"But, you're the county sheriff. You can't be doing recreational reading at work. It's not right. What kind of example does it set for the other officers?"

"Relax, love," I countered. "Aurelius deals with human nature and man's relations with other men. Now, if that isn't what law enforcement deals with every day, I don't know what is. Listen to this. 'How is it that every man loves himself more than all the rest of men, but yet sets less value on his own opinion of himself than on the opinion of others.'[1]

"Besides," I continued, "Kay is the only one who knows what I read in here."

"Let me see that book," asked Connie, extending her hand.

I handed her Aurelius and took a few moments to straighten up my desk while she paged through the text. "Now I know why you like this guy," she said brightly. "He understands you perfectly. 'Wipe out fancy; check desire; extinguish appetite, keep your ruling faculty in control.'"[2] With that Connie shot me a big smile and said, "Boooor-ing. But you are my little bore, my OTL."

Usually that meant "one true love," but from time to time, "out-to-lunch."

"You used to think I was exciting," I retorted, slightly peeved.

"And you still are, darling," answered Connie as she turned up her smile. "Only, you're not exciting as often as you were twenty-five years ago."

I walked right into that one. You'd think by now that I would have learned not to get into a verbal sparring match with my bride. This is the woman who once introduced me to her book club as a "middle-aged woman's dream husband." I puffed up with pride until Connie added, "He works steady, doesn't drink too much, and is too tired for sex."

Connie stood up and leaned over me to give me a quick peck on the lips and turned toward the office door. "Oh, I almost forgot," she said turning back to me. "We're going to have dinner in Butte. There's a tuna casserole and some pasties in the freezer if you boys don't go out. I'll be home around eight."

"Yeah," I replied. "Have fun." I rose, grabbed my coat, which it turned out I didn't need since it was an exceptionally warm and bright April day, followed Connie out the door and made it to the Apex in an elapsed time of three minutes.

The Apex anchors the southern end of Rodgersburg's business district. Access to the bar is from Main Street while a side door on Rodgers Street leads directly into the restaurant. I invariably use the restaurant door. Although no one has ever said anything to me about it, I just don't think a law officer should be going into a tavern in uniform during the day unless there is a clear reason for him to be doing so.

Stepping through the side door, one encounters a bank of video poker and keno machines on the left. Under Montana law a party with a casino license can operate up to twenty video machines. Virtually every establishment with a liquor license now has video gaming as well. It's become an important revenue stream for the bar owners—and local government.

Also to the left, lining the wall that separates the restaurant from the tavern, is a set of twelve booths with Formica-topped tables. Other dining tables occupy the center of the room. To the right of the side door is a U-shaped counter. The top of the counter carries the coffee makers, a milk shake mixer, chilled display case for pies and pastry and related equipment. Underneath is storage for the clean dishes, silverware, and other paraphernalia for restaurant service. Here the waitresses prepare salads, dish up desserts, and fill soup bowls.

Immediately adjacent the counter and stretching toward the kitchen door is a tall, refrigerated display case with an array of soft drinks, fruit juice, and bottled water.

Directly across from the doorway is the lunch counter with stools for eight. The counter makes a 90-degree bend passing through a wide entryway into the saloon and becomes the bar. Another set of tables for patrons fills the middle of that room. Centered high on the wall looking back toward the bar is a 54-inch flat screen, plasma television perpetually tuned to ESPN or Fox News. The folks in Rhyolite County are serious about their news and their sports.

After stepping in the back door it took my eyes a few seconds to adjust to the darkness. The gaming machines were silent for the first time that I could ever recall, the flashing lights failing to entice players with a mad desire to part with their cash. There was a good crowd for a weekday, and the place had a buzz to it which was atypical. When my eyes focused, who should I see but "Pug" McKenney and his ever present companion, Roddy Johnson. They were leaning against the bar, surrounded by a group of onlookers. Pug got his nickname from his pushed in face, apropos that breed of dog, the pug. Pug was retired but had spent his life around Rodgersburg working as a ranch hand, lumberjack, miner, truck driver, and finally, as a mail carrier. He was a full-time raconteur who held court in at least one of the area saloons every day. Notwithstanding the look of his face, Pug had a heart of gold, and for years he and Roddy coached the local Legion baseball team.

"Sheriff Pete, c'mon over and see this. I was just showing the boys," Pug said as he waved me in his direction.

I worked my way past a couple of tables of coffee drinkers offering a salutation to one and all. "Whatcha got, Pug?"

"Hold it, Pug," commanded Gil Stewart, owner of the saloon and day shift bartender. "We've got traditions to uphold. It's wisdom time!"

"Oh m'God," replied an apologetic Pug. "In my excitement I plum completely forgot. Sorry, Gil."

Then Gil rang a bell that he keeps behind the bar, acquired specifically to announce wisdom time. The room quieted down quickly and Gil shouted, "Anybody got words of wisdom they want to share?" No one answered. Gil asked again, and then turned to me. "Sheriff Pete, the floor is yours."

I paused for a few seconds, then remembering the past few minutes with my wife said, "Happy is he who dwells with a sensible wife."[3]

My comment drew a low level of laughter and nods of agreement from several of the female patrons.

"Who said that?" asked Gil loudly.

"Sirach," I replied.

"Who's Sirach?" countered Gil quickly.

"He wrote the Book of Sirach. It's in the Catholic bible."

"You ain't Catholic," answered Gil. "How would you know that?"

"I'm very ecumenical."

"What's that mean?" asked Roddy to Pug.

"It means Sheriff Pete likes everyone. Ya know, they're all voters," answered Pug with a knowing glance to which Roddy nodded in agreement.

I started wisdom time quite accidentally during football season about two and a half years ago. I was with a table of fellows discussing the relative merits of offensive versus defensive play in winning football programs when I was asked what I thought. I replied quoting Napoleon, who once was alleged to have said, "The whole art of war consists in a well reasoned and circumspect defense, followed by a rapid and audacious attack."[4]

That comment drew extensive discussion but in the end it was dismissed by Billy Goodyear, a true football aficionado, who said, "What does some Frenchy general know about football anyway? He was dead before the game was invented."

Gil was greatly amused by my quote and Billy's concluding remark. He wrote them down on index cards and posted them on the bulletin board at the end of the bar. Every weekday thereafter we've had wisdom time at three o'clock coffee although, practically speaking, it only ends up happening a couple of days a week when someone finds a quote especially appealing. Gil turned it into a promotional effort for the bar. All the quotes are written down and posted on the bulletin board. Once a month, the staff at the Apex selects the quote of the month and the winner receives a free dinner for four. Truth is, there's nothing scientific or objective about how Gil picks the monthly wisdom winner. A lot of people in town play the game primarily by pulling quotes off Internet websites. Gil is smart enough to make sure that the same people don't win too often. So he keeps up player interest by picking winners from every sector of the town's population.

With wisdom time concluded, I turned back to Pug. "Where were we, Pug?"

"I found a broach, Pete, an old timer. It looks like hammered silver with a nice piece of turquoise."

"Where'd you get it?" I replied.

"In my backyard, this morning. I started to turn over the dirt out there. Annie wants to put in a real big garden this year."

"Well you've sure got the space—must be an acre, acre and a half."

"Little more, actually, but as I was saying, Pete, I was digging along, shoveling the dirt onto a screen to get rid of the rocks and weeds, and I found this piece."

"What can I say, Pug? They tell me that when you were mining, you had a great nose for ore. Looks like you haven't lost your touch."

At that point Roddy spoke up. "Pug, he don't believe it, but Sheriff, I'm a thinkin' that brooch is a part of the Mendenhall Treasure."

"Ah, Roddy," answered Pug with some irritation, "don't be saying no such thing. Them jewels been gone since the turn of the century. If they was just laying around on the ground, somebody would have found 'em by now. Ain't that right, Sheriff?"

"Makes sense," I observed objectively.

But Roddy wasn't about to have his opinion ignored. In a bold yell he said, "That's from the Mendenhalls, I knowed it! That jewelry there is like all that stuff you see down in the southwest and Mexico. Before Amos Mendenhall come here to run the Galena Queen, he run a mine in Sonora 'bout a hundert miles south of the border. Old Mrs. Mendenhall had lots o' that kind of jewelry."

"Now, how are you knowing that, Roddy Johnson?" asked Pug pointedly.

"From my grandmother, Pug. I told you before. She used to talk all the time 'bout the Mendenhalls and the missus' treasure. She worked as a maid in their home before she married Grandpa Luke."

"Well," I injected, "for your sake, Pug, I hope Roddy's right and you find the treasure. Good digging. Now, if you'll excuse me, I've got a cup of coffee waiting."

The coffee was good but the conversation was a bit monotonous. Everybody was talking about Pug's find and speculating whether he had, in fact, found the Mendenhall

Treasure. I cut coffee short and went over to the high school for a little workout.

Rodgersburg isn't big enough to support a health club but we've got the next best thing, a well-equipped weight room at the high school courtesy of three years of fundraising by the Miners Booster Club. The school opens the weight room and gym to the general public in the early morning, late afternoon, and on weekends as long as there is no conflict with the school's schedule. I try to get there at least two days a week to keep the body firm. Pushing fifty, I probably should be in there three days. I was on the bench working the second set of presses when I heard someone approach me from behind.

"Seven, eight, nine, ten. You've got a great set of pecs there, Pete."

I hung the iron on the rack, sat up and turned toward the voice I well recognized and was greeted by the cheery smile of Mandy Lynn Marks. It was pure Mandy Lynn standing there in a tight blue-gray workout suit that hugged every curve on her body. The workout suit seemed to be the perfect complement to her short, softly curled, platinum hair and, as for Mandy Lynn's curves, let's just say that she was generously proportioned where a woman should be. Mandy Lynn was the kind of woman a man had to look at but not see, if he didn't want trouble in his life. Mandy Lynn and Kay Best were the two most attractive women in Rodgersburg. They were classmates growing up and remain good friends to this day. They also couldn't be any more dissimilar. Kay was a model of stability and fidelity. Mandy Lynn had left a trail of bruised hearts and broken marriages in her wake.

"Mandy Lynn!" I tried to act surprised. "I just left your father and the ever-faithful Roddy down at the Apex."

"So what are those two old coots up to today?" Mandy Lynn's voice was light as she stepped over to the bench press and mentally calibrated how much I had been lifting.

"Pug showed me a silver brooch that he found in the backyard this morning. Roddy thinks Pug's on to the Mendenhall Treasure."

"Shhh," hushed Mandy Lynn. "Pete, that's nothing to be blabbed about. Someone gets the idea my folks have got money in that house of theirs, it could be trouble."

"Too late for that," I said as I got up and started to disassemble the weights. "Pug was flashing the brooch around the Apex. It's already the talk of the town."

"I better go get it from him and take it to the bank."

"Good idea, Mandy Lynn, but it's too late today. The banks are closed. But, you're right. If he finds any more jewelry, it's best kept quiet."

"Not with my father. Every discovery will become an epic tale, told in every bar in town. My poor mother."

"Don't worry. After all, this is Rodgersburg, not San Francisco. Your folks will be all right."

"Yeah, you're probably right," agreed Mandy Lynn as she quickly nodded her head.

"Say, not to change the subject, you must hoof it ten miles a day at the restaurant. What are you doing here?"

"I come every day," replied Mandy Lynn.

"No kidding. I don't think I've ever seen you."

"I come in the morning."

"You're one of those people who are up at five and pumping iron by six."

"That's me."

"I am impressed. Couldn't do it myself. Too much of a night owl."

"Well, that finishes it for sure."

"Finishes what?" I asked.

"The chance for us to have an affair. Morning girls and night guys just don't work."

Mandy Lynn looked me straight in the eyes, flicked her right eyebrow up and quickly ran her tongue between her lips. With her, you could never tell if she was serious or simply having fun with you. "Quit trying to embarrass me," I said. "Save it for the guys with the tips."

"Sorry, Pete. I saw those pecs." She gave me a big smile again. "Must have turned my head. See ya."

"Good plan," I replied, happy to have the weight room back to myself as I watched her tush disappear into the women's locker room. Spandex was made for Mandy Lynn.

The next day I woke up early and made it to the office before eight, which is not customary. I met the two night-shift deputies in the parking lot as they headed home for a little shuteye. They gave me a quick once over of the previous evening's activities. Essentially, nothing happened but wherever people congregated the talk was all about Pug discovering the Mendenhall Treasure.

I stepped into the office a few moments later and called out "Good morning, Kay." Then I noticed my coffee cup on the end of the front counter with a waft of steam rising above it. "What's this?"

"Coffee," replied Kay as she stepped out of the supply closet with a ream of paper for the copy machine.

"I'm never here this early, how could you know I was..."

"Woman's intuition," came her cheery reply, "coupled with Johnny calling me on the radio from the parking lot. Oh, and nice pecs. I never noticed before." Then she laughed, not a light laugh or a polite laugh, but a deep belly laugh.

"Don't get me started on that woman."

"She had a good time, Pete," laughed Kay again, a bit more restrained. "Mandy Lynn says you're adorable when you blush."

"I don't mind the flirting around the restaurant when it's in full view and happening to every man in the place, but over at the weight room...never mind." My tone was serious. "You know what I mean."

"Yes, I do," responded Kay. "Rodgersburg's most interesting divorcee was getting a little too close." She laughed again. "The male ego never ceases to amaze."

"What's the male ego got to do with it?" I answered, puzzled by Kay's comment. "On second thought, don't tell me. But, what is it with her—the guy thing I mean."

"It's not what most people think," she replied as she sat down at her desk.

"And what's that?" I answered.

"That Mandy Lynn is some type of nymph," Kay replied. "No, Mandy Lynn's problem is that she's in love with love."

"Huh."

"Pete, remember when you and Connie got married—the intensity of your feelings toward one another?"

"Sure I do. Connie still refers to that as the 'touching stage of life.' I don't think I had my hands off of her for more than fifteen minutes for about six months."

"Yup. And then the hot romance faded and you moved into everyday, stable love and marriage. The boys came, you both got jobs. You don't love Connie any less than during the honeymoon, do you?"

"Heck no, more, in fact, much more."

"Well, Mandy Lynn can't get there, Pete. It's like she's addicted to the intensity of, for lack of a better term, 'honeymoon love.' When it's time to move on to 'routine love,' she loses interest in the guy and the marriage falls apart."

"Has she told you this?"

"Not directly," answered Kay. "It's not something she really wants to admit—not even to herself."

"Well, what you're telling me makes sense. I guess I just assumed that..."

"That Mandy Lynn can't get enough of men," said Kay finishing both my thought and sentence. "No. Mandy Lynn can't find love and she's been on an emotional roller coaster for twenty years trying for it."

With that statement, Kay stood up, grabbed the ream of paper from her desk and turned toward the photocopier. She took a couple of steps and started to giggle again. I thought I heard her whisper "great pecs."

"Don't run away," I replied firmly. "In fact, get a cup of joe for yourself and join me in my lair. I have some other questions—and not about Mandy Lynn."

Kay didn't get there right away. The phone rang, someone came in the front door to file a complaint about a pack of dogs running loose, and then she went to the radio. I had time to finish my first cup while looking over the night shift's log book and I was refilling my cup in the kitchen area when she walked in and handed me her mug to fill. Instead of going back to my office, we sat down at the dinette table.

"Okay, now what can I, hopefully, answer?" asked Kay. Before I could respond, I spotted a bag of trail mix and compulsively scooped out a handful. Once my palate was satisfied I asked, "Given your vast knowledge of the history of the area, give me a short course on the Mendenhall Treasure."

"Oh, sure," said Kay. "I was going to ask you about that anyway. When I was at the market yesterday afternoon, the place was humming over the fact that Pug McKenney had found the treasure."

"Treasure? Pug found one silver brooch."

"Apparently he found a lot more. I heard it was an old leather bag full of jewelry," Kay said as she swiped a couple of M&Ms from my remaining trail mix.

"Give the rumor mill until noon and it will have grown into a chest full of Spanish doubloons and gold bars from Coronado's expedition," I answered. "But, back to the facts."

"I think you know most of the story, Pete. Amos Mendenhall ran the Galena Queen. His wife Florence was the leading lady of Rodgersburg, patron of the arts and mistress of the town's intellectual life."

"Yeah, that much I do know."

Kay continued, "The Mendenhalls came to Rodgersburg from Mexico. He had managed a mine down there and that's where Florence was supposed to have acquired most of the jewelry, including some pieces of Aztec gold."

"Come now." Aztec gold in Rodgersburg, Montana, was a bit much for me to fathom.

"You remember that history of Rhyolite County that Grandma Wakefield compiled a few years ago?" Kay asked while she filched some more M&Ms.

"Can't say that I do."

"If you're that interested, I'll bring in my copy tomorrow. There's a long section in the book on the Galena Queen and the Mendenhalls. There's a picture of Florence wearing her jewelry at some kind of party. That's where I saw the reference to the Aztec gold. The picture was taken sometime in the early 1900s. I'm guessing maybe 1910 to 1912, before the fire, anyway. That was in 1914."

"Is that when her jewels disappeared?" I asked.

"Yes. The Mendenhalls lived in the mine superintendent's house on the hill next to the mine. The house caught fire at night and burned to the ground. They found three badly burned bodies in the rubble the next morning. One was clearly a woman. The other two were men. One was presumed to be Amos Mendenhall. The other was a mystery. The Mendenhalls didn't have any children and had no houseguests at the time."

"A butler?"

"No. Florence employed a couple of local women as domestics, but they lived in Rodgersburg and were safe and sound."

"So the third body could have been a burglar," I offered.

"That's the most common theory. There was also speculation there might have been two thieves and that one took the jewelry, double-crossed his partner, and set the house on fire to cover his tracks."

"Sounds plausible, but how does a piece of jewelry end up in Pug McKenney's backyard? The Galena Queen's at least a half mile from Pug's place."

"That's true now," replied Kay before pausing to take a drink from her coffee mug. They sunk a new shaft in the late

1940s and ended up moving the whole mine. Pug's house is just down the hill from the original mine. Fact is, his backyard is where the bone yard and dump for the old mine used to be located."

"Now that's interesting, very interesting. Can you bring in that article? I want to see the jewelry Mrs. Mendenhall was wearing in that photo."

After lunch I took a drive up to Pug's house. He and his wife Annie live a bit less than four miles southwest of Rodgersburg along Tower Creek Road. The road links Rodgersburg with Moonlight Lake which is cradled in a cirque at the base of Mount Rodgers. The lake is the headwaters of Tower Creek and serves as the town's water supply.

Tower Creek also bisects the Galena mining district. The ruins of the old mines dot the hillsides above the stream. Pug and Annie's home sat between the remnants of the Constellation and Galena Queen mines.

The house looked about thirty years old, a small rectangle with a hip roof and cedar shakes for siding, painted light brown. To the left of the house was a combination garage and shop building tied to the house by a wide deck with a large barbecue built from field rock and brick.

I could tell that no one was home when I drove up and parked. Annie's Subaru and Pug's Dodge Power Wagon were conspicuously absent from the driveway, so I took a look around. In the backyard I spotted two pits where Pug had been digging and, apparently, where he found the silver brooch. From there I wandered up the hill to the old mine area. You'd never know it from the road; the trees have grown back in and largely obliterated all trace of man's former presence. About halfway up the slope, directly above

Pug's place, I discovered a large foundation, the remnants of two fireplaces, and a few chunks of charred wood, all that remained of the Mendenhall home. Water flowed off the home site through a wide but shallow incision directly onto Pug's backyard. It was nearly three o'clock so I decided it was time for coffee. The odds were good Pug would be at the Apex.

I took a seat at the counter and was greeted by Mandy Lynn as she returned from the milkshake machine with two strawberry shakes, which she set on a tray near the end of the counter. As usual her white blouse was too tight, showing off that aspect of her femininity to full effect.

I nodded, encouraging her to come over and visit at the same time hoping that she'd give the flirting a rest. "A little late, isn't it? I thought your shift ended at two."

"Normally, it does," replied Mandy Lynn, "but Dad came here all charged up and I made the mistake of thinking that, if I stayed, I could keep him under control."

"What's got him going today?"

"Same thing as yesterday. He went out digging this morning and found another piece of jewelry—an earring with a green stone in it, an emerald according to Roddy."

"What does Roddy know about gemstones?"

"Nothing. Just like he knows nothing about almost everything, but that never stopped him from having an opinion."

"Gotcha. So where's Pug now?"

"Went over to Goodyear Ford to buy a radiator hose and show Billy his latest find. He'll be back in a few."

"Sheriff Pete!" yelled Pug McKenney from someplace behind my back.

"He's back now," said Mandy Lynn, shaking her head and giving me a rueful glance.

I turned around just as Pug reached my stool. "Sheriff, boy am I glad to see you. You gotta see this." Pug paused to catch his breath. "Roddy thinks it's an emerald. I figured you might know."

"Nice piece of jewelry, Pug, but I've got to be honest with you. I don't know anything about gems."

"Oh." Pug seemed disappointed. "I was thinking from your time on the Seattle PD, you probably saw..."

"Sorry, Pug," I interrupted, "I mostly worked vice and homicide. Stolen goods wasn't my beat. Take it down to the pawn shop. I bet Marty can tell you in an instant."

"Already tried that. His brother passed away in Oregon. They closed up and left for the funeral two days ago."

"Then you'll just have to wait a few days or drive into Copperton."

"I ain't going nowhere now. This clinches it. Roddy's right. I've got the Mendenhall Treasure in my backyard. I gotta find it."

"Will you knock off that nonsense about the Mendenhall Treasure?" Mandy Lynn said sharply. "That craziness has Mother very upset and half the town thinks you're a fool."

"Well, my own flesh and blood's a skeptic, going around town telling people I'm crazy," answered Pug.

"You're damn tootin' I am," responded Mandy Lynn. "The traffic in front of the house is already ten times higher than normal. Mom can't open a window for all the dust."

"That's right." Roddy Johnson weighed in with a comment that drew an instant glare from Mandy Lynn.

27

"Butt out, Roddy. You got this whole Mendenhall thing going. I don't know which of you two is crazier."

"I ain't crazy and neither is your dad," said Roddy defensively. "We just bought a metal detector so we can find them jewels fast."

"We?" Mandy Lynn sounded incredulous.

"Of course, we," replied Pug matter-of-factly. "Roddy's in for twenty-five percent."

"What? Does Mom know?"

"Well ..." Pug's voice trailed off into silence.

"That's what I thought. You'd better be telling her your plans and that means tonight, or..."

"Much as I love standing in the middle of a family fight, it's time to go," I said. "Good luck on the treasure hunt, Pug." I got up from the counter, never having given my order, and retreated out the back door to the peace and quiet of my patrol car.

I was watching the 10 o'clock news when the phone rang. I didn't even get out a hello before Pug's voice came over the wire.

"Sheriff, it's me, Pug. Can you come up? We've had an intruder. Annie's pretty scared."

"What happened?"

"I let my dog out about 9:30. I hadn't shut the door but a few seconds when he starts barking his fool head off. I figured it was a coyote or a bear so I got my 357 and went out for a look see."

"Yeah?"

"Didn't find me no bear or coyote. Old Buck led me to a hole back in the shadows behind the house. Some two-legged varmint was up here trying to dig up my treasure."

"You got any yard lights?"

"Nah. Just a light on the garage and by the back door."

"Turn them on and put the gun away. I don't want you doing something stupid. I'll be up in a few minutes."

I didn't expect to find anything at Pug's house except another hole in the ground, which was exactly what I found. Whoever had been digging in the yard hadn't done much work, maybe a dozen shovelfuls of earth and then hightailed it once the dog started barking. I spent a little time talking with Annie. She was visibly upset, but I suspected more so with Pug for bringing the attention on them than from fear of an actual intruder.

The next morning I walked into the office just as Kay took a call.

"Rhyolite County Sheriff's Office, Kay speaking." She flipped it on the speaker so I could hear.

"Morning, Kay. This is Mandy Lynn. Is Pete in?"

I shook my head "no" and Kay obliged.

"No. Sorry, Mandy Lynn. He said something about driving over to Ajax this morning. I could try and raise him on the radio for you, at least find out when he'll be back in town."

"That won't be necessary," answered Mandy Lynn. "Could you ask him about putting a deputy up at Mom's house or, at least, run patrols by there pretty often? After last night, my mother is just petrified."

"Was there a problem?" asked Kay.

"You don't know?" Mandy Lynn sounded confused. "No, of course you wouldn't. Sorry. Someone was up at the house digging in the backyard last night."

"Does Pete know?"

"Oh, sure. Dad had him come up last night."

"Listen, Mandy Lynn, I'll have Pete call you when he gets in. I've got to run."

"Okay. I'll be at the restaurant until two today. Thanks."

I walked over to Kay's desk and said, "I am not sure I want to talk to Mandy Lynn just yet. What do you think she really wants?

"Just a guess," replied Kay as she twisted an ink pen in her hand, "I think she really wants you to post a deputy at the house to look after her mother. I don't think she has any other agenda, Pete," she added grinning.

"Well, she might as well ask for the moon. I've got eight deputies to cover close to five thousand square miles and I'm supposed to dedicate one or more to looking after Pug and Annie McKenney. They could solve that problem in a heartbeat if he'd quit running off at the mouth about all the jewels he's found."

"It's Pug you're talking about," Kay said with a chuckle. "The only way you'll ever stop Pug's mouth from running is when he's six feet under."

"You're right. How about Annie moving in with Mandy Lynn for a while?"

"That wouldn't work."

"Why not? Mandy Lynn has a big house."

"Mandy Lynn got engaged a couple days ago. She's in the passion stage again."

"How come I didn't know that?"

"This one will be number eight. It's hardly news, Pete."

"So who is it this time?"

"Some guy from Copperton. Grew up there, went to

California and decided he had enough of the big city. Mandy calls him 'Doc' but he's not a doctor."

"Pug and Annie must have never told her that marriage is supposed to be a distance event, not a set of sprints, but I understand. She doesn't want her mom getting in the way right now. So Annie will stay home with Pug and there'll be no police protection."

"Fine, now call Mandy Lynn and tell her," said Kay. It wasn't quite an order. Kay wouldn't do that. It was more of an imperative statement, the kind a woman gives to a man she knows well.

But I had no intention of taking on that duty so I pulled rank. "Nope, not me. I just delegated that little chore to you. I feel the need to check in with the county coroner."

"Are you feeling okay?" asked Kay.

"Yeah, why do you ask?"

"You've got that pale look like you get when you haven't had much sleep."

"You're right about the sleep," I replied. "After I got back from Pug's, I had a hard time shutting off the brain. I think I drifted off around 4 or 5 A.M."

"Pete, you need to quit fighting it. Take a sleeping pill. You need the rest."

"Look, Kay, I really appreciate your concern, but I am not getting hooked on sleep aids just to avoid a little insomnia. When I can't manage it with exercise I'll seriously consider it, but not until then."

"I thought you had a basketball game today," retorted Kay quickly, still maneuvering for the last word. "You can't run the court after being up close to forty hours."

"The game's tomorrow," I answered as I moved toward

the front door. "We're just playing some of the guys from the bank and they're not that good. I could sleepwalk through a game with them and we'd still win. Bye. Remember—call Mandy Lynn."

I made a tour around the village for the rest of the morning checking in with the coroner, ambulance service, and fire department. We had a joint training exercise scheduled for next week and it gave me a chance to ensure that everything had been coordinated. Then I went home and had lunch with Connie. Typically she eats at the elementary school where she works but had taken the morning off to get some dental work done. Lunch together was a rare treat. She confirmed that the town was alive with excitement over the prospect of the Mendenhall Treasure being found. As a native of Rodgersburg, she knew the story by heart and added a few details which Kay hadn't mentioned.

When Pug didn't show up for afternoon coffee at the Apex, I decided to stop by his house and see how things were going. As I pulled in to park in front of his garage, I saw him walking around his backyard looking at the ground. He heard my vehicle and signaled for me to meet him on the side deck of his house. I moved a chair out into the sunlight and waited for Pug to join me.

After pulling off his denim jacket and pushing his ever present Mariners baseball hat farther back on his head, Pug asked, "How's she goin', Sheriff?"

"I should be asking that of you," I responded.

"Not as well as I hoped. The metal detector Roddy and I got doesn't work so good. Let me say that again. It works too good. It picks up every bottle cap, tin can, nut, bolt—everything."

"That's too bad. Looks like you'll have to do it the hard way and dig it all up."

"Yup, but that's all right, especially when you find one of these things now and again." Pug reached into the breast pocket of his blue-green flannel shirt, an omnipresent part of his wardrobe, and pulled out another piece of jewelry.

"What's that?"

Pug held it up for me to see. "I think it's a piece of a necklace. Gold, too. Feel how heavy it is." With that he handed me a short piece of gold chain with four small globes attached. It was heavy.

"It looks and feels like the real McCoy," I said and handed it back to him.

"So, what brings you by?" asked Pug.

"Just wondering if you had any more problems last night?"

"No, but we sure got lots of traffic on the road in front of the house. People drive up, slow down, point. It's enough to make you wonder—"

"Why you didn't keep the discovery to yourself?" I interrupted.

Pug affected a sheepish grin and said, "That's what Annie was saying, but it's too late for that now."

"Well, don't hesitate to call the office if you have any more trouble."

"Thanks, Sheriff. I appreciate it. I really do." Then Pug looked down at his feet. I could tell he wanted to tell me something but seemed to be struggling for words. I waited but he never said anything more other than to offer his thanks again, so I left wondering what he had on his mind.

The stop at Pug's was my last official act of the week. After getting a good night's sleep without the benefit of a sleeping pill and leading my team in a rout of the local bankers, Connie and I drove over to Helena on Saturday afternoon and spent the weekend. I set Pug McKenney and the Mendenhall Treasure on the back burner until Monday morning.

"Good morning, Kay," I said as I stepped through the front door of the office. "How was your weekend?"

"Mine was fine," answered Kay, "but the deputies got a steady workout going up to Pug's. It might be easier on everyone if you just stationed a deputy on site."

"What happened?"

"Three calls Friday night, after you went home. More people digging in the backyard."

"Why didn't Pug just put that hound of his out back?"

"He did, but someone must have come prepared. They found the dog sound asleep next to an empty package of hamburger."

"Slipped the pooch a tranquilizer. Smart move." That's the beauty of television crime shows, I thought to myself. They upgrade the skills of garden-variety criminals.

"Must have," replied Kay. "Then on Saturday we had two disturbance calls. People showed up wanting to dig and Pug ended up calling us when they wouldn't go peacefully."

"And Sunday?"

"More of the same. We got calls from Pug complaining of nocturnal visitors, and then one of Pug's neighbors called, claiming that he heard gunfire. Pug denied it came from his place, but I don't believe him."

"I'll talk to him. This thing is beginning to get out of control."

After Kay left I quickly pawed through the file folder she'd given me a couple of days earlier containing several old photographs of Florence Mendenhall bedecked in her jewels and newspaper accounts of the fire which had cost the Mendenhalls their lives. The photos were grainy and it was difficult to clearly see the distinctive features of the jewelry but one brooch appeared similar to the one Pug had discovered. Perhaps the old boy was on to something after all.

I spent the balance of the morning searching for Pug but without success. I knew his usual haunts, but no one claimed to have seen him, and he wasn't at home. Finally, I just decided to wait until afternoon coffee to see if he would show up. There was a good crowd in the restaurant when I stepped inside, and it was inordinately noisy for that time of day. Pug was sitting at the bar talking with Gil Stewart, the proprietor.

As I slipped up on the stool to Pug's left he said, "Howdy, Sheriff. Let me buy you a drink."

"Thanks, but not when I'm on duty, Pug. You seem to be in an excellent mood despite all the action over the weekend."

"You'll never guess what happened this morning."

"Don't keep me in suspense." Gil placed a cup of coffee before me and then moved away so Pug and I could talk in private.

"This real estate agent from Missoula came by and offered me $100,000 for my house and land."

"That's one heckuva price for property around here," I offered.

Pug leaned over conspiratorially and in a low tone said, "Yeah, but it's nothing compared to the Mendenhall Treasure. I found some more stuff the last couple of days. No, I'll not be selling."

"Pug, I am not interested in your real estate, just your safety, and I..." Before I could finish, Pug's cell phone rang. It was his buddy Roddy. Pug listened intently for about half a minute and then excused himself and cruised out the front door of the saloon. For the second time in as many meetings, Pug left me wondering what was going on.

After Pug left, I asked Gil, "Who won last month's wisdom contest? It is the first, isn't it?"

"Yup," answered Gil as he lit a Marlboro. "Billy Goodyear, with a quote from a book Lou Holtz wrote, 'People don't care how much you know until they know how much you care.'"[5]

"That's good," I answered. "I like it."

"But, I tell ya, Pete, that quote of yours about being happy with a sensible wife came in a close second. The ladies really liked it."

"Second," I echoed. "Close, but no cigar."

"Not this month, Pete," replied Gil as he moved down the bar to take an order from a couple of fellows who'd just climbed aboard the bar stools.

A cold front blew in Monday night bringing rain mixed with snow. Pug disappeared for several days and with him, most of the talk about the Mendenhall Treasure. Then, he called me at my house in the middle of the night.

"Sheriff, it's me, Pug." He was clearly excited but this was no time or way to report his latest discovery, even if it was antique jewelry.

"Pug, it's 2:30 in the morning," I lectured. "What now?"

"I caught him."

"Who?"

"The damn varmint who's been sneaking around up here at night trying to steal my treasure."

"Look Pug," I replied between yawns. "I'll call the deputy working graveyard. He can be there in a few minutes."

"No, I want you, Pete. This is too big for your deputy."

"Okay. Give me twenty minutes. Can you safely hold him that long?"

"No problem. I've got the S.O.B. hogtied. He ain't goin' nowhere, no how."

Twenty minutes later to the minute I was walking through Pug's front door. He was brimming with excitement.

"Thanks for coming so fast, Pete. If I had to wait much longer, I might have killed the snake. This way. He's in the kitchen with Annie."

We crossed the dining room and went through the kitchen door where I got a big surprise.

"Well, I'll be," I observed. "Helluva way of being a friend, Roddy." I sat down at the table across from Roddy Johnson. Pug stayed by the door.

"And I had already cut him in for twenty-five percent, just for being my friend. Well, he ain't no friend anymore and he's not getting a cent, I tell you," growled Pug with an angry slur.

"What have you got to say for yourself, Roddy?" I asked.

Roddy looked down toward the floor hoping, I'm sure, that his eyes could dig a hole in it. "I've been a fool," Roddy answered. "I saw those jewels Pug was finding in the yard and, I guess I lost my head."

"And you lost your friend of over forty years, you damn polecat!" yelled Pug from his territory across the room.

"Where's your car?" I asked.

"My pickup's in the campground," answered Roddy. "I walked from there."

"C'mon," I said. "I'll take you to the car and you can drive it home. You can come by the jail tomorrow and we'll do the paperwork then."

Pug was aghast. "You mean you're not taking him to jail now?"

"What's the point, Pug? We know who he is, and besides, where is he going to go?"

"He's a felon! He could try to escape!" shouted Pug in reply.

"You better take me in, Sheriff," said Roddy meekly. "Pug already called Alice. She'll kill me if I go home. Just lock me up until she cools down."

"Well, knowing Alice...all right, but I am only going to hold you until morning."

"What?" yelled Pug for the second time.

"Pug, I know you're mad, mad as hell," I answered, "but I'm running the jail, not you. Let's go, Roddy. And Pug, you better get a fence up around your property. It might save you from a few sleepless nights."

"Already looked into it, Sheriff. It'll cost four thousand bucks. There's no way I can come up with that kind of money, leastwise not until I find the rest of the treasure."

The news of Roddy's arrest spread like wildfire and only added momentum to the theory that Pug had, indeed, found the Mendenhall Treasure. The townfolk reasoned that if Roddy was willing to risk his friendship with Pug over it, there had to be a lot of jewelry buried in Pug's backyard. Over the next several days, the department responded to several more calls regarding intruders or disturbances on Pug's land. Then, quite unexpectedly, Pug showed up at the office.

"Pete!" shouted Kay. "Pug McKenney is here to see you."

"Send him in," I said coldly. The Mendenhall Treasure was taxing the department's resources and I was more than ready to have it go away.

Pug caught me by surprise. He was dressed up in his Sunday go-to-church gear, a pair of dark blue Dockers and light blue sports shirt. Something was up.

"Pug, what can I do for you?"

"I'm going to do it. I am just exhausted trying to watch the place. Annie is scared to death some real bad guys are going to show up and Mandy Lynn is madder than all hell at me. It's the only way out."

Now I was a bit confused. "What's the only way out?"

"That guy from Missoula you arrested on Wednesday when he wouldn't leave."

"Yeah, what about him?"

"He offered me $1,000 if I would let him dig in my backyard for one day."

"So?"

"It gave me an idea, Pete. I'm going to auction off the rights to dig in my backyard with me and the digger splitting the value of anything he finds 75-25, like I was going to do with Roddy."

"So why are you coming to me? That's something you should get worked out with a lawyer."

"I already done that. Saw Steve Fenton this morning. The paperwork will be ready this afternoon. I came to talk to you about crowd control." Pug wiped his brow with his red handkerchief.

"Oh?" I said, somewhat stunned by the request.

"Yeah, I got about an acre and a half back there. I'm going to divide it up into two hundred square-foot parcels and sell them for a hundred dollars a parcel. That's 326 parcels. Figuring two people to a lot, we got quite a crowd. And..."

"And they might get a bit unruly, if some folks are finding jewels and others are not." I ventured to complete Pug's sentence.

"Probably. People get greedy, like my old friend Roddy," offered Pug matter-of-factly. "I floated the idea at the Apex this morning. Between there and the calls I've been getting, I've already got forty-three parcels committed for. I'll advertise it in Missoula too."

"I'll have to charge for the deputy's time."

"Fine," came Pug's quick reply. "If I sell out the parcels, I should have over thirty grand to pay expenses.

It took Pug until the third week of May to get everything set up. Once the word got around that Pug was going to sell off digging rights, everything seemed to calm down. The traffic by his house more or less returned to normal and Pug didn't have any more late night visitors.

Pug's rules for the diggers were simple. Each digger had to supply his own picks, shovels, and wheelbarrows. The dirt was to be hauled to a set of screens and sifted for jewelry. Any junk—nuts, bolts, beer cans—were to be disposed of in a refuse pile.

Pug had Dennis Ward, the local surveyor, lay out a grid

of digging squares whose boundaries were marked with lines sprayed on the ground using surveyor's marking paint. Never one to miss a chance to be theatrical, Pug stood atop a step ladder with a starting pistol borrowed from the high school's athletic department. After wishing everyone good luck, Pug fired the pistol promptly at 8:00 A.M.

It was a sunny, but cool Saturday, perfect weather for manual labor. The diggers moved quickly to their assigned squares and began shoveling. Folks were in a festive mood and it wasn't but a few minutes into the dig when Mike McCarthy, a highway department employee from Rodgersburg, made the first discovery, a silver pendant with a set of three sapphires. When Mike yelled and held up the pendant, a cheer went up from the crowd. Everything seemed to be in good hands so I left about 10:00 and spent the day doing springtime clean-up chores around my house.

The dig finished in the late afternoon and the deputy there reported that it had wound down quietly as relatively few of the diggers actually found any treasure. After dinner I went up to Pug's house to see how things turned out. I found him sitting on the back deck having a beer with Mandy Lynn and, of all people, Roddy Johnson.

"Good evening, Sheriff," offered Mandy Lynn while she winked her right eye at me and motioned for me to come and sit down next to her.

I stayed on my feet and walked over next to Roddy. "Mandy Lynn, Pug, and Roddy," I said. "Now here's a trio I wouldn't have expected in a million years."

"All's forgiven," answered Pug as he hoisted his beer glass in salute to his friend Roddy.

"Yeah," I replied. "The word is that the dig wasn't too

successful. A few people found a few pieces of jewelry, but the elusive Mendenhall Treasure remains, well, elusive."

"That's about it all right, Sheriff," answered Pug with a gleam in his beer-shot eyes, "but I wouldn't say the dig was a failure. Any time you can get people to pay you thirty thousand, to till your own garden, well, that's a successful dig in my mind."

Pug started to laugh a deep belly laugh, and he was quickly joined by Roddy and Mandy Lynn.

I could feel my temperature rise. "You old buzzard. The three of you made up the whole thing. The Mendenhall Treasure—it was just a scam. I ought to haul you in for fraud."

"That won't do you any good, Pete," answered Pug confidently. "After I return the money to the locals..."

Mandy Lynn interrupted. "Now Sheriff, nobody's gonna convict these old goats for conning a few bucks out of some city folk from Missoula."

"Yup," Pug agreed with a grin that seemed a foot wide. "I figure Roddy and I are goin' to be folk heroes. Don'tcha think, Sheriff?"

Well, you should have heard the laughter on that deck. Eventually, it was enough to bring a smile to my face, as well.

CHAPTER THREE

One Saloon Too Many

I was at home, plopped in front of the television watching a piece on the Discovery
Channel about the development of the solar
system. It was about nine o'clock on a Thursday night in
late April. Then the police scanner went off.

"Dispatch to Car Six, dispatch to Car Six, over."

"Car Six, over."

"Where are you, Car Six?"

"Assisting Winslow Ambulance with a house call."

"We've got a single car rollover at Boulder Lake near
mile post thirty-seven. The ambulance has been dispatched.
Can you assist?"

"Negative. Have you tried Car Three?"

"Yes, he's out of radio range up Madison Creek."

"You'll have to get Pete."

"Okay, over and out."

In the next few seconds I would receive a phone call
mustering me out of my home to the reported car wreck at
Boulder Lake. I was reaching down to get my boots when
the phone rang. My wife Connie answered and told the dispatcher I had heard the scanner and was on my way. Another day in my life as Sheriff of Rhyolite County, Montana.

It was a cool evening. The wind was blowing in from the west at about ten miles per hour, fast enough to wring all the heat from one's exposed skin, and slow enough to lull you into thinking that you didn't need a hat. There had been a cold rain earlier in the day and I felt the chill as soon as I stepped outside through the back door of my house, but I forgot my hat anyway.

It's about twenty miles from Rodgersburg to Boulder Lake, but it's a slow ride even with a siren and flashing lights to clear the traffic. The highway is a narrow, two-lane affair that twists, turns, switchbacks and gains fifteen hundred feet in elevation to cross Quartz Pass. The highway was wet, and as I climbed higher there were fresh patches of snow on the ground.

The "Lake" and its surrounding environs have changed dramatically since I moved to Rodgersburg and became sheriff. Once the exclusive province of people from Butte and Copperton, the area gained national attention about ten years ago when it was featured in a magazine article entitled "Little Known Treasures of the Rocky Mountains." The next year, the subdivision on Big Rock Point was platted and it's been non-stop land development ever since.

Land around the lake is expensive, not nearly as rich as it is around Flathead Lake in northwestern Montana, but pricey by Montana standards. Most of the new homes are big and infrequently used by their out-of-town owners who want this part of Montana as their personal Shangri-La, a respite from the urban world where they live and work. The outsiders' presence is both a blessing and a curse to Rhyolite County. Local residents are generally resentful toward the rich outsiders who have bought land in the county, but thankful at the same time for the few jobs they provide.

It was 9:40 P.M. when I reached the accident scene. A late model, beige Ford Taurus was parked on its roof in the ditch alongside the road. The Rodgersburg ambulance was on site, led by Charlie Roper who also serves as Chief of the Rhyolite County Sheriff's Reserve. He's a retired hospital administrator from Oklahoma.

Several cars, some with their hazard lights flashing, were parked along the sides of the highway, and a small group of onlookers, about fifteen to twenty people, were watching the EMTs work.

"Charlie, what have we got?"

"One dead, severe head injuries, Pete. There's beer in the car so he might have been drinking and, as you can see, the highway's wet. I think he lost it right after he came across the North Fork Bridge. Looks like he slid down the roadway sideways for a hundred and fifty feet or so and he might have made it except the rear wheel caught the curve sign. That spun him into the ditch and he rolled."

"Any passengers?"

"Nope," answered Charlie while he fished around the inside of his jacket for one of his little cigars.

"Wearing a seat belt?"

"Nope."

"Do we have a name?"

"Jeremy Ryckman, age thirty, lives in Helena. Couple of folks over there by the ambulance said they knew him."

I looked at the ambulance where most of the gawkers had stationed themselves. Several I recognized; several more I did not. "Which ones?"

"The guy in the brown sport coat and that tall blond fellow next to him, for sure. Maybe some of the others," answered Charlie as he finally put a match to his cigar.

"By the way, how did you get here so fast?"

"Dumb luck. We took Mrs. Ferris into the hospital at Copperton. We were about ten miles east of here when we heard the call."

"Too bad there wasn't something you could do," I answered.

"I hate it when they're so young," said Charlie with a clear look of dismay.

I went over to the group Charlie had pointed out and got their names and addresses. It turned out three men admitted knowing the victim. The leader of the group was the guy in the tweed jacket, Lee O'Leary, also from Helena. O'Leary was clearly the most senior of the group with a hint of gray hair around his temples, with some mixed in his well-trimmed moustache. When I had initially walked toward the group, O'Leary was talking to the other men and they were nodding their heads in agreement. It reminded me of a coach talking to his team.

"Mr. O'Leary, did you see the wreck?" I asked.

"No, I didn't see the accident. We drove up on it not long after it happened. Russ went back to the bar to call it in."

"Russ?"

"Russ Swanby. I was riding with him."

"I don't recall meeting Mr. Swanby."

"He hasn't come back from the bar. He was terribly upset. They were very close friends. Russ and Jeremy, I mean."

"What were you folks doing up here?"

"Having dinner."

"And a few drinks."

"Yes, a couple." I was getting the impression that the interview might take some time. O'Leary was being cooperative but clearly not saying very much. That bothered me.

"It looks like your friend had more than a couple."

"Could have. I wasn't paying any attention to what the others were drinking."

"Are all of you folks from Helena?"

"Just Russ and me—and Jeremy. Two more are from Washington, D.C."

"Both places are a long ways from the lake. What were you doing up here?"

"Having dinner and talking some politics. Sometimes it's good to get away from Helena. You get a fresher perspective."

"What do you do for a living, Lee?"

"I'm a campaign consultant, as are these two gentlemen from D.C." O'Leary pointed toward the two men he'd stepped away from at my approach. Both were wearing sport coats, no tie. They were pressed against the ambulance to get out of the wind, their collective shivers a gauge of their distress. Most interesting, I thought to myself. Three high-powered campaign consultants in Rhyolite County, which has more cows than voters. Something doesn't figure.

"And the other two gentlemen with you?"

"Jeremy and Russ both work for Governor Summitt." Now I knew something didn't figure. Rhyolite is a solidly Republican county; Governor Summitt is a big-time liberal Democrat. Why would his people come here?

"So, I assume you were having a little strategy confab."

"That's right," continued O'Leary, the man of few words.

"The election is coming up."

"Where did you have dinner?"

"At the Evergreen Saloon."

My ears were freezing and I was really wishing that O'Leary would be a little more forthcoming so I could get back to the warmth of my patrol car. "The fare's a little simple there for a high-brow meeting."

"Well, but the food's good and this time of year it's nicely private."

"Can't disagree with you there. So you all drove over from Helena?"

"No, we met the others here. They're staying down the road at the Mountain View Inn."

People from Washington, D.C., come to this part of Montana to vacation in July and August, not April. My sense of disquiet continued to grow. "What time did you get here?"

"Around 6:30."

"When did Mr. Ryckman leave the bar?"

"We started to break it up around 8:45. Jeremy was the first to leave, so it must have been around that time."

"Did you discover the accident?"

"Yes. We were only here a couple of minutes when that big fellow in the green coat drove up. He helped pull Jeremy away from the car."

"That guy? Bill Dortmund?"

"Yeah, but I didn't know his name."

"You were driving home as well?"

"Not directly. We were going to take a quick look at a house for sale by the lake. My wife has been nagging at me to get a summer place while the kids are still with us. I was going to show it to the D.C. boys."

"Good. You answered my next question. I was wondering how a couple of men staying at the Mountain View could be here. It's a few miles out of their way."

"We were together in my car."

"Back to the dinner. What was the deceased drinking?"

"He usually drank beer. Once in awhile, gin and tonic."

"And tonight?"

"I'm not sure. He was on the other end of the table from me. I'm trying to picture it — I'm guessing he was drinking gin. I don't recall seeing a beer in front of him."

"How many did he have?"

"I don't know. It was a long dinner and several rounds were bought, but not everybody was drinking every round. I only had two glasses of wine."

"Did everyone have wine with dinner?"

"I did, but we didn't order a bottle or anything like that."

After finishing with O'Leary I talked with each of the fellows from D.C. and learned little. Their answers were nearly identical to O'Leary's and it didn't take long to realize that he'd coached them about what to say. But why? This was an automobile accident, not a criminal investigation where they were suspects. As for their little political meeting, I found it puzzling but it certainly wasn't criminal.

I went back to visit with Charlie Roper. I had noticed him taking a large number of photographs, far more than usual for a simple rollover.

"Charlie, why all the photographs?"

"It doesn't add up, Pete."

"What doesn't?"

"The blood and tissue in the car. We're finding it in places it shouldn't be if there was just one occupant."

"Show me."

"Right here." I followed the beam of light from Charlie's flashlight to the passenger door. Sure enough, there was a large swatch of blood on the interior of the door and more on the dashboard, but nothing on the steering wheel.

"The driver could have bounced all over when it rolled."

"Maybe. Billy Dortmund pulled him from the car. He said the body was doubled over on the passenger side."

"Anything's possible in a rollover. You've told me that a dozen times, if you've told me once."

"Maybe. The floor mats on both sides are damp. Someone sat on the passenger side today. And there's this," Charlie said holding up the driver's side seat belt. It was loose, not retracted like the seatbelt on the passenger side.

"Someone was wearing it?" I asked.

"Maybe," said Charlie again.

"Well, discretion is the better part of valor. Let's treat this as a crime scene. Get Goodyear's wrecker up here and have them impound the car inside tonight. I'll get Deputy Titan over there first thing in the morning to check for prints. If the ambulance crew doesn't need you, why don't you talk with the deceased's other companions while I go down to the Evergreen and see what I can learn down there. We'll catch up later."

The Evergreen Saloon is up the North Fork Road about two hundred yards off Highway 47, which follows the eastern shore of Boulder Lake. Built of logs darkened by more than a hundred years of varnish and cigarette smoke, with a massive field rock fireplace, the Evergreen is variously home to fishermen, hunters, and snowmobilers, depending on the season. The bar is a half log cut from a giant fir tree just shy of three feet across. Behind it one could usually find owner Al Nelson.

I entered the front door, paused momentarily to let my eyes adjust to the dim interior and the multi-colored menagerie of dozens of neon beer signs hung throughout the room. A television above the far corner of the bar was tuned to the remnants of the Sonics–Nuggets game but no one was watching. There were two solitary drinkers at the bar and a party of three women at a nearby table, about average for a cold spring night.

"Sheriff, be right with you," said Nelson as I moved over toward the bar. He was putting some drinks on a tray.

"No hurry, Al." I found a perch where we could speak privately. Al joined me a few seconds later and started to pour me a Coke but I waved him off.

"I see you've got a little activity down on the highway," he said.

"Yes, a rollover."

"Is it bad?"

"About as bad as it gets. The victim was dead by the time Charlie got there."

"And now you're coming here to see if he or she might have been patronizing my establishment."

"He and I already know that. The dead guy's name is Jeremy Ryckman. Short, kind of pudgy fellow with black hair. He was in here with a group from Helena."

"I know who you mean. They used the private dining room."

"They drink quite a bit?"

"Nothing out of the ordinary. They were here two to

three hours. I probably sent back five or six rounds. Nobody looked drunk to me."

"You recall what Ryckman might have been drinking?"

"Gin and tonic."

"How many did he have?"

"I'm guessing here. Four, maybe five." Al pushed the jar of pickled eggs in my direction. He knows I am a sucker for both pickled eggs and pigs feet. At that point the conversation paused while I fished out a couple and put them on the napkin Al placed before me.

"Somebody run a tab?" I asked.

"Yeah, the older guy, but I didn't track it by the drink, just a total for each round."

"How many were in the party?"

"Six."

"You sure? I was told five."

"Wait, I'd better check that."

I ate another pickled egg while Al checked his receipts.

"Yup, six of them."

"All men?"

"Yup."

"What time did they leave?"

"They left in two groups. The guy that you say is dead left with another fellow about a quarter to nine, the rest of them a few minutes later."

"So two cars?"

"I think they came in three. Before the second bunch left they were talking about looking at some house one of the guys was going to buy. The older fellow."

"O'Leary."

"If you say so. O'Leary told two of the fellows to get in

his car and he'd bring them back so they could get their car."

"So one of the cars is still here."

"Probably. The cars were in the parking lot on the east side. I haven't checked the lot."

"O'Leary told me one of the guys drove back here and called 9-1-1."

"Not here. None of those guys have been back since they left."

"Can you describe the other four guys in the party?"

"Not really, Pete. You know how it is. You look at folks but don't really see them. Besides, I had a bar full when they showed up and I never paid all that much attention to the group. I remember the old guy 'cause he paid the bill and the fellow you said was dead bought a six pack for the road."

"So how do you know none of the others came back to the bar?"

"I know everybody else who was in the bar tonight. They pretty much cleared out between 8:30 and 9:00 so someone coming in to use the phone would have been noticed."

I visited with Al for a few more minutes, then checked the parking lot. It was empty. By the time I returned to the accident site the ambulance was gone, as were the onlookers. The wrecker was loading what was left of the Taurus onto the back of a flatbed truck for the trip back to Rodgersburg. Charlie Roper was waiting patiently for me to return.

"Learn anything?" I asked.

"They've all got the same story. Left the Evergreen to look at some house. Driving down the road they discovered the accident. Billy Dortmund showed up a few minutes later and helped them with the body. They knew he was dead when they found him."

"Did you get a chance to talk with Billy?"

"No. He left right after you."

"And everyone says there was only one person in the car."

"You got it. Pete, I've been around enough accidents to know that no two people tell the same story. Now there's three guys all with the same story, almost word for word. In my opinion, it was rehearsed. I think someone else was in that car and they got him out of here."

"My sentiments exactly. Did someone pick up the three who stayed behind?"

"Yeah. Not long after you left. It was a red Buick."

"Did you get the license number?"

"No, ah shit. I wasn't thinking. I was more concerned about clearing the accident site."

"That's okay. According to Al at the bar, nobody came in to call 9-1-1, so I'm left to conclude that he either drove to another place to make the call, or used a cell phone."

"And he didn't come because he was hightailing it out of here, maybe with whoever else was in that car," Charlie injected.

"Yup, that's what I am thinking."

"The phone call should be easy to sort out," added Charlie. "Dispatch will have a record of who called."

"I know it's late, but let's take a ride down to the Mountain View and talk with those fellows from D.C. O'Leary said they were staying there."

It was just past midnight by the time we reached the Mountain View. I talked with the night clerk to find out what rooms the D.C. guys were staying in, but he told me they loaded the car and left a half hour before we arrived.

I called the Ponderosa Sheriff's Department in Copperton to see if Ponderosa might be able to intercept them. Then we quickly checked the two motel rooms. Both were empty, but I picked several plastic drinking cups out of a waste basket to check for fingerprints. Charlie and I called it a night and returned to Rodgersburg. We never heard from Ponderosa.

The next morning I called the Governor's office to talk with Russ Swanby. I was told that he wasn't available. Then I asked if Lee O'Leary was there and received the same reply.

My deputy, Johnny Titan, pulled several sets of fingerprints from the plastic cups taken from the motel rooms and sent them to the state crime lab and FBI. Then he went down to Goodyear Ford to examine the wrecked vehicle for additional evidence. Fred Early, our County Coroner, had notified the next of kin late last night. It didn't take long before reporters got wind of the story and were calling the office. I handled each of the calls and carefully limited what I said to the facts. We didn't have the lab work completed and I wasn't going to speculate on what might have happened.

After completing my calls to the reporters, I drifted into the kitchen to refresh my coffee cup and help myself to another piece of banana bread which one of the deputies had brought in that morning. Kay joined me. It was time to fill her in on what had happened at the lake.

After providing her with a complete description punctuated by my analysis of the situation, she asked, "What's your next move?"

"I'm not sure, probably a trip to Helena for follow-up interviews. Finding the missing sixth man is a priority."

"How about the money?" Kay asked.

"What money? I never said anything about money."

"I know you didn't, Pete. But it was a bunch of political types having a meeting so it had to be about money."

"How did you reach such a conclusion?" I asked, not quite following the logic that led to Kay's conclusion.

"From you Pete, Mr. Politician, who has observed on more than one occasion that 'money is the mother's milk of politics.' And further, that 'clean money is better than tainted money, but tainted money is better than no money at all.'"

I have said that, exactly that, and was astounded to see that Kay had remembered. Usually she gets about half the quote or cliché correct and then adds her own special twist. The boys around the office call these malapropisms "Kayisms."

"At this point, Kay, I don't have any reason to believe there is any money involved, but I will consider it as we move the case along."

"Okay," answered Kay happily as she poured the remnants of her coffee into the sink and started to return to the dispatch area. "Glad I could help."

Saturday's newspapers were full of the story. The deceased, Jeremy Ryckman, had been deputy campaign manager for Governor Summitt during the last election. The other individuals listed in the story had also been involved in the campaign. Apparently, they were working on the next election, which made sense since it was only six months away.

I decided to hold up the investigation over the weekend pending results from the crime lab. I was perplexed over the missing "sixth person" and why Ryckman's associates departed the area so quickly on Thursday night.

Tomorrow was Saturday and I had to deal, once and for all, with my seventeen-year-old son's desire to purchase a car. Last fall Phil, who is a junior in high school, started bugging me about allowing him to buy a vehicle. Several of the boys he hangs out with have their own wheels and Phil wants to join in the fraternity. I've told him numerous times that he isn't equipped for the responsibility of owning a car. But my intransigence on the issue has only stiffened his resolve. Finally, after several months of his badgering I gave in and told him that I would let him buy a car if he would take care of our pickup, the vehicle he drives most of the time, and pay all of the costs associated with owner-ship for one month. He readily agreed and has done a good job checking the oil, seeing that it's full of gas, and keeping it clean. Tomorrow the month is up and I have to face the music.

"Phil, whatcha doing?"

"Nothing right now, Pa. Jimmy's coming over around 6:30. We're taking the girls to the movie."

"C'mon with me. I've got some errands to run."

"Is this going to be one of those father-son conversation things?" The kid is used to my methods. I like to get him alone, in the car at sixty miles per hour. He can't leave and Mom isn't there to facilitate the conversation in ways which only make sense to a woman.

"Only if you want to talk. C'mon, let's go."

A few minutes later I turned the GMC half-ton in to Jack's Exxon and drove it into the lube bay. Ronnie Hale, co-owner of the station, greeted us as we climbed out of the cab. "Sheriff Pete. Oh, and I see you've got Mr. Handsome with you."

"You got that right, Ron," said Phil lightly. Phil is handsome. Six feet four, two hundred five pounds, dark blue eyes, dishwater blond hair, a ready smile for everyone he meets, and devil may care attitude. He's a male version of his mother and the tempestuousness of their relationship is testimony that like temperaments repel.

"Did those tires I ordered come in?" I asked Ronnie while Phil yawned.

"Yup, gonna run $315.80, mounted and balanced."

"Slap 'em on, and I'll take Phil over to Carmichaels. I'm feeling like a dish of butter brickle."

"Fine, Pete. See you in about twenty minutes."

Phil and I had moved toward the garage door on our way to Carmichaels across the street when I turned back to Ronnie. "And, Ron," I said loudly so Phil couldn't miss hearing what I had to say, "prepare an invoice for Phil. He's paying for the truck this month. I am sure his credit will be good with you."

"Can do," shouted Ronnie as he slipped into the back room where the tire inventory was housed.

Phil was strangely quiet as we walked the block to Carmichael's front door. I reached and pulled it open only to have Tara Visser, one of Phil's classmates, step out into the sun.

"Hi, Philip," greeted Tara as she elongated the "hi" and flashed him a seductive smile.

Phil slips a barely audible "hi" out of his mouth in return, walks past Tara, and leads me to a booth in the café.

"What was that all about?" I asked after we'd taken our seats.

"Whaddya mean?" answered Phil with a quizzical look.

"You," I said, "brushing off Tara. That's the first time in your life you bypassed a pretty girl to talk with your parents."

"Tara is kind of poison now," answered Phil matter-of-factly. "I talked with her at the prom last week and Lynette got a little pissed."

"Oh."

"You saw Marcie in the hall behind Tara, didn't you?

I nodded yes in reply.

"If I had stopped to talk with Tara, Lynette would already know about it."

"You went to the prom with Lynette, so why were you talking with Tara?" I asked.

"I went up to get some punch and Tara came over to the table and says 'hi.' She had this dark green strapless dress on, real short, not a formal like the rest of the girls were wearing. I don't know what you call it."

"A cocktail dress," I offered.

"Yeah, okay. Tara looked incredible," continued Phil.

"And you paused for a moment to visit with the cleavage," I replied.

"How did you know that?"

"As the old saying goes, 'the apple doesn't fall too far from the tree'" I answered, "And then Lynette showed up wondering what was keeping you."

"Right on," answered Phil the anxiety evident in his voice.

"Let me guess, back at the table a bit of an arctic front blew in as you tried to make some excuse which sounded pretty lame, even to you."

"Right again. How do you know this stuff?"

"A few more years of dealing with women than you." I continued. "Since then, Lynette has wanted to discuss the issue, several times."

It was Phil's turn to nod yes in reply.

"Welcome to relationships, son. I had a similar experience not long ago with your dear mother after I made some comment about Mandy Lynn's backside."

"Mandy Lynn," answered Phil with newfound energy, "for an old gal, she's pretty hot."

As the conversation with Phil proceeded, I was becoming more and more astounded. I have a good relationship with my son, conventional in every way for a seventeen-year-old and his father. Our normal conversation consists of the daily clichés and platitudes of life ("How ya doin?"), some dialog about sports, and a series of grunts, shoulder shrugs, and blank stares if I actually try to inquire about what's really going on in his life.

And now he's sitting here telling me about his prurient interest in a woman better than twice his age. I understand that many if not most teenage boys have fantasies about sleeping with an older woman. It's personal testimony to their sense of maturity and belief in their manhood. At my age, the process is inverted and men fantasize about sleeping with a younger gal, testimony to a belief in their boyhood.

After Phil's observations about Mandy Lynn had run their course, I said, "Phil, let me give you a little advice. Some women are best admired from afar, that is, if you don't want trouble in your life."

I left the lecture at that, knowing full well that it was generally pointless to try and talk to a teen-aged boy full of testosterone about the perils of sex. At that age they're in the Ichabod Crane stage of life—a headless creature riding through the night, striking fear into the hearts of their parents at the mere thought of what he might be doing in some back seat.

"C'mon, let's go get the truck," I said as I started to pull myself out of the booth.

"Pa," answered Phil. "You win."

"Win what?" I tried to act puzzled.

"The car. I can't afford the tires, even if Ronnie gives me credit."

"I know that, son, but you had to experience it for yourself. Cars are a big responsibility."

"Okay, okay."

"You'll get a car when you're off to college. Just like Tom."

Late Monday afternoon we received several faxes from the crime lab but the information was mixed. All of the blood samples from the wrecked vehicle matched the deceased. If someone else was in the car, there was no telltale evidence. In addition, the only fingerprints on the steering wheel came from the deceased. It was beginning to look more and more like Ryckman had been alone, notwithstanding Charlie's and my observations in the field. Ryckman's blood alcohol came back point-oh-five. He wasn't legally drunk. The fingerprints from the drinking cups found at the Mountain View Inn were much more helpful. We got six good sets. Four matched the names of individuals at the dinner meeting, one was unidentified, and one set belonged to Gary Summitt, the Governor's grown son and most likely our mystery man, and I thought I knew why: Summitt had been in the news for multiple DUIs. It was time for a trip to Helena.

I started by meeting with Lee O'Leary at Democratic Party headquarters, an old mansion converted into offices a couple of blocks east of Helena's historic Last Chance Gulch, site of one of the earliest gold discoveries in Montana. O'Leary came into the conference room, took a seat at the end of the table, and opened a notebook.

"Coffee, Sheriff? We just made a fresh pot."

"No, thanks. Had plenty at lunch."

"What can I do for you, Sheriff?" O'Leary's tone was quite businesslike.

"I need to clean up some details from the events surrounding last Thursday's accident."

"I'll help, if I can."

"For starters, you told me there were a total of five people in the party; the two political consultants from D.C., two people from the governor's office, one of whom is the deceased, and yourself. But Al Nelson, owner of the Evergreen, said there were six people in the party."

"He's mistaken," answered O'Leary quickly as he turned his face just enough so that I lost eye contact.

"I don't think so. We have a copy of the dinner order, the one you paid for with your credit card. Now, unless you want to tell me which of your associates ate two dinners, it appears as if six meals were served."

"I'm shocked by Mr. Nelson's action, padding a dinner tab," answered O'Leary. "I didn't notice." The answer was pat and without emotion, another lie.

"Al Nelson didn't pad your bill. If he said he served six dinners, he served six dinners. Now, do you want to cut the crap?" I raised my voice. It was time to push him for the truth.

O'Leary responded angrily, "There's no crap to cut. There were only five people in our party."

"Nelson also told me that you folks left in two groups. The first group consisted of the deceased and the mystery man, with your group of four following a few minutes later."

"There is no mystery man, Sheriff. Jeremy left the bar with Russ Swanby but Russ joined us in the parking lot and rode with me to see the cabin."

"Why did you folks depart the scene so quickly?" I changed the subject. I could see that O'Leary had thought this situation through very carefully and it was going to be difficult to get the truth.

"If waiting for the ambulance to pick up Jeremy and then staying around to answer questions from law enforcement is leaving too quickly, what can I say?"

"I wasn't referring to your actions at the accident site. I meant your friends from D.C. checking out of the motel around 11:30 that night."

"We thought it best to return to Helena," answered O'Leary confidently. "We needed to prepare for the media."

"Oh, really," I answered cynically. "Needed to get the right spin on the incident."

"Something like that."

"You've got another problem, Mr. O'Leary."

"What's that, Sheriff?"

"In one of the motel rooms we found six plastic drinking cups in the garbage can, and we lifted six different sets of prints. You want to clear the record now?"

"Sheriff, good luck with your investigation. I'm sorry I can't be of more help."

O'Leary didn't have to tell me anything more. His reaction when I mentioned the six sets of fingerprints told me I was right on target. His stonewalling was only going to bring him a lot of trouble.

After leaving O'Leary, I did some shopping for my wife Connie, had dinner with a friend from the Department of Justice, and stopped by the home of Gary Summitt, the Governor's son, for a quick interview. Summitt lived in a brick home on Highland Street about three blocks from the Governor's Mansion. I had met him once a few years before at a Sheriffs and Peace Officers Association convention when he was campaigning for his father. Summitt had a law degree from Yale and served as in-house counsel to the governor's office.

I pressed the door chime and could hear it ringing inside the house followed by a heavy set of footsteps to the door.

"Gary Summitt?" I asked after he'd opened the door.

"Yes."

"Sheriff Pete Benson, Rhyolite County. I've got some questions in connection with Jeremy Ryckman's death."

"I don't know anything about it," answered Summitt hesitantly.

"I have a set of your fingerprints from a motel room at the Mountain View Inn and a bartender who will say you were at the Evergreen Saloon that night," I said, and waited for my revelations to soak in. "Now, you can talk to me, or you can do so in front of a grand jury."

Summitt adopted a thoughtful look and said, "Come in, Sheriff."

Summitt ushered me into his living room, which was dominated by a 54-inch television. It was tuned to MSN-

BC, but given whom he was and who he worked for, I wasn't surprised.

"Have a seat," said Summitt cordially while he directed me toward a floral patterned sofa. "Let me shut off the TV." After moving a throw pillow and nestling in the soft fabric of the sofa I said, "Thank you. Mr. Summitt, I've talked with several of your companions that night. They insist there were only five people at the meeting, but we know there were six. You were there."

"Yes, I was. I wasn't supposed to be, but I was there."

"You want to explain that last comment?"

"I've been in the papers some. I am sure you know that."

"Yeah, you've got a problem with drinking and driving."

"I made a deal with the prosecutor the last time I was arrested to go into alcohol treatment and stay completely out of all establishments or functions where liquor is served."

"So by attending the dinner last Thursday you were breaking the terms of your probation."

"Yes. I didn't drink, but I wasn't supposed to be on the premises."

"When did you leave the Evergreen?"

"Just before nine. I left with Jeremy." A few short hours ago, O'Leary was telling me that Russ Swanby had walked out of the bar with Ryckman.

"And you weren't injured in the accident?" I asked.

"I left the building with him, but I had my own car. Last I saw of him was in the parking lot."

"Where did you go after you left the bar?"

"Into Copperton. I stopped at Ned Pittman's house to drop off some political materials."

"I trust you mean State Senator Ned Pittman."

"The same. I was there about a half hour until around ten. Then I drove back to Helena."

"When did you hear about the wreck?" I asked.

"That night, Sheriff. Russ Swanby called me on the cell from the motel. He told me what had happened and how Lee thought it best to try and keep my name out of it."

"You're sure there was no one with Ryckman?" I was still having a hard time believing that Ryckman was alone. I had become convinced that Russ Swanby had taken the other person in the car back to the Evergreen where he picked up the third vehicle and departed. And, I really liked Gary Summitt as a candidate for the mystery man. The problem was, Summitt looked just fine, not a bit like someone who had been in a serious rollover. There should be some bruises, at a minimum.

"Absolutely. He was alone and planning to go to Missoula that night. That's why he was headed toward Rodgersburg."

"Why were your friends from D.C. so anxious to clear out of the motel room?"

"Running for cover. They all got together on Friday, here in Helena, to craft a media strategy. I wasn't involved. I was told to keep my head down and my mouth shut."

"Your father know of your role in this thing?"

"Not from me, but I don't know what O'Leary might have told him. I haven't talked about it with my father."

"If what you've told me is true, I'd advise you to call the County Attorney and make a clean breast of things. I have reports to file and the press is dogging this investigation. Sooner or later your role will come out anyway. Then, you're probably going to jail and your father will be publicly embarrassed by you and his aides."

I headed back to Rodgersburg and managed to climb into bed just before midnight. I spent the next morning writing up my report on the case and gave it to Kay to type. "Thanks for the counsel the other day, Ms. Best. But, as it turns out, we had a bunch of politicos hunkering down in private and it wasn't about money."

"Just trying to be helpful," volunteered Kay sheepishly. She never says anything, but it irritates her just a little when she gives me advice and I don't take it. But she hates it more, if it turns out that her advice was bad.

"Just a case of the governor's son trying to hide from the legal consequences of violating his probation," I answered matter-of-factly, knowing full well that any form of gloating would chill the atmosphere of the office considerably.

Gary Summitt surprised me. By the time I called the Lewis and Clark County Attorney, Summitt had already contacted him and described his role in the affair. My office coordinated the investigation with the State Highway Patrol and the Lewis and Clark County Attorney's office. The media had their feeding frenzy for a few days, but in the end, no criminal charges were filed. The coroner's jury ruled that Jeremy Ryckman had been alone in his car when he lost control and ended up killing himself.

It was good to have the entire incident concluded, and I was glad that my suspicions of the political operatives turned out to be over a matter which was rather benign in the end. The election came and went. Governor Summitt was reelected in a squeaker. He had a lot more money for the campaign than his opponent. Otherwise, he'd be unemployed.

I'd long since forgotten the incident, only to be reminded of it several months later when I found myself talking with former Senator Ned Pittman at a fishing access site on Upper Madison Creek. He was coming back after fishing in the morning and I was getting ready to go out that afternoon.

"So why did you quit politics, Ned?"

"Sometimes even things you love end up tasting bitter after awhile, Pete."

"Bitter?"

"The governor and the way he ran that last campaign."

"It was a bit on the negative side for Montana."

"That's not the half of it. Remember the night the Ryckman kid was killed?"

"Yeah."

"O'Leary and the boys from D.C. came to my house that night around midnight."

"Oh?" I wondered where this was leading.

Ned continued, "They said they were having car trouble and needed to get back to Helena, so they borrowed my car. Later on, I learned you had put out an APB on them."

"That's true," I replied, "but we caught up with them and the truth finally came out in the wash."

"Not the whole truth," answered Ned calmly as he looked me straight in the eye.

"What's missing?"

"The money. The D.C. boys dropped off a half million in cash with O'Leary that night. They called it an anonymous campaign donation. But, I am sure it came from a coal company which is very interested in trying to reduce its operating expenses in Montana. Ryckman was taking it to Missoula when he had the wreck. The governor's boys recovered the cash and sent Swanby back to the motel with it. Then they blew the scene and used my car to get past any police surveillance."

I was stunned. "The governor?" I stammered. "The populist scourge of corporate America? And, you're telling me he's on the take from King Coal. In all honesty Ned, I am finding that just a little hard to believe."

"Believe it, Pete. That anti-big business tune is just campaign rhetoric. It keeps the lefties happy and right now, they control the party. But when someone can pile on greenbacks, you can count on most any politician being all ears. Cash is the mother's milk of politics, Pete, you know that," answered Ned, more dismayed by my apparent naiveté than by the incident he'd just described.

Then it hit me. Kay was right. I should have looked for the money. My lord, I am going to get those "told you so" looks for a month. My first instinct was to handle this impending situation like any red-blooded American male would—by taking it, unspoken, to my grave. Unfortunately, with my job and personal ethics at play, I couldn't do that.

"Ned, you should come forward," I said angrily, but at this point I couldn't tell if I was agitated over the political hypocrisy or because I'd been completely flummoxed by the politicos.

"No, Pete, I can't do that. I might not be a part of the system anymore, but I'm still invested in it," said Ned quietly as he put away his fishing gear.

"I hope you change your mind, Ned. This is important."

"I should mention there's another reason I left politics."

"What's that?" I pressed.

Ned got into his car and started the engine. "I can't seem to remember what I said from one minute to the next. See you around, Pete."

I looked at Ned, intending to reply but, instead, accepted the cold fact that no testimony meant no evidence, and no evidence meant no case. I watched Ned drive away and realized there was nothing I could do. Machiavelli was right. "Politics has no relation to morals."[1]

CHAPTER FOUR

A Real Pretty Picture

A lot of people think that living in a rural area or small town must be boring—nothing ever seems to happen. As a county sheriff in Montana, I can tell you that's just not true.

It was a stunningly beautiful Monday morning in mid-July. The air was crystal clear with just a hint of breeze from the west, the sky a deep azure blue, and the sun's rays beaming off the snow fields still remaining on the north slope of Quartz Peak above Rodgersburg. I'd risen at 6:30 a.m. and taken a long run before breakfast. I generally run every day and pump iron over at the high school gym two or three days a week. I'd like to claim that it's keeping my physique chiseled like the statute of a Greek god, but the truth is, I didn't look all that good when I was twenty and still don't today. But the exercise is good for my job and good for my sleep.

Later at the office I was having a cup of coffee and looking over the shift reports from the previous weekend when Kay Best, my chief dispatcher and office manager, came into the office.

"So how was the weekend?" she asked.

"Great," I replied. "Connie and I went to the theater Saturday night. It was a great show."

"What was playing?"

"*Broadway Extravaganza.* They started with Rodgers and Hammerstein and worked their way through the sixties and seventies and then finished with several songs by Andrew Lloyd Weber. Two members of the cast had really good voices, particularly the soprano."

"Well, glad you had a good time. I am too much of the cowgirl for that long-hair stuff."

"Each to his own," I replied. Kay's choice in music is country western, country western, and country western. I'm not terribly partial to it myself. After three or four songs it all sounds the same to me, but it is Montana and I keep my mouth shut lest the town folk think I am some kind of traitor or, worse yet, a liberal.

"You know how the cast goes out into the audience to pull some unsuspecting patron into playing some part in the show?" I asked.

"Yeah."

"Well, this time it was me."

"You're kidding!" Kay exclaimed, a smile spreading across her face.

"No, it's true. All of a sudden I'm up on the stage and Carolyn, the troupe's artistic director, says to me, 'Sheriff Pete, I hear you sing a mean version of "Old Man River."'" I momentarily paused and said, "I've been wondering how she knew that, Ms. Best." I gave Kay the evil eye. I saw a fidget. Then she looked me straight in the eye and started to giggle.

"I figured it was you," came my quick retort.

"I did it to prevent a jail break," answered Kay with a coy smile. When I didn't rise to the bait she added, "Last week when you were in the wash room toning your pipes, the prisoners could hear you through the wall. They complained about the racket and wanted me to stop your singing. I knew I could never confront you. It would hurt your feelings."

"Yeah," I said nonplussed, "as if that ever stopped you before." If there is one thing that Kay has no problem doing, it's confronting me.

Kay continued. "So I called Carolyn over at the theater and asked her assistance in setting up a momentary embarrassment for you, all for the greater good of mankind." Kay really loved this. Nothing more fun than pulling off a practical joke on the boss.

"And, no doubt, Carolyn jumped at the chance," I quipped, knowing full well the degree to which the women of Rodgersburg will conspire to give the rhubarb to a man.

"Of course," came Kay's response, accompanied by another light giggle, her green eyes alive with glee.

"Well, it didn't work," I said matter-of-factly. "I got a standing ovation, the only one that evening."

"Oh, my God, what kind of beast have I unleashed?" said Kay rhetorically, her joy undiminished by my attempt to let the air out of her balloon.

"Hear this," I said as I sang out the first stanza of Old Man River[1] in deep bass.

"Not bad," admitted Kay, adopting a bit more serious tone. "But don't give up the day job just yet. At least wait until you've found an agent."

Just then the telephone rang in the outer office. "I'll get it," Kay said as she turned to the door. "While I'm gone, why don't you practice an aria or whatever it is you bassbaritones sing?" Then she giggled again.

I pulled out the pile of paper which had built up in my inbox over the week and started to sort through it when Kay returned.

"Pete, that was Wilma Johannson. She and Harold got home real late last night. This morning they found that someone had broken in through their back door. She's pretty upset. Harold is checking the house to see what's missing."

"Well, we'd better go down and see what we can do."

"We?" Kay asked.

"Yes, we. You know we'll look at things for a minute or two, and then we'll have to have coffee. Harold will want to show me what he's made in the shop and talk some football or about Butte in the old days. Then Wilma, not to be outdone, will drag out her quilts. I just don't do quilts well—but you do. C'mon."

It was only about two minutes to the Johannson home, a three-story brick affair with a wide verandah that wrapped around three sides of the house. Josiah Wakefield, son-in-law to Clyde Rodgers, after whom the town was named, opened a brick works in 1888 to meet the construction needs of what was then a rapidly growing community. The demand for his product escalated rather sharply following the great flood of 1897. Virtually every building in the town's business district and two-thirds of its older residences are either brick or fieldstone.

Harold and Wilma are both retired, but you'd never know it from their activity level. Harold ran a welding and machine shop while Wilma stayed home and raised six kids. Wilma is sixty-eight but looks twenty years younger. Medium height, trim, with a full head of brown hair which, admittedly, only her hairdresser knows for sure, more energy than most women half her age, and a smile for everyone she meets. The most amazing thing is her hands. They're small with pudgy fingers and you'd find it hard to believe she could hold a cup of coffee, much less sew. But, give Wilma a piece of cloth and a sewing machine and magic happens. She has a wall of blue ribbons for her entries at quilt shows and fairs across the Northwest and a file full of thank you cards from the drama departments of five high schools in this part of Montana for helping them with costume construction.

Wilma was waiting at the door when we drove up. "Oh, Sheriff Benson, we're so glad you could come. Kay, I'm delighted you're here too. I've just finished a new quilt you must see."

"I'd love to, Wilma," replied Kay, "but we'd better let the sheriff conduct his investigation first."

Wilma led the way to the back door. From the looks of it, the burglar had pounded on the lock from the outside with something like an axe or sledgehammer until the catch ripped off the door frame. That surprised me because the lock was a cheap spring-loaded latch whose only purpose was to hold the door closed from the wind or to keep pets outdoors. It was the kind you could pop open with a credit card or long-handled screwdriver. The burglar must be a real amateur. Anyone who knew what they were doing would never have taken the risk of pounding on the lock. Too much noise; too much of a chance that a neighbor would hear. Just a guess, but the perp is probably a local who knows the comings and goings of residents.

"Whoever it was knew that Harold and Wilma were not at home," observed Kay, reading my thoughts.

"And the neighbors on either side of the house," I replied. "My guess is that it happened either sometime Saturday night or Sunday afternoon when most folks were down at the Winslow rodeo. Well, we're not going to learn much from the door. Let's see what's missing." I turned to move toward the front of the house just as Harold Johannson entered the kitchen. He was wearing his signature uniform—blue jeans, khaki shirt, and a Green Bay Packers baseball hat. In the winter he switches to a Packers stocking hat. Harold is a lot like me—just a bit over six feet, stocky, with powerfully built arms and serious by nature. He was all business today.

"I've already called the lumber yard," Harold said, with a tone of annoyance that couldn't be missed. "The door's beyond repair."

"That's true. Have you figured out what's missing from the house?" I asked.

"Near as I can tell, only one thing, a painting from the living room wall," answered Harold.

We followed Harold through the house until he stopped and pointed to a small square of discolored wallpaper on the living room wall. "It's been hanging there a long time," I observed.

"It belonged to Harold's father," Wilma said. 'He brought it home from Europe after World War II."

"What kind of painting was it?" I asked.

"An oil," Harold replied. "A picture of a vase of flowers on a stone wall. I called it fuzzy art." Harold must have read the confusion on my face and continued, "When you look at it from a distance, it's real clear what the picture is, but up close, it's hard to tell. The lines aren't real distinct."

"Oh," I replied, still not sure what he meant. "Was it valuable?"

"I don't think so," answered Harold. "It had great sentimental value for my dad. He found it in an estate that had been a German command post. He said they fought like hell to take the place and he lost a couple of good friends. I think that's why he kept it—a memorial for them."

"What kind of a frame was it in?"

"Oak, with a dark stain. Dad made the frame."

"Have you or Wilma touched the wall here since you discovered it was gone?"

"No, we thought you might want to check for fingerprints."

I nodded in reply, and Wilma sensed that this phase of the investigation was over. She herded us to the dining room for a repast of coffee, cake, and an assortment of cookies. After biting into an oatmeal chocolate chip cookie, I asked Harold, "Would you make me a list of all the new people that have been in your home over the past several months?"

"New people?" He asked with a perplexed look on his face.

"People you've met for the first time, someone who hasn't been here before. Maybe a new delivery boy for Homer's IGA. Get my drift?"

"Pete, we don't get many visitors. Just family and the same old friends we've had for thirty years."

"Think about it a little and let me know what you come up with."

After we'd had coffee, Kay looked at the quilts and I toured the wood shop. Harold's hobby is making toys and furniture for his grandchildren. His current projects included a gun cabinet for his oldest grandson, Danny, and a family of wooden ducks on wheels to be pulled around the house by Carly, the newest granddaughter.

Kay and I returned to the office about eleven o'clock. Deputy Nick Colusa was helping out this week while my chief deputy, Johnny Titan, was on vacation. Normally, Nick works out of Winslow, a town of about 500 people about twenty-five miles east of Rodgersburg. I sent him down to Johannson's to dust for prints, but I didn't think he'd find anything. Actually, it was more for show, to let Harold and Wilma know we were taking the investigation seriously.

Just as I reached the front of the office on my way home for lunch, Kay called after me softly. "Pete."

"Yeah?"

"If you'd like to see how you did at the theater Saturday, Connie left a copy of the DVD by the TV."

"Connie!" I thundered. Actually, it was more of a loud expression of surprise. "My own wife was part of the conspiracy?" I asked. "I should have known. She probably initiated the whole thing." Kay shrugged her shoulders and shot me a dumbfounded look, making it clear that there's honor among practical jokers.

In the mid-afternoon I took a trip up Madison Creek to drop off a summons. Madison Creek starts on the far western end of the county near the base of Cathedral Peak and flows almost due east past Rodgersburg to Winslow where it meets the Clark Fork River. I had just returned to the squad car when Kay called on the radio to tell me Harold was waiting in the office with the list of "new" people I had asked for. It took about fifteen minutes to get back.

Harold was still there when I arrived. "Harold, you didn't need to come in. I'd have stopped by."

"I got that list you wanted, Sheriff. Wilma and I thought about it hard, but we could only think of three people."

"What have you got?"

"Bridget Clews. She's a home health nurse from Butte. Came up twice a week to help me with Wilma's therapy after she cracked her hip back in January. Really was a big help and very kind. I don't think Wilma would have mended nearly so well without Bridget pushing her through all that therapy."

"How's that?"

"The best way I can describe it, Pete, is that she's like a good coach. Wilma was in a lot of pain but Bridget would coax her through her exercises, asking Wilma to move that leg and yet never overdoing it. When I first saw Wilma struggle to get back on her feet, I was afraid the pain would shut her down and she'd refuse to do the therapy. But Bridget got her moving and kept her going. She's good people, Pete."

"We'll put her on the list anyway, but burglary doesn't tend to be a woman's crime."

"Maybe so. But of the three, she's the only one we can remember looking at the painting. She told Wilma she admired it."

"She say anything else about it?"

"No, just that it was a nice painting."

"Who else you got?" I asked.

"Brett Schuler. He's a friend of my grandson Danny. Came down with him from Missoula a couple of weekends last fall, and he's working in town for the summer. Not my kind of a kid."

"How so?"

"He's mannerly enough, but he has real long hair and wears earrings. I know it's just a teenage thing, rebellion and all, but I think he looks like a freak."

"Did you or Wilma ever see him eyeballing the picture?" I asked while fishing through my pants pocket for another ink pen to replace the one whose ink flow had abruptly stopped.

"Not really," answered Harold thoughtfully. "Brett's been in the living room several times but never seemed to pay particular attention to anything but the TV. Come to think of it, there is one thing I like about Brett."

"What's that?" I asked innocently, although I was certain I knew the answer.

"He's a Packers fan," replied Harold with a wry smile. Harold knows I favor the Seahawks and looks forward to giving me a little jab when the Seahawks lose. Funny thing is that whenever the Packers lose, it's almost impossible to find Harold around town for the next several days, to give him what for in return.

"Who's the last name?"

"Rob Barker. He's a carpenter and came in a couple of months ago to fix the banister to the upstairs. I didn't know him until then. Got his name from Freddy Martin, who said he was an excellent finish carpenter."

"Rob Barker. The name sure sounds familiar. Where would I know him from?"

"He's from Ajax."

"Okay, now I know who you mean. He's the scrounger. His place is full of junk, looks like he's living in a landfill. I didn't know he ever worked for a living."

"He did good work and was neat as a pin. Didn't talk much. Seemed kind of shy. He didn't even warm up to Wilma, and Wilma's friends to everyone she ever met."

"You said he never showed any interest in the painting?" I asked.

"Not when we were around. But we went to Will Cook's funeral for about three hours that day he was working at the house."

"He was only there one day?"

"Yeah, that's all it took."

"It's a good start, Harold. We'll talk to each of them soon. Thanks for bringing in the list."

"I've got something else, Pete."

"What's that?"

"A picture of the picture."

"Oh."

"See, here, Wilma is standing beside it with our granddaughter Carly. I took a close-up to get the baby's face and got the picture real good too. It's a real pretty picture."

It was hard to see the detail of the painting on the small photograph Harold showed me. There was a rounded deep green vase holding a bouquet of yellow and purple flowers sitting atop a rock wall near a wooden gate. Harold's description of it as "fuzzy art" was right on target. The painting's lines were not distinct and objects seemed to mesh together.

After Harold left, Nick came in to report. As suspected, no usable fingerprints were found on the wall. He'd also called several pawn shops in the area to see if anyone had been trying to sell a painting—no one had, and called the Missoula and Butte police departments and asked that they check the hock shops there.

Nick had to go to Missoula the next afternoon to pick up some firearms we had repaired at the gunsmith, so I gave him Harold's photograph and asked him to stop by the art department at the university to see if someone could identify the painting.

"Pete, I called the hospital as you requested. Bridget Clews is over there now and has an appointment for the rest of the afternoon," Kay said as she brought a cup of coffee and small plate of trail mix to my desk. It was heavily loaded with M&Ms, which I love, so I took her gesture as a small peace offering. "So how was the video?" she asked sweetly.

"I didn't watch it," I said, trying to appear indifferent.

"Don't lie to me, Pete Benson. I haven't worked with you for close to twelve years without learning something about how you operate. Now, tell me the truth. You watched the video before you ate."

I wondered how she knew that. "Okay," I confessed. "Tell you the truth, I sounded a lot better than I thought I did."

"Yeah, Connie said it was good. Pastor Saltman told me the same thing. I'm surprised you haven't heard from more people around town."

"No doubt I will, thank you very much."

Just before five I went over to the hospital to interview Bridget Clews. I found her in an office outside the emergency room. She was an attractive brunette, about forty. Her voice was husky for a woman, and she was untroubled by my presence in her office. After the necessary introductions and two minutes of ritualized small talk, I cut right to the chase.

"Ms. Clews, I am investigating a burglary and I have a few questions for you."

"Does this involve one of my patients, Sheriff?"

"Yes."

"I'm sure you're aware of HIPAA regulations. I cannot divulge information about my patients' medical problems or treatment."

"I know, but that's not why I'm here, Ms. Clews. I'm interested in what you might know about the victim's home, their possessions, your acquaintances, and things of that nature."

"What...do you think I might be involved? I'm a nurse. I've spent my entire professional life helping people." Ms. Clews was obviously stunned by my question. I gave her a few seconds to compose her thoughts.

"I don't think anything, just yet. I'll make my mind up after I get the facts."

"Well, I'll tell you right now, I'm no thief. I drive a little fast once in a while, but that's the limit of my law breaking."

"That's good to know, but right now I'm interested in your relationship with the Johannsons."

"There's no relationship other than nurse-patient, Sheriff. I went to the house to monitor Wilma and help her with her physical therapy when she broke her hip. I was there twice a week for nine weeks starting, I believe, the last week of January."

"Harold said you were very good with Wilma, pushed her along and got her to do the therapy."

"That's true, Sheriff. It's what this job is all about, but we didn't become friends. Mrs. Johannson is a fine lady, but a little too talkative for me."

"When was the last time you were at their house?"

"It must be three and a half months ago by now. Let me check my calendar...yes, I was there the first week of April."

"I understand you admired their artwork?"

"I remember the Johannsons had a number of pictures, mostly landscapes I believe, and lots of pictures of their grandchildren."

"How about a painting on the living room wall?"

"I'm sorry, Sheriff, you're going to have to remind me. It's been a while since I was there."

"Some flowers in a vase on a rock wall."

"Oh my, yes. I remember that one. Is that what's been stolen?"

"Yes," I replied.

"It was quite nice," replied Ms. Clews. "I don't recall all the details, but it had an impressionist style to it."

"Do you know art?" I asked.

"I took an art appreciation class in college but I am hardly a connoisseur."

"Did you think the painting was valuable?"

"Oh, I wouldn't know. I just thought it was a nice, colorful picture. It's hard for me to believe it could be valuable."

"Why's that?"

"Well, look where it's at. In the home of a retired welder in Rodgersburg, Montana."

"There's a first time for everything."

"Maybe so. I don't think I thought about it, being valuable, I mean. I certainly don't know anyone with expensive art so I'm not sure I'd have the slightest clue about what it would look like."

"Could you tell me where you were at this past Friday, Saturday and Sunday?"

"I was out of town. My husband and I took one of those gambling excursions to Elko. We left Friday afternoon and got back late Sunday night, just before midnight."

I visited with Ms. Clews for a few more minutes but didn't learn anything of value. It was late so I called it a day. I got an early start the next morning. In fact, Kay was surprised to see me.

"Pete, did Nick get hold of you last night?"

"No."

"He called right after you left and said he struck out at the Art Department. The guy he needed, a Professor Rasmussen, left for Europe last week and will be gone for several weeks. Every summer he takes a group of students to Europe and visits art galleries."

"Tough duty, but I'm sure someone has to do it," I observed.

About that time Nick came through the door. "It wasn't a complete waste," he said. "The secretary of the Art Department gave me the name of another professor, guy by the name of Weir who'll be back in a couple of days. She thinks he'll be able to help. More importantly, I stopped by Brett Schuler's home. His mother told me he was here in Rodgersburg with Harold's grandson."

"Sorry," I replied. "Harold told me that Schuler was working here this summer. I forgot to pass it on."

With Nick's information, I decided to go over to Bob Johannson's home and find out where Brett Schuler was staying in Rodgersburg. Bob is Harold's oldest son. He was already at work but his wife Joyce met me at the door. After explaining the purpose for my visit, Joyce told me to sit down and she'd wake Brett. He joined me on the front porch for coffee and conversation. I could see why a man Harold Johansson's age wouldn't take to Schuler. He was a little hard for me to like as well. I took the long hair and earrings in stride, but he had a surly way about him and I found it hard to believe he could be friends with Danny Johannson, one of the most likeable kids Rodgersburg ever produced.

"Brett, I'll get right to the point. I am investigating a burglary. You were among those seen at the subject premises. So, where were you this past weekend?"

"Right here," he replied confidently. "Danny and I have been working at Carmichaels. I work in the RV Park. He works in the restaurant."

"Where were you at on Friday night?"

"Danny and I were out with the Moseley twins. We dropped them off about midnight and came straight home."

"Saturday and Sunday?" I asked.

"Same thing. On Saturday we all went to the rodeo in Winslow and stayed there for the street dance. Got home around 1:00 A.M. I got up and went to church with Danny's family Sunday morning, then we all went on a picnic and did some fishing on Big Antler Creek."

"Catch anything?"

"A mess of small brookies. Enough for supper."

"So Danny can vouch for your whereabouts all weekend?"

"Yes, yes he can. You said I was at the place that was robbed. Where's that?"

"The Johannson place," I said.

"Oh yeah, Danny's grandparents. What was stolen?"

"A painting of flowers on a rock wall. Remember it?" I asked.

"Nah," answered Brett slowly. "I've only been in the house a couple of times when Danny's had to drop something off. Never there for more than a few minutes."

"All right."

I paused momentarily and Brett asked, "Do you have any more questions, Sheriff?"

"No, good enough for me," I said as I got up to leave. The Schuler kid was pretty relaxed. I contrasted his style with that of Bridget Clews. She was poised; this guy, supremely confident. If he was involved, he was a good liar.

After interviewing Schuler, I decided to take a ride down to Ajax to visit the last suspect, Rob Barker.

Ajax is about fifteen miles east of Rodgersburg, a little more than half the way to Winslow. Just west of Ajax, the mountains come together to form a narrow canyon barely wide enough to accommodate Madison Creek, the railroad track and the highway. Limestone cliffs 200 feet high tower above the road. The locals call it "the Gap," and for the sixty seconds or so that it takes to pass through at highway speeds, it feels as if you're driving down the Grand Canyon. Then, suddenly, you're out of the canyon and into the lower valley. Ajax sits off the highway about a hundred yards, a hamlet with about seventy-five souls and twice as many dogs. Its business district includes the Ugly Bull Bar and Café and Freddy Martin's garage. Freddy is a diesel mechanic by trade, and an outstanding one at that, I am told. Every trucker and contractor in the county takes their big rigs to Freddy when they need to be repaired.

Rob Barker's place was about a half mile up the road from Freddy's. It backed up against a hillside thickly covered with lodgepole pine, of which over half were red instead of green. They were dead, victims of the mountain pine beetle which infested the area two years ago.

Barker's backyard was, literally, just junk from one fence line to the other. Old cars and trucks, equipment from the mines, timbers of all sorts, logging machinery, furniture, windows and door frames, the old steeple from the Marcusville church, and the list could go on. Barker had a ghost town in his backyard, disassembled for sure, but all of the pieces necessary for a town. And, he never paid a dime for any of it. Just helped himself, and nobody ever complained.

No one was home, so I backtracked to the Ugly Bull for a cup of coffee and to talk with Skinny Pinkerton, the owner. Skinny saw me at the door and had the coffee poured by the time I reached the stool.

"Sheriff, to what do I owe the pleasure?"

"I came down to visit your neighbor Mr. Barker, but he wasn't home. Have you seen him around?"

"Should be, unless he's out on one of his foraging expeditions. A good place to find him is the old Winslow dump. Sometimes he goes up Nugget Gulch around those old mines."

"I don't know him. What's your take on the guy?" I asked.

"Most people think he's a weird duck. But hardly anyone, including me, really knows the man. He keeps to himself...never comes in here."

"Oh?"

"About the only one he gets along with is Rasmussen. He's got that big, fancy cabin on Wolf Ridge."

"Rasmussen, where do I know that name from?"

"He's an art professor at the University in Missoula."

I felt a little tic of excitement, like the tumbler of a combination lock falling into place. "That's interesting. He hangs out with a guy like Barker?"

"Oh, yeah. They're good friends. About the only time Barker leaves here is to go shopping in Missoula on Saturday and have dinner with Rasmussen."

"Skinny, I thought you didn't know him that well."

"I don't, but Rasmussen comes in with his wife once in a while for dinner and I've overheard them talk about Barker. I remember, because I thought it odd that they would be breaking bread with Barker."

I made arrangements with Skinny to call the department when Barker showed up. Back at the office Kay handed me a note from Wini Ferkin, who has a little business doing clothing alterations. I didn't know her well, but Connie was a regular customer.

"What does Mrs. Ferkin want?" I asked.

"You. Specifically, she wants Pete Benson, renowned local vocalist, to sing at her daughter's wedding next month."

"Oh, great," I said with a combination of surprise and dismay. "Call her back and tell her that my repertoire consists of Old Man River, and Music of the Night."

After Kay departed, hopefully with enough information to kill my unwanted singing career, I picked up a biography of Henry Ford, which I had been picking through for the past several days, and finished the last twenty pages.

We didn't make much progress on "the case of the missing artwork" for the next couple days. Things were quiet except for a traffic accident when a truck plowed into a cow loose on the highway at night. Finally, on Friday Skinny

Pinkerton called to say that he'd seen Rob Barker on the road that morning.

I'd made the mistake of betting Kay lunch on the outcome of the Mariners–Yankees series, so I brought her along to have lunch at the Ugly Bull when we were through talking with Barker. When we drove up he was watering some plants in a flower box in his front yard. After the introductions, Barker invited us into the house for coffee. He was a short, wiry fellow with a full beard and it, like his hair, was salt and pepper, more salt. His hands were calloused but clean, as were his clothes. Given his local reputation, I expected much less.

When we stepped inside his house I was surprised again. Outside it looked like a shack, but inside it was spotless with some of the finest woodwork I'd ever seen. The kitchen cabinets were cherry; the living room done in oak. There were several large bookcases filled with books, a computer on a desk in the living room, but no TV. A number of paintings decorated the walls, mostly wildlife scenes and western landscapes. Barker came into the living room with a tray containing the coffee. After we'd all taken a cup Barker sat down on the couch opposite me.

"I trust this is not a social call, Sheriff. How can I help you?" His voice had a little edge to it. Maybe hesitancy would be more accurate.

"You're correct," I replied. "We're investigating a robbery at the Johannson residence where we understand you've done some work recently."

"They've been robbed! I am so sorry to hear that. They seemed to be very nice people. Can you tell me what was stolen?"

"Some art work. Can you tell me where you were at last Friday, Saturday, and Sunday, Mr. Barker?"

"Friday night I was here—alone. Saturday I went to Missoula to do my shopping. I usually have dinner with my friend Roy Rasmussen, but he's currently traveling in Europe. I got back here about 6:30. I saw Mrs. Quigley on the road coming in. She can verify that."

"Anna Quigley?" I asked.

"Yes, she and one of her daughters, Megan I believe, have been up at their cabin all week."

"Rasmussen? That name sounds kind of familiar."

"He has a cabin up on the ridge, Sheriff. I met him several years ago when he was building it. I sold him some barn board and did some finish carpentry for him. We've been friends ever since."

"Oh yeah, the guy from Helena whose place got vandalized last year. I was on vacation at the time—"

"No, you're mistaking him with the Bennings. Their place is up the road about another mile."

"Like I was about to say, I was on vacation and didn't actually meet the folks. Say," I said offhandedly, "where's this Rasmussen fellow from?"

"Missoula. He teaches at the U."

I paused momentarily to decide where to take the questioning, and Kay, as if on cue, started to ask Barker about the house. It gave me a chance to think. Barker was certainly congenial. The hesitancy I first noticed had disappeared. In fact, every one of the potential suspects in the case has been relaxed and straightforward. Typically, although not exclusively, when someone has something to hide, they get nervous, edgy, defensive, call it what you wish, and they telegraph it with their body, if not their speech. When you've been in the business as long as I have, you develop a good sense of when people are either lying or have something to hide.

After Barker finished explaining how he salvaged his hardwood flooring from an old school building which was being demolished, I restarted the interview by asking, "And how about Sunday, Mr. Barker. Where were you?"

"I got up late, had breakfast, then hiked to Alpine Lake to go fishing. Spent the day and came out in the evening, before dark."

"Anyone see you?"

"No one that would know me. I passed a couple from Butte in an old pickup and a big SUV with New Mexico plates."

"Mr. Barker, I'm picking up the trace of an accent in your voice," Kay said. "Where are you from originally?"

"Boston. I came out here when I was twenty-two and never went back except to visit family," Barker answered.

"You certainly seem to be a reader," she replied. "Some of the books here look like old college textbooks."

"They are. I went to Dartmouth. Studied philosophy."

"Tough degree to find work in hereabouts," I interjected.

"I never tried, Sheriff. I like wood work and my needs are pretty simple. I work a few days each month to get by."

At that point, Kay started to cough and between spasms asked Barker for a glass of water. When he had left the room she motioned toward the bookcase behind me. I turned around for a quick look and there on the two bottom shelves were forty or fifty volumes with the words art or painting in their titles. Barker returned with Kay's water, and once she'd settled her cough, I began questioning him once more.

"I couldn't help but admire your artwork, Mr. Barker. I particularly like that set of four paintings with the wolves. Did you do them?"

"No, I wish I had that kind of talent, Sheriff. I purchased them at an estate sale in Bigfork several years ago. My contribution was to reframe the pictures so they would match the interior of the room."

"You did a nice job." I replied. I looked for a painting in the same style as the one stolen and finally saw one. "What's that seascape?"

"It's a print of a painting entitled 'The Harbor at Lorient.' It's a Morisot."

"Morisot?" I asked with a puzzled tone.

"Berthe Morisot. He's a French impressionist. Personally, I've never much cared for that style of painting but my mother dearly loved it. I brought that one with me three years ago, after she passed away."

"I am so sorry for your loss," injected Kay quickly.

"Thank you," he said. When no one spoke, Barker continued. "She suffered horribly. A gas barbecue exploded and she was badly burned. I think death was a comfort."

"That's terrible," I added.

We made small talk for a few more minutes, thanked Barker for his cooperation, and departed. As we started down the sidewalk to the car, I shot a last glance into the living room window. Barker was standing deep in the room away from the glass, watching us. I suspect he never took his eyes off us until we reached the county road.

Once we were safely away, I announced, "Fifteen minutes

ago I had Barker as a potential suspect just because of his relationship with Rasmussen. Now, I think he's our man."

"Because he reads art books?" asked Kay in response.

"Well, yes and no. The art books are part of it. So is the fact that he's a masterful frame builder. I've tried building picture frames and it's no simple task. And then there's Rasmussen."

"Sounds pretty flimsy to me, Pete," answered Kay with what I've come to know as her cynical voice.

"There's more," I replied. "What does it for me is his knowledge of art. That takes us back to the books but particularly his experience with French impressionists."

"He said he didn't like impressionists," Kay said.

"But he knows what they are," I answered. "It would take a trained eye to recognize a genuine piece of that type of art, particularly out here, next to nowhere. Now, it's a matter of putting Barker at the scene of the crime or finding the painting and tying it back to him some way."

"No small task, Pete," observed Kay as I turned the squad car into the parking area in front of the Ugly Bull.

True to my word, I bought lunch and while there, I hired Skinny's fourteen-year-old son to watch Barker's cabin for the next few hours until I could organize a more thorough surveillance. I gave him an extra cell phone and told him to call us if Barker left the house. Kay and I returned to the office and I rounded up some members of the Sheriff's Reserve to keep a watch on Barker.

Nick came in around 4:30 p.m. and reported on his meeting with Professor Weir earlier that morning.

"The Professor said the painting looked as if it were done by a French impressionist," Nick said.

"Is it valuable?" I asked.

"Could be if it's an original."

"Did he name an amount?"

"No, but I told him it was an oil painting, not a print, and that Harold's dad had brought it back from France after the war. He told me there was a lot of art that was either destroyed or stolen by the Germans, but if this painting were an original, it might be worth several thousand dollars. Professor Weir said he'd check into it and see if he could get a line on the painting. He'll let us know next week."

"Sounds to me like motive enough for burglary," Kay added.

Following our conversation, I walked over to the County Attorney's office to get a search warrant. While the paperwork was being prepared, I called Judge Pollard's office to let him know what was coming. The judge's secretary reported that His Honor had slipped out early for a round of golf and wasn't expected back at the office. With that advice Tom Wilson, our County Attorney, and I drove over to Cottonwood, a town about fifty miles distant, where the judge lived. After I explained the situation, the judge approved the search of Barker's home but thought it too much of a stretch to enter Rasmussen's residence. We parted with the judge's promise that if we could find something to tie in Rasmussen, he'd be happy to revisit the issue.

When I got back to the office I found a note from Kay. It said, "Wini was delighted that you will sing at the wedding. It will be on Saturday, August 29th at St. Bart's. She'll send over the music. Joanie Claridge is the accompanist."

All of a sudden, I had this empty feeling in my gut. What had I gotten myself into? I'd have to deal with it later. There was a search warrant to execute.

After getting a bite to eat, I drove back to Ajax and met my posse consisting of Nick and two men from the Sheriff's Reserve. We showed up at Barker's home about 9:30 P.M. He was clearly surprised by our visit but remained cordial. As we entered the house, he stepped over to his computer and shut it off.

"I am perplexed by your action, Sheriff. I was completely forthcoming with you the other day when you visited with Ms....Ms. Best, is that right?"

"Yes, Kay Best," I replied. "She runs the office." I paused, saying no more with the expectation that my silence would cause Barker to continue talking. Instead, he bobbed his head a couple of times and turned toward the kitchen.

"Mr. Barker," I continued, "would you mind if I looked through your art books? I don't know much about the subject."

"No, fine, help yourself. Just leave them on the desk. I'll reshelf them." Barker moved into the kitchen, poured himself a glass of water out of the tap, leaned back against the sink, and watched me as I started to comb through his bookshelf.

The books were arranged in groups by time period or type of art. There were several books on Western art and I took a few minutes to look through a book about Frederic Remington. There were several volumes on Charlie Russell, Montana's most famous painter. I found books on Baroque art, Renaissance art, the American School, Expressionism, and finally two volumes dealing with French Impressionism. I pulled out both, climbed into a nearby easy chair and slowly paged my way through the contents. The color reproductions of paintings were first class and, in short order, I became superficially acquainted with the works of Monet, Degas, Cezanne, Gauguin, Seurat, Renoir, Matisse, and numerous lesser known artists. But, I never saw anything resembling a vase of yellow and purple flowers on a rock wall.

One of the books was published in 1936, the other in 1977. If the Johannsons' painting was important, surely it would be represented in one of the volumes. There were prints of over 200 paintings between them. I felt a sense of defeat course through my body. Why I talked myself into believing the Johannsons' painting was valuable, I'll never know.

Barker poked his head through the door of the kitchen and asked if I wanted anything to drink. I said no, and then Barker came out and sat down in the chair across from me.

"What do you expect to find from your search, Sheriff?" Barker asked softly. He didn't display any hostility or irritation, which was surprising because every other time I've been involved in a search, the homeowner gets anxious, some because they're guilty of the crime, others because they're fearful the search team will break something, and still others because we'll find something that causes personal embarrassment. You'd be amazed by the number of people who have extensive lingerie collections and various instruments crafted from latex to enhance their bedroom gymnastics.

"To be truthful with you, Mr. Barker, something that ties you to the Johannsons' missing painting," I said in reply to his question. "You're the only person who has been in Harold and Wilma's house who knows anything about art."

"So that makes me a suspect?" asked Barker as he looked me directly in the eyes. His eyes had that "deer in the headlights" look, as if he continued to be surprised by our search of his home.

"Well, yeah," I answered. Think about where we're at—Rhyolite County, Montana—mining, logging, and ranching country. Not too many people in this part of the world know anything about art. It would be easier to find someone who knows about diamonds."

"I get your point. Hopefully this will be over soon and my innocence established to your satisfaction, Sheriff."

"We'll see," I replied.

The boys searched the house for a good hour and a half, but to no avail.

"I think we're about done here, Mr. Barker, except for one thing."

"What's that, Sheriff?" he asked.

"We're going to impound your computer and look over the files."

"You can't do that. It's my only way of communicating with the outside world."

"You can use the phone for a day or two—I see you've got one."

"But what if you damage it? What if my files are lost?"

"Don't worry, we'll take good care of it."

Barker's hurry to shut off the computer and his subsequent agitation over our wanting to check its contents told me there was something he didn't want us to see. Finally, a crack in his veneer. Throughout the search Barker had remained completely composed, too composed if you ask me. He knew there was nothing in the house for us to find but he didn't count on us taking his computer. I moved from a gut hunch about Barker being the perp, to a strong belief that he was our guy. Now all I needed to do was find some real evidence to prove it. No small task, but I'd have to think my way through that tomorrow.

My suspicion of Barker was confirmed the next afternoon when Frank Morgan, the computer whiz-bang from the state crime lab in Missoula, opened up the e-mail files. There were two short e-mails to Rasmussen at his University address. The first, from Wednesday before the crime said, Project on schedule.

And, the second from Sunday afternoon read, Parcel delivered.

It was a skimpy tie, but the judge gave us the okay to search Rasmussen's cabin in Ajax as well as his home in Missoula. To my surprise, the search of the cabin turned up nothing, so Nick and I went to his house in Missoula, picking up a couple of Missoula police officers along the way to assist us with the search.

Mrs. Rasmussen answered the door. I handed her the search warrant and explained its purpose. She was clearly shaken by the reason for our visit but invited us in without a fuss. I stayed with her while the officers started the search.

"Sheriff, what you're saying doesn't make any sense. Roy has spent his whole life either conserving art or teaching others about it. He's never stolen a thing in his life. What could he possibly gain by doing such a thing?"

"Money, Mrs. Rasmussen. I never met a thief yet who stole something just so that he could have it around and enjoy it. Things get stolen and then they get sold for cash. That's the long and short of it, ma'am."

"We have no need for money, Sheriff. Roy's salary is decent and I have a substantial inheritance from my father."

I was about to ask what would happen to the money if she were not in the picture, but just then one of the Missoula police officers assisting our search team interrupted. "Sheriff, is this what you're looking for?" he asked. "Heavens no," replied Mrs. Rasmussen. "That was done by our friend, Rob. He delivered it here Saturday evening." "Rob, Rob Barker?" I asked. "Yes," answered Mrs. Rasmussen. "I ran into him at the hardware store that morning. He told me he had a painting for my husband and was planning to stop by. I had some other errands so I told Rob to come by after four." "I thought your husband was in Europe, Mrs. Rasmussen." "He is, Sheriff, but Rob is an old and dear friend. He frequently dines with us when Roy is in town."

I took a few seconds to examine the painting. It was a landscape of an alpine lake not far from Barker's home, and very well done, I might add. I turned the painting over in my hands to look at it from several angles. The frame seemed to be stouter than normal. Then I spotted it, a little bubble at the edge of the canvas and what looked like another piece of canvas below it. It took a while to remove the top layer, but sure enough, the Johannsons' painting was underneath.

All of the color drained out of Mrs. Rasmussen's face. She muttered a low "excuse me" and walked, unsteadily, over to a buffet and pulled out a bottle of Maker's Mark.

I called Captain Kelly at the Missoula Police Department and asked him to go through Interpol and have Rasmussen arrested. I then called Kay at the office and told her to have the reserve deputy who was watching Barker's house arrest him. Nick and I took the painting back to Rodgersburg. Harold identified the painting as his and we put it in the evidence vault until we could sort everything out.

Even though we had found the painting, I was troubled about the case. If Barker had the painting on Saturday as Mrs. Rasmussen said, then he either did the job Friday or someone else did. Somehow I couldn't see Barker beating in the back door. He would have found an easier and less noisy way of breaking in.

Sunday and Monday, Nick and I both worked the case, principally checking and rechecking alibis. On Tuesday morning, Professor Weir called Nick with the information on the painting. We were ready to put the case to bed. Nick pulled all of the suspects in for another interview. We started with Brett Schuler.

"Sit down, Brett. I have some more questions about the Johannson burglary."

"I told you where I was," he replied.

"Yeah, you did, but you also left out some important details. Now, because of your age, I am willing to cut you some slack, but if you don't want to play ball, you'll be going to the state penitentiary for a long time. This is grand theft, kid, and that means a lot of time. If you're lucky you might be out before you're thirty."

"I've already told you everything I know." Schuler didn't have the same sense of confidence I'd seen in our previous conversation. It was time to press hard.

"Not good enough, Brett," I said loudly. "I know you were at the Johannsons Friday night with Danny, and I am sure you were there again on Saturday night after you got back from Winslow. According to the Moseley girls, you left the party at the campground for about a half hour to buy beer. That was plenty of time to break into Johannsons' place. Do you want me to continue?"

"I didn't do anything," he protested.

"Look, Brett, we've already got Barker and we know he didn't do this alone."

"I think I need a lawyer," he responded, but I could see he didn't have the stomach for hard ball.

"That's up to you, but I am prepared to go to the county attorney and ask for probation in exchange for the rest of the information."

"For sure, no jail time?"

"That's right," I guaranteed.

Brett swallowed hard. "Okay, Sheriff, here it is. I took the picture Friday night before we met the girls. Danny and I stopped by to help his grandfather load the car for their trip. When they were in the front yard saying goodbye, I went back in the house, took the picture, and slipped it outside the back door when Danny locked up the house. I put it in the trunk of my car. Danny never noticed it was missing."

"Then what?"

"Just like I said before, later than night Danny and I went to Ajax with the Moseley twins. I stepped out of the bar for a few minutes and put the picture next to the side wall of the saloon and called Barker on the cell phone to come by and pick it up."

"How did the door get busted?"

"I did that Saturday night to make it look like a break-in."

"And Barker was to sell the goods?" I asked.

"No," Schuler replied, "he was just the runner."

"Responsible for getting the painting to Rasmussen," I added, largely as a guess.

"Right. Rasmussen was supposed to sell the goods. He told us it would bring $10,000 and we'd split it $2,500 each."

"Each? Who got the other quarter?" I asked, clearly puzzled by his previous statement.

Brett shook his head. "I don't ..."

"Who, Brett?" I demanded as I slammed my hand on the desk.

"My aunt, Bridget Clews. She spotted the painting in Johannsons' house and put the whole thing together with Rasmussen. She's been seeing him on the side for a couple of years, after she met him at the Ugly Bull."

"Brett, your mother is going to be very disappointed in you."

"Not as disappointed as Mrs. Rasmussen. She's been such a sucker."

"You've done pretty well in that regard yourself, Brett."

"What do you mean?" he asked.

"The painting. You were going to get $2,500. It's worth a fortune."

"What?" Brett gasped.

"Truth is, it's an original by some guy named Henri Fantin-Latour, a famous French artist. It's been missing since World War II, but according to Professor Weir, who's a colleague of your friend Rasmussen, the painting is worth at least a million. You work too cheap, Brett."

CHAPTER FIVE

A Concert for One

It was a beautiful Tuesday afternoon in early October. I had just returned to the office after lunch at the Rodgersburg Elementary School. As Sheriff of Rhyolite County, I try to visit both the grade and high schools once a month. It gives me a chance to talk with the staff about children who are having problems and who may be headed for a showdown with the criminal justice system. More importantly, it gives me the opportunity to get to know the kids and, hopefully, help a youngster avoid meeting me in the professional discharge of my duties.

Kay Best, my office manager, handed me a stack of invoices for approval and I was thumbing through them at the counter when the front door opened and I was face-to-face with a hysterical Philomena Corrigan.

She was out of breath. "Sheriff...Sheriff...I am so glad you're here. You must help me."

"Kay, could you get some water for Miss Corrigan?"

"Certainly."

I took Philomena by the hand and escorted her to a chair. "Come in, Miss Corrigan. Sit here. Take a few seconds to catch your breath."

"Thank you, Sheriff," she replied, more composed. "You must help me."

"Now, what's the problem, Ms. Corrigan?"

"My harp! It's been stolen, Sheriff!" Ms. Corrigan's face was a portrait of fright, almost to the point of panic. She took a deep breath and was about to say something when Kay returned with the water.

"Miss Corrigan, here's some water," said Kay softly. She then put her hand on Ms. Corrigan's shoulder to steady her.

Philomena is a relative newcomer to Rodgersburg, arriving three years ago from Chicago where she had retired as harpist with the Chicago Symphony. She's a tall woman, nearly six feet, with short, almost uniformly white hair. I would guess her somewhere between sixty-five and seventy years of age. You wouldn't call her pretty; perhaps striking was the better word. She lives quietly with a big Saint Bernard and an extensive flower garden. Each December she puts on a concert to raise money for the Rodgersburg Hospital Auxiliary. She's a virtuoso on the harp and the concert attracts people from miles around.

"Now Ms. Corrigan, please slow down for a minute and tell me what happened from the beginning."

"I'm sorry, Sheriff, and please call me Philomena. My harp. It means so much to me."

"Certainly," added Kay, "but the sheriff can't be of much help if you're upset.

Ms. Corrigan stood up, smoothed her black wool skirt, sat down, and turned to me. "I'm fine now...let me think... what happened. I got up this morning at the usual time, about 7:30, had breakfast and fed Russo, that's my dog. I wrote a couple of letters to friends back in Chicago—email, actually. Then I went in and practiced on my harp. I do that every morning when I'm home.

"So the harp was still safe this morning?" I asked to verify the facts.

"Oh, yes. After practicing, I changed clothes and went to the Garden Society meeting at the Huggy Bear. We meet once a month for lunch and have a guest speaker."

Philomena's mention of the Huggy Bear Café brought a smile to my face. The restaurant's name was the creation of Caroline Mathers, daughter of the owners, Jake and Marissa Mathers. When Caroline was a toddler she dragged a small black teddy bear with her wherever she went. She frequently hugged the bear and it soon became known as Caroline's Huggy Bear. Caroline's now in college and the bear sits in a glass case hanging on the wall above the restaurant's cash register with a brass plaque affixed which says "OUR FOUNDER."

The Huggy Bear is a favorite eating place for the ladies of Rodgersburg. The menu features a wide variety of salads and ethnic foods not found in the town's other cafés, which tend toward man-sized meals, with an emphasis on meat and potatoes.

"When did you leave the house?"

"I think it was about ten minutes to twelve, Sheriff, and I got back home around 1:30. That's when I discovered it was gone. I had bought this tole painting of a little girl with her dog and took it into the solarium. My harp was gone."

"Had you left the doors open or were they forced open?" I inquired.

Philomena suddenly looked puzzled. "Oh, my. I guess I don't know. The front door was fine. I went through it when I came home, but I didn't look at the side door. I just panicked and came rushing down here."

My first thought was to send a deputy down to her house in chance that the thief might still be in the neighborhood, but then realized that all of the officers on duty were working in the nether parts of the county. The only staff I had in town was Kay and myself. Instead, I asked, "Can you describe the instrument?"

"Certainly Sheriff, it's my baby. It's a custom built Style 26 Concert Grand Harp, made by Lyon and Healey. The forepost is hand-carved maple with relief work at the top and bottom of the column. The relief has a Gothic look to it."

"Oh," I replied, not quite sure what Philomena meant. Gothic cathedrals I might be able to recognize; gothic harps were another matter. Fortunately, I don't think there will be much of a problem picking it out from all of the other harps likely to be floating around Rhyolite County.

Philomena continued talking unaware of my momentary lapse of interest. "The harp is gilded with 23 karat gold leaf and there are a number of delicate floral decorations made of rosewood inlaid on the sound board."

I didn't like the sound of 23 karat gold leaf. Usually, we don't have sophisticated criminals who would know the full value of an expensive instrument. I visualized the harp in someone's garage with a couple of dirtbags using a chisel to scrape off $50 worth of gold. I didn't want to go there.

As I came back to the moment, I heard Philomena say, "It has forty-seven strings stretching from zero octave G to seventh octave C."

I felt myself crack a smile at the thought of putting that information into a description to be sent out to all of the law enforcement agencies in the northwestern United States. Perhaps Philomena thinks we're going to have the musicians' union investigate the case. Stop being cynical, I told myself mentally. She's a charming lady, an expert in her field and she just doesn't realize that detailed technical information about the instrument's qualities isn't helpful to us.

"There are seven foot pedals and each pedal has three positions which you use to control the tone of each note from sharp to flat," continued Philomena. "The tonal quality ..."

"Excuse me, Miss Corrigan...sorry, Philomena, you're getting a little too sophisticated for me here," I interrupted. "My deputies tend toward twangy guitars and drums and I don't think they are apt to appreciate the tonal qualities of your instrument."

"Sheriff, I..." Then Philomena broke out into a big smile and chuckled lightly, saying "I suppose you're right. I got a little carried away."

"No problem, Philomena. How about some more basic information. How tall is it?"

"Seventy-four and one-quarter inches," she said, smiling.

"Okay," I replied, flashing a smile as well. "A little over six feet. How wide? Weight?"

"It weighs eighty-one pounds and is thirty-eight and five-eighths inches wide. You can't get it through a standard doorway, width-wise."

"Thank you. How about a serial number?"

"It's on a little brass plate down near the foot pedals and, sorry, but I don't know the number. I'll have to get it from my insurance policy."

"That's fine, you can always call it into the office. Is there anything else that would help us identify it?"

Philomena paused for a moment. "Oh, yes, my name is on it, inlaid in the bottom of the sound box, about chest high. It says Philomena Corrigan, Chicago Symphony."

"Where is the sound box?" I asked. I thought a harp was just a bunch of strings pulled tight between two boards.

"Sheriff, the very top of the harp is a very strong piece of curved wood referred to as the neck, and sometimes as the gooseneck. The harp strings extend down from the neck to the sound board which makes up the sloping bottom piece of the harp. The sound board is also the top of the sound box and makes up the belly of the harp. It's the part right next to the harpist."

"I see," not quite sure if I did or not.

"When a harp string is plucked it causes the sound board to vibrate. The sound box is also called the resonator and it causes the sound to reverberate. Harps work on the same acoustic principles as do the violin, cello, or guitar."

"Okay, now I get it," and finally did. "What is the estimated value of the instrument?"

"About sixty thousand dollars."

"Now I better understand your anxiety. I was thinking it was maybe ten grand."

"Ten thousand can buy you a smaller instrument, something like you might find in a university music education program, but true concert harps are much more expensive. Actually, my harp is only a mid-range model, at least in terms of price. Lyon and Healey produce an instrument called the 'Louis XV' which retails for about $130,000."

"Must be nice," is all I could think to say, feeble as it sounded to me.

"Nice doesn't begin to describe it," replied Philomena lightly. "It's unbelievable. The tonal quality is simply exquisite. Far better than my...sorry again, Sheriff. You don't need a lesson on harps."

"Oh, quite to the contrary. I am certain that in the last ten minutes I just became the harp expert among Montana's law enforcement officers."

Philomena chuckled again. Then her face got more serious. "Why would anyone steal a harp?"

Kay brought herself back into the conversation. "Most thieves try to sell what they steal. I don't think we've got too many frustrated harpists in Rodgersburg looking for a good instrument to play."

"Oh, my God!" came Philomena's panicked reply. "That harp is my life."

Kay made Philomena a cup of tea. After Philomena regained her composure, Kay drove her back home. I followed in the squad car, bringing along the evidence kit to conduct an on-site investigation. It didn't take too long to figure out what had happened. The side door opening into the kitchen was secured with a flimsy lock set. A couple of wood shavings at the foot of the door indicated that the thief had pried the door open using a knife with a fairly stout blade. Russo, Philomena's dog, was lying on the floor inside the kitchen. He raised his head, looked at me for a second or two, and put it back down. Not much of a watchdog, I thought to myself.

"Russo must like you, Sheriff," said Philomena. "He barks at most men."

"That's Pete," injected Kay lightly, "friend to all of the creatures of God's realm, except during hunting season."

Once inside, it was about twenty steps to the solarium where the thief picked up the instrument and carted it out through the kitchen door. Kay asked Philomena to brew a pot of coffee and she disappeared into the kitchen while we looked over the crime scene.

"Two things right away," commented Kay nonchalantly.

"What's that?" I inquired.

"The thief was a stout male, strong enough to pick up a heavy, awkward contraption and carry it out the door. Look at the carpet. There is no indication the harp was dragged across the floor. No woman, at least no woman from around these parts could have moved the harp that way."

"It could have been two women," I said casually just to bait Kay along a bit.

"Uh, no," came Kay's matter-of-fact reply. "Women only play harps. They don't steal them."

"I am detecting just a trace of gender bias in that statement, Mrs. Best, but I am willing to accept your premise as a working hypothesis, at least for the moment."

"A working hypothesis my foot. Nothing but the facts, Sherlock," she answered lightly as she beamed me a big smile.

"Okay, Watson, and your second observation would be?"

"The thief is a local. Look here." Kay stooped down and showed me a small clod of mud on the edge of the carpet. It had a rich brown texture but the giveaway was a piece of straw embedded in the mud.

"I defer to your investigating prowess, Watson. Looks like one of our local ranch hands has taken a liking to string music."

"One who appreciates fine tonal quality," whispered Kay with a smile and a hint of guilt while she looked toward the kitchen to insure that Philomena hadn't heard her. I struggled for a moment trying not to laugh.

I excused myself and checked the side door for fingerprints, finding and lifting several, but after quickly inspecting Philomena's hands decided they were most likely hers, although I would do a full comparison back at the office.

Kay stayed to have coffee with Philomena while I walked around the neighborhood to find out if anyone had seen anything. There was no one home at the two houses on either side of the Corrigan residence. I had better luck across the street.

"Sheriff, good afternoon. How may I help you?"

"Mrs. Elkins," I replied, "I am working on a little matter of a break-in at Ms. Corrigan's home earlier today, sometime between noon and 1:30 P.M. I was wondering if you happened to see anything?"

"Philomena, is she all right?" Mrs. Elkins asked in reply, a look of concern crossing her face.

"She wasn't hurt," I tried to reassure her. "Ms. Corrigan was gone at the time of the break-in but she's obviously very distressed."

"I must go to her," answered Mrs. Elkins.

"And, I want you to, Mrs. Elkins, but right now you could help her most by telling me what you saw, if anything."

Mrs. Elkins relaxed a bit and then rubbed her chin while she tried to recall the past couple of hours. "At the noon hour... hmm...come to think of it, I did. The UPS man was here about that time. I was standing here on the steps just like I am with you. There was a truck parked in Philomena's driveway."

"Can you describe it?" I asked hoping that we might get a decent lead.

"I'm not real good with cars and trucks Sheriff, but I remember it was white and it had one of those campers on the back."

"The camper, anything special that you can remember?"

"No," answered Mrs. Elkins quickly, "except that it was also white."

"Did you see anybody around the house?"

"No, but it was odd about the truck. It was backed in the driveway at an angle like someone was going to load something from the back step of the house."

"That's what they did, Mrs. Elkins. They loaded Ms. Corrigan's harp."

"Oh, my!" exclaimed Mrs. Elkins. "That'll about kill Philomena. The harp and Russo, her dog, they're her children. I must go help her, Sheriff."

"I'm sure she'd love your company, Mrs. Elkins, and thank you for your assistance. It was very helpful."

Rather than wait for additional information about the truck, I went back to the squad car and radioed the office with instructions to put out an APB, asking that all white trucks with white campers be stopped. I then went back to my canvass of the neighborhood and picked up another clue at the Klein house two doors down from the Elkins place.

"Did I see a white truck at Ms. Corrigan's place today?" answered Ben Klein echoing the question I put to him a few seconds before. "I'm sure I did. Yeah. I did," confirmed Ben thoughtfully. "It was in the driveway. I didn't think much of it. Miss Corrigan has some friends from Missoula that have one of those big Fords with duals on the back."

"With a white camper?" I probed.

"No, with a white topper," answered Klein. "I was walking home, oh, maybe six or seven weeks ago...maybe like around Labor Day. I know it was hot, and when I came by Philomena's house that dog of hers started to bark. She was with a couple by her back door and she yelled at the dog to stop. All of them came walking out to the sidewalk and she introduced me to them. Like I said, friends from Missoula. I think the rig I saw today was the same one I saw then."

"You wouldn't happen to remember their names?" I asked.

"You would ask me that," Klein replied again, pausing to ponder his answer. "Not exactly. It was something like Parsons, Pearson, Parkinson, Rierson. I know it ended in 'son' and was a P or an R word. He was a good-sized fellow, looked to be quite a bit younger than Philomena and the woman he was with, who I took to be his wife, she was pretty big too."

"Did you find out anything else about them?" I continued.

"Not really. It was one of those ritualized meetings where you both say you're glad to meet the other, but neither of you ever expects to see the other party again. About the only thing Philomena said was 'Ben, meet my friends,' whatever their names were, 'they're from Missoula' and then that damned dog of hers started to bark again, so I took off."

It was after 4:00 P.M. when Kay and I returned to the office. I decided to accelerate the search process so I called Bob White at the Rhyolite News and Shopper and gave him the story. His paper appears weekly on Wednesday, and he promised me a front page headline the next day. As I hung up the phone, Kay buzzed me from her desk and said, "Call from Jim Watters, insurance adjuster from Missoula."

Watters wanted to talk with me about Philomena's harp. She had called him earlier in the afternoon. I explained that Ms. Corrigan had reported the harp stolen and that we had started an investigation and had a couple of leads but no suspects.

Before he hung up, Watters made an interesting comment. "Well, Sheriff, I hope you find the darned thing. This company is getting tired of paying for new harps. This is the third time where one of her harps has either gone missing or was seriously damaged."

"What can you tell me about that?" I asked.

"Nothing," replied Watters. "All I have access to in the computer is her claim history. There's no explanation of the claims other than the amount and date paid."

I repeated Watters' information to Kay as well as Ben Klein's report about Philomena having friends from Missoula who drive a white truck with a similarly colored canopy.

"You don't think..." Kay started to say and then stopped.

"Think what?" I replied.

"That Philomena could be involved in this some way. I mean, she was really upset about the harp. I don't think that was something she could fake."

"Well, that's the way I read it too, but we have to look at all angles. Maybe we have a situation where the friends lift the harp and Philomena files an insurance claim. She gets the harp back later, tells the world it's a new machine, and splits the insurance proceeds with her friends. There are cons like this all the time."

"But, this is Philomena, Pete," continued Kay. "I can't see it."

"I respect your opinion, Kay, but check her financial records anyway. Let's see if she needs money," I instructed.

Just then the phone rang again. It was Nick Colusa, my deputy based in Winslow. "Wait a minute," I said. "I am going to put you on the speaker phone so Kay can hear you as well and we can make a note or two. Can you hear me okay?"

"Loud and clear," Nick replied.

"So give it to me from the top," I directed.

"There's a white pickup and camper parked on Harrison Street next to Winslow Park. It's got a Billings license plate," answered Nick.

"Maybe you found our harp thief."

"It gets better, Pete. Guess whose truck is parked right alongside—Fred Shandy's."

I shuddered, a momentary flash of apprehension. "You mean, Freddy the Wolf?"

"The very same."

"Anybody around?"

"No," replied Nick. "I think they're inside the Hideaway having a few beers, or maybe over at the Homestead getting a bite to eat."

"Any backup available?" My brain went into high gear. I am not sure I'd send three men against the Wolf, much less one.

"No. That's why I called. The Highway Patrol is tied up. Can you send some help?"

"I'll get a team rounded up. We should be there in forty-five minutes. Meantime, pull out of sight, but stay where you can watch the camper. If they come out of the saloon, keep on the camper and let us know where you are going. We can always find the Wolf."

Nick was playing heads-up ball. The prospect of having Wolf Shandy involved in this thing was a decided turn for the worse. Wolf was aptly named. He was a violent predator who'd spent most of his life since age twelve either in reform school or prison, the last time for aggravated assault. It should have been a murder rap, but his victim was too tough to die. Between prison stays the Wolf bunks with his aged mother in Winslow. He got out of prison eight months ago and had been a good boy since then, but I knew it wouldn't last.

I quickly rounded up two reserve deputies and the two Rodgersburg deputies on duty, and the five of us made the trip to Winslow. Before leaving town I called County Attorney Tom Wilson to get us a search warrant for both vehicles. We had probable cause to search the camper but I wanted the I's dotted and the T's crossed, if there was any prospect that Wolf was a player. We met up with Nick behind the Hideaway Bar. He already had the search warrant which the County Attorney had faxed to Nick's patrol car.

"Any developments?" I asked.

"Nothing much," murmured Nick quietly. He always seems to power down just before we make a bust, particularly if it's likely to get ugly. I think it's his way of getting focused. Nick is six feet four inches tall, two hundred forty pounds of muscle, packs a smile as big as the outdoors, and is almost impossible to anger. The people who know him think of Nick as a big teddy bear. But when he puts on his game face, Nick is all cop, and there is nobody I'd rather have at my side than Nick, especially when I've got to quell a brawling bunch of drunks in a tavern.

"I called the saloon and the café to find out where Wolf was at," he continued. "According to Sheila, he's in the café with some bearded guy, having dessert with coffee and a pack of Marlboros."

"That's too bad," I observed. Unlike Nick I get excited and tend to speak faster as I get ready for action. "We could have busted him for violating his parole, if he'd been in the Hideaway."

"Well, we won't have to wait long," interjected Nick. "The Homestead will be closing in about twenty minutes."

I stationed one of the reserve officers in an unmarked car outside the Homestead Café with instructions to radio us as soon as Wolf and his companion left the restaurant. Nick took up position behind a large ash tree in the park while I waited between the two vehicles. The other officers were stationed nearby to cut off any escape routes. The minutes ticked by slowly. Then, the speaker on my hand held radio came to life. "This is Car 9. The two suspects are on their way."

I could hear both their footsteps on the concrete sidewalk as well as their conversation. Wolf was in an expansive mood. Long a Green Bay fan, Wolf was recounting the highlights of last Sunday's game to his walking partner.

"Evening, Wolf," I said forcefully. "I don't think I've met your companion here." Wolf drew his eyes into tight slits and the vein on the right side of his neck started to bulge out from the skin. "Don't even think about it, Wolf. Nick's behind you with a thirty-eight pointed at the middle of your back and there are several more boys nearby."

Wolf just continued to stare. The bearded fellow backed up to the door of his pickup and put his hands into the air. "Nick," I shouted, "the Wolf man doesn't believe me."

"Go ahead, Wolf," answered Nick, just loud enough so that Wolf could hear.

"I can take a hint," snarled Wolf as he slowly raised his hands.

"Now back up slowly, Wolf." Nick spoke very calmly. "Now, down on your knees...Good, Wolf. Now down on your stomach with your hands behind you."

When Wolf was down, I stepped behind him and locked the cuffs in place. We then repeated the process with his partner, a fellow who said his name was Jason Stillson.

As we stood the two of them up in the dim orange light of the nearby street lamp, Wolf very much resembled his namesake, with high cheek bones, an angular face, and sharply pointed nose. I was once told that he was nick-named Wolf as a youngster because he had two oversized canine teeth in his upper jaw. For as long as I'd known him, he sported a pasty complexion commonly seen in convicts who spend most of the daylight hours indoors. Wolf was slender but his entire body was a rope of muscle and sinew, and the man seemed oblivious to pain. I had once seen him hit across the face with a bar stool. The blow slammed him back against the wall, and then he shook it off as if he'd only been slapped and jumped back into the fray. It took four men to get him in cuffs that night.

If Nick hadn't had the heat pointed squarely at Wolf's back, there is no telling what would have happened. With the steel bracelets on, we could all rest a little easier.

"Mind telling me what this is all about, Sheriff?" Wolf sounded almost cordial.

"Got the word that a white pickup with a camper was parked outside the scene of a burglary a few hours back. Seeing your truck here tonight, just naturally raised our curiosity. So now we're going to take a thorough look."

"That ain't my pickup, it belongs to Jason," answered Wolf with a smug look on his face. "You ain't got probable cause to search my rig."

"Might be true, Wolf, but when the Judge heard you were parked right next to it he gave me a warrant for yours too."

"Son-of-a-bitch," growled Wolf.

"I'm sensing a trip for you back to the gray bar hotel, Wolf. You must miss the place."

Nick popped open the door of the camper while I kept Wolf company. He wasn't into the search more than a minute when he called out. "Pete! Here in the camper."

"What have you got, Nick?" I answered.

"No harp, but plenty of bags of Mary Jane. I'll bet there's two hundred pounds of pot in here."

We didn't find Philomena's harp, but it was a successful evening for law enforcement. The search of Wolf's truck recovered an assault rifle and some burglary tools, but no drugs. Turned out that Stillson was Wolf's old cell mate from the Montana State Prison. At a minimum, both were going back inside for parole violation.

It was almost midnight by the time we brought our prisoners and their vehicles back to Rodgersburg. Wolf surprised me with his almost lackadaisical attitude about being sent back up. As I turned him into his cell for the night he said, "Ya know, this parole is harder time than being inside, Sheriff. In there, at least I can get some liquor to drink."

Midnight is past my normal bedtime and morning came early. I wanted to stay in bed but duty called. Bob White's newspaper story about the theft of Philomena's harp would appear on the townspeople's doorsteps about 6:30 A.M. Would it generate any leads for us to follow? That I didn't know, but I did need to address the issue of Philomena's possible involvement in the disappearance of her harp.

By the time I reached the office we'd already received some calls. "Morning, Pete," Kay said as I came through the front door. "I see that you and Nick were busy last night."

"Yup. It was a good bust but it didn't find us a harp," I replied.

"Maybe you'll have more luck with these," offered Kay, holding a sheaf of phone messages. "Got a report of a vehicle matching the description at Clearwater Campground."

"Thief steals harp and drives three miles to a campground where he serenades himself by the light of a campfire. Doesn't sound too promising to me."

"But you have to check it out anyway," answered Kay matter-of-factly. "Maybe you'll like the second call better. Todd Brantly called from the Mountain View Inn. He's got a guest from Idaho driving a white half ton with a topper over the back end."

"Not a camper?"

"No, but don't take Mrs. Elkins' description of a camper too literally. She's in her seventies and women of her generation aren't terribly into cars. Camper or topper, it may all be the same to her."

"Good point," I conceded. I headed back to the kitchen to pour myself some coffee. After taking a couple of deep swallows I returned to the dispatch area. Kay was talking on the radio with my chief deputy, Johnny Titan. I heard him say that he was driving on the back side of Boulder Lake, so I interrupted and told Johnny to check out the Idaho truck at the Mountain View Inn.

When we finished our three-party conversation I told Kay that I would check out the rig at Clearwater and stop by for a little visit with Philomena. But before I left the office Kevin Donaldson came in carrying a big box. Kevin and I are teammates in a Fantasy Football League. He's a logger by profession, and like me, a high school football player whose talent never lived up to our aspirations. Nonetheless, Kevin knows the game and together we've been league champions three times in the past six years and never finished worse than third. His girlfriend, Mary Cahill, works with Connie and we see a fair amount of Mary and Kevin on a social basis.

"What's in the box?" I asked after Kevin had plopped down in the chair next to my desk.

"Books. Mary is cleaning out Megan's room now that she's found a job and is heading west to the bright lights of the big city. Megan said she didn't want the books anymore. They're mostly college books, but I thought you might want first pick."

"Thanks. I'll do that. So, where is Megan going?" I inquired. Connie probably had told me about her travels but frankly, keeping track of other people's kids isn't high on my priority list. That is, unless they've made some bad choices.

"Portland. She got a job at an advertising agency. The important thing is that she's in the same town with Johnny," answered Kevin. "My guess is a wedding next summer but, what do I know, except that I saw a couple of wedding magazines at Mary's when I went over to get the books."

"Might as well get it over with. They've been going together since high school. Ya know, Connie and I had only gone out two weeks before we got engaged. Got married two months later."

"You're kidding?" Kevin said.

"No. It was a good thing, at least for me. If she'd known me any better she might have said no."

"Not to change the subject or anything, but could I ask you a personal question?" asked Kevin hesitantly.

"Well, pard, you can always ask. I might not answer."

"It's not about the marriage or anything. I was kind of wondering about..." Kevin paused, as if he was searching for words. "Pete, uh, you read a lot, heavy stuff too. And, I was wondering, uh, with your intellect, how come you're a cop? You could be a professor or a lawyer, ya know."

I smiled. "Thanks for the compliment and, Kev, you're not the first to ask me that question. So, here's the simple answer. I enjoy the job. Always have. Every day I go to work, it's something new. Lots of problems to solve, some big, others little, but there's always something challenging my mind. I never get bored with my work."

"Oh. Okay."

"I also like helping people," I added. "That's what this job is all about."

"But, the books?"

"I wasn't always a reader. Fact is, in high school I was a pretty indifferent student. My favorite subjects were basketball, football, and psychology."

"You took 'ball' as a class?"

"No, that's not what I meant," I answered. "If it wasn't for sports, I might have dropped out of school."

"And the reading?"

"I started that much later. I was on a stakeout in Seattle. We were watching a house up in Wallingford, west of the University, and my post was in this professor's garage which he had converted into an office. I was supposed to watch the alley. It was unbelievably boring. I was sitting in a room full of books and I picked up one on the history of warfare. It was pretty interesting and that's what got me started. Of course, I would have been fired if the lieutenant had caught me with my nose in a book during the stakeout and, if that had happened, I doubt I'd have picked up anything heavier than *Sports Illustrated* ever since."

"Okay. Sorry for being such a snoop, but I was...well...I was just interested, ya know," answered Kevin. "Well, I've got to run. Take what you want from the box and, if you don't mind, take whatever's left over to the library."

"Okay, see ya," I replied to the back of Kevin's head.

My curiosity was aroused. The job could wait a few more minutes while I pawed through the box. Herman Hesse's *Steppenwolf*, Ernest Hemingway's *A Farewell to Arms*, and Virgil's *Aeneid* shared space on the top layer of the box with *Introduction to Marketing* and *Kinesiology*. Quite the combination, I thought to myself. Maybe Megan had taken a double major—business with what—phys ed, philosophy, literature? No doubt I'd find something of interest in the box.

After a short side trip up to Clearwater Campground to check out the report of a white truck with a camper, I arrived at Philomena's home about mid-morning. She looked anxious as she peered at me through the storm door.

"You've found my harp, I hope," asked Philomena rhetorically.

"No, I'm sorry to say that we haven't, but we've got a few leads, which is a lot better than where we were yesterday."

"Well, how can I help you? And please excuse my manners. Come in out of the cold. I have coffee."

After we'd settled down at the kitchen table I asked, "Do you know anybody who drives a white truck with a white camper or topper on the back?"

"Why, is that who took my harp?"

"I don't know. One of your neighbors said she saw a white truck with a camper in your driveway about noon yesterday."

"I see," answered Philomena thoughtfully. "I don't pay a lot of attention to what people drive. I can't think of anybody here in Rodgersburg. My friends are mostly older women, some couples. We're past the truck and camper stage of life. I guess I'll have to say no."

"Anybody from out of town—Butte, Missoula, Copperton, Cottonwood, Winslow?"

Philomena hesitated a few minutes and then said, "No. My answer's the same."

"I take it the harp was insured?" I asked, changing the subject.

"Certainly, and I called the insurance company yesterday when Kay was here. She told me to. I'd totally forgotten. But money can't replace my harp, Sheriff. I might be able to buy another one but I can't replace that one. It was very special to me."

"Why would anyone steal a harp?" I asked. "Is there a black market for stolen harps?"

"I'm sure I don't know," came Philomena's reply accompanied by a questioning look on her face.

"Let's think about this for a minute, Philomena. We're in Rodgersburg, Montana, and Seattle, Spokane and Salt Lake City are the three closest cities where there is likely to be any kind of market for a harp. True?"

"True."

"So you'll agree that it's not likely that anyone would steal the harp to sell to another harpist around these parts."

"Agreed."

"Now, does a harp have any value broken up? Are some parts particularly valuable?"

When I said the words "broken up" Philomena turned positively ashen. "Oh my God, no!" she exclaimed. "The value of a fine harp is in its craftsmanship. They are all made of fairly common materials. The strings are usually made of steel, gut or nylon, nothing special there. My harp had some gold leaf on it but even if it were all carefully removed, I doubt it would add up to half an ounce."

"But someone who wasn't too knowledgeable about a harp might not know that. He might see that glitter and think there was a fortune to be found."

"I'd never thought of it that way, Sheriff," said Philomena, her voice becoming taut with fear.

"You know lots of harpists, don't you?"

"Certainly, Sheriff. It's my profession."

"Ever know anyone who had a harp stolen?" I asked quietly.

"Only one, me."

"Oh?"

"Yes, it happened in 1992. The orchestra went on tour. We had finished a concert in the Quad Cities, packed up and went up to Madison, Wisconsin, only my harp never made it. It disappeared into thin air and was never found. That's when I purchased my current instrument.

"Ever have any other problems with your harps?"

"Yes, one was badly damaged in the back of the concert hall in Chicago. One of the stagehands may have hit it with a forklift but no one ever admitted responsibility. Personally, I always thought it was done by the set builder named Frank Boharsky. He had a bit of a drinking problem. I think he accidentally hit the harp. No one was around to see and he denied doing anything."

Philomena's answers to my questions seemed sincere except for her claim that she didn't know anyone who owned a white truck with a camper unit. That bothered me, but I decided on one more question and then I'd leave. "Philomena, how much insurance did you have on the harp?"

"Eighty thousand dollars. I updated the policy last year. It's what I think it would cost to fully replace the instrument."

I was gone from the office for a little over two hours. When I returned Kay was just hanging up the telephone. "Your timing is perfect," she said. "That was Johnny calling in from the Mountain View."

"Anything worthwhile?"

"Not for the case but Johnny had a great time. The vehicle is owned by some fellow named Walter Dorrance. He's from Coeur d'Alene. The guy apparently makes fly fishing videos and he's here scouting out some locations for next season's work. I think Johnny finagled himself into being a model of some kind. How did you fare up at Clearwater Campground?"

"I got a chance to meet and have coffee with Chuck Carpenter. He's retired and lives in Helena, and was over doing some late season fishing, but not for harps. Did we get any other leads?"

"Just one. A woman on East Appomattox reported a truck matching your description backing into that old building where Kenyon's garage used to be located."

Rodgersburg's street names may be its quaintest characteristic. Clyde Rodgers, the town's founder and its mayor for many years, had been a Union artillery officer during the Civil War. He was also highly educated by the standards of the day with a classical education from Otterbein College in Ohio. When Clyde laid out the avenues of his new town he named the north-south streets after prominent military commanders and the east-west thoroughfares after famous battles, with a decided preference for honoring his Union compatriots, which is why Rodgersburg has streets named Sherman, Sheridan, Farragut, Rosecrans, Shiloh, Antietam, Gettysburg, and Appomattox.

In 1927, the city council broke with tradition and re-named Saratoga Street, a pivotal American victory in the Revolutionary War, in honor of Clyde Rodgers. At the same time, two streets named after senior Union commanders, Grant and Halleck, became Main and Park streets respectively. Since then, Rodger's original naming scheme has been faithfully followed.

"I thought that place was abandoned?" I asked.

"That was my reaction too, but apparently not," Kay answered just before she drained her coffee cup. "Someone is using it for a garage or storage of some type."

"Do we know who?"

"No, but the caller described them as a couple of rough looking characters."

"Are they at the place now?"

"No. The caller said they backed the truck into the building, closed the door, then came out fifteen to twenty minutes later. The two men got into an older model red car—a Ford, she thinks—and left. She said she's seen the car parked there quite a bit lately."

"Is it there now?"

"No. She hasn't seen it today."

"Not to change the subject, but did you look into Philomena's finances?"

"I'm not done."

"Anything of interest?"

"Some. No major debt. Her house is paid for. She gets Social Security and a pension from the symphony. Her savings account has been drawn down quite a bit in the past several months. That's as far as I've gotten."

"Hmm, spending money a lot faster than she's taking it in. That can be a prescription for trouble." I said it more to myself than Kay.

"You learn anything in your talk with her?" asked Kay.

"She admitted that she had one harp damaged and one went missing, probably stolen. Claims she didn't know anyone with a white truck and camper. That troubles me."

"It shouldn't," came Kay's assertive reply. "Tonight when you go home for dinner ask Connie to name the make or the color of her friends' cars. I'm telling you, she won't know many. Cars are a guy thing. The only vehicles most women pay any attention to are the ones in their own driveway."

Kay turned to answer the telephone and I retreated to my office where I called Tom Wilson, our County Attorney, to get us a search warrant to investigate the inside of the Kenyon building. That done, I planned its surveillance. I also called the County Treasurer to have her go through the property tax records to find the current owner of the building. She informed me that the tax notices were being sent to an address in Racine, Wisconsin. Kay found a number but no one was home.

After I returned from lunch, I found a note from Kay. It read, "Wolf Shandy wants to talk about the missing harp." I checked my gun belt with the dispatcher and went into the cell block. Wolf was lying on his back.

"I hear you wanted to see me, Wolf."

"Sure 'nuff, Sheriff," Wolf said. He got up and walked over to the bars. "I've been hearing things about a missing harp."

"That's why we stopped you last night, Wolf. Finding the drugs and the assault rifle just turned out to be a little extra frosting."

"But you ain't found no harp yet, now have you?" The Wolf was actually trying to be agreeable. He wanted something.

"No, we haven't," I replied.

"I could help," offered the Wolf.

"What's going on, Wolf? You having a crisis of conscience?"

"Don't you wish," answered Wolf flashing a surly grin. I caught a glimpse of his unusually large eye teeth. "This is purely a business deal."

"So you'll return the harp in exchange for what?"

"First thing is, I don't have the harp 'cause I didn't cop the thing, but I've got a good, no, excellent idea as to where it is."

"And second?" I asked.

"I gotta get something," responded the Wolf. "You drop the parole violation charges, I fix you up with the harp."

"It's tempting, Wolf, that I've got to admit. But there's a little problem. For most people around here, if finding the harp means letting you back on the streets, they'd rather see that harp be lost forever."

Wolf was not about to be put off. "The newspaper says that harp is worth about sixty K. You don't want to deal, fine. I have some friends that would like to get into the music business, and they'll pay a finder's fee."

"I'll run your proposal in front of the County Attorney," I said. "In the meantime, I'll know where I can find you."

Wolf's proposal caught me by surprise. And I believed him, at least the part about knowing where the harp was. I wasn't convinced he was innocent of the actual crime, but the trouble was, I didn't have any evidence against him.

I visited with Tom Wilson about Wolf's offer and we decided to sit on it for a few hours to see if anyone showed up at the old Kenyon Garage. If we didn't have any visitors by sundown, we'd go ahead with a search of the building and reconsider what to do about Wolf in the morning.

When I returned from the courthouse, Kay handed me several sheets of paper and said, "These just came in from the

Motor Vehicle Division. It's all the white trucks registered in Missoula County, alphabetically by owners' last name."

"There must be a thousand," I said somewhat disheartened. "I thought computers were supposed to make things easier."

"They do," came Kay's quick reply. "When you know exactly what you're looking for. Montana doesn't register truck canopies anymore, so the search can't use that parameter. But, not to worry. Assuming Ben Klein was correct about the name starting with a P or an R and the fact that it ended in s-o-n or s-e-n, there are only four entries that match up. There's a Carl and Anita Parkinson, Francis Person, William Parson, and a Jason Reardon."

"You call them and see if they know Philomena. Use the neighbor throwing the surprise party ruse."

Just then the telephone rang. It was Charlie.

"Pete, two guys just showed up at Kenyon's Garage. C'mon down."

After hanging up I told Kay to radio all the deputies and have them meet me there.

Kenyon's garage is a tall, single-story brick building with a rounded, barn style roof running its length. It originally housed a livery stable complete with hay loft. In the middle 1920s, when the folks of Rhyolite County finally substituted the automobile for the horse as their preferred source of locomotion, the building was converted into a bus and truck garage jointly used by the local school district and a couple of logging companies.

Alf Kenyon owned and operated a body shop in the place when Connie and I moved to Rodgersburg. He was killed in a boating accident not long afterward and the building had been used only intermittently since then. There was a twelve-foot garage door in the center of both the front and back walls. To the left of the door a brick chimney rose above the front wall venting gas from the boiler room immediately below. On the right side, a man door opened into a small room which Alf had used as his office. All of the windows of the building had been boarded up long ago. The roof was missing a lot of shingles and I am sure it leaked like a sieve. I hadn't been in the building in years but if memory served me correctly, behind the boiler room and office were a large space where the vehicles were repaired and a paint booth in the far back corner.

As I approached the man door I could hear two muffled voices followed by hearty laughter. I knocked on the door softly and to my surprise heard, "C'mon in. It ain't locked."

I did just that, followed by Charlie and the team of deputies who immediately fanned out to search the premises. Two men dressed in hunting attire—wool pants, heavy sweatshirts, and wool caps and gloves—were sitting around Alf's broken down desk with a couple of six-packs of Bud Light between them. There was fresh blood on the shirt of a blond headed guy who looked familiar but I couldn't recall a name. The other was heavy set, with a gorilla type body and a big bushy beard. The blond uttered something softly to himself which sounded much like, "son-of-a-bitch." The bearded dude started to stand but I strongly suggested that he sit back down and that they both keep their hands on the table. That done, I presented the blond with a copy of the search warrant.

We searched the building finding a white truck with a camper and, back in the paint booth, discovered exactly four times the allowable limit of elk. We made the arrests but never found a harp. Unlike Wolf Shandy, these jail-bound characters had plausible alibis for their whereabouts yesterday about noon. Unfortunately, I was no closer to solving the case of the disappearing harp now than I was twenty-four hours ago.

It was after six when I returned to the office. My stomach started to remind me that it was time for dinner. I was dismayed about the lack of progress in the harp case, yet pleased about the arrests we'd stumbled into. Maybe in the future, as a routine part of office policy, I should put out an APB on a different kind of vehicle once a week just to see what kind of wrongdoers we could snag.

Kay surprised me by still being on duty. She typically leaves at 4:30 to get back home and get dinner on for her four kids.

"Any luck?" she asked.

"Yeah. Two poachers and eight confiscated elk, but nothing that will make Philomena Corrigan happy. Did you get anything with those names?"

"Yes," answered Kay. "I connected with two and neither professed to know anyone in Rodgersburg. So I called Philomena and simply asked her straight out about some friend whose name ended in a 'son' from Missoula. It turned out that her friends were the Parkinsons, Tom and Mary Lou. They are the parents of Carl Parkinson, one of the names on our list. The parents had borrowed their son's truck the weekend they visited Philomena."

"That helps," I replied, quietly pleased that I could relax my suspicion of Philomena.

"There's more," added Kay. "The kids took the truck

to northern Canada on a hunting trip a week ago. They couldn't have been here on the day of the burglary. I can verify that with the border patrol if you want."

"No. We're good. Let's the two of us get out of here before I melt into nothing from starvation."

Kay laughed, "You melt? Maybe in about sixty days. See you tomorrow."

I went back to my office to get my coat. I saw the box of books which Kevin had brought by earlier in the day and took a few minutes to finish the browsing I'd started earlier and ended up finding four gems that captured my fancy.

The evening was quiet. Connie usually sews on Wednesday night. My son Phil was actually in his bedroom doing homework—trigonometry and chemistry, at least based on the moaning he did at dinner.

I went downstairs to the rec room, tossed another couple of logs on the fire that Connie had started after school and planted my backside in Grandma's rocker, an antique salvaged from my grandmother's home after her death. I had disassembled and completely rebuilt the chair a couple of years ago, complete with leather upholstery. Around the house it's known as Dad's chair, but Phil, if ever there was a guy into creature comfort, has established co-occupation rights. But since he was doing homework at a desk, imagine that, I could comfortably have my place for an hour or two. I started reading Steinbeck's *East of Eden* but the book didn't hold my attention, and I kept drifting back to Philomena's harp. My ruminations did little good, however, so I put down the book and surfed the TV channels for a few minutes hoping to find something of interest on ESPN. That effort also failed, so I turned to the Discovery Channel and watched a show about the construction of the Roman Coliseum.

I didn't sleep well; I rarely do when I am in the middle of a big case. My mind gets going as I process and reprocess what we know and what we don't, looking for that little factoid which leads us to a solution. Sounds stupid, I suppose, but it usually helps me develop a plan. However, not this time. That night I was haunted by the idea that I was going to have to make a deal with Wolf Shandy to retrieve Philomena's harp. I rose, fatigued and pensive, and made my way to the office, fortified by a double espresso which I had picked up at the Burger Haven Café during my five minute commute to work.

All morning I procrastinated, hoping we'd get something that would help us find Philomena's harp. I did not want to deal with Wolf Shandy and neither did the County Attorney's office. We were running out of time. Wolf hadn't had any visitors, not even an attorney, but that wouldn't last forever. If he knows where the harp is, he'll make arrangements through one of his dirtbag friends to get it, possibly by harming someone else. Then, we'd really be in a quandary. I was stewing over it, drinking a lukewarm cup of coffee, completely oblivious to the departmental financial reports I was supposed to be reading, when Nick called in from Winslow.

"Pete, I've found the harp," he said, "but you need to come down here and see this."

"Can't you handle it?" I felt a tingle of anxiousness run up my spine.

"Nothing like that. You just got to see it. I'm at 316 North Harrison, just up from the Hideaway a couple of blocks."

"All right. I'll be there. Give me a half hour."

"No rush. The harp is fine."

I guess Wolf did have something to trade after all, I thought to myself as I stepped into the patrol car and started toward Winslow. That address is only two blocks from where we picked him up.

The traffic was light and I drove fast, making it to Winslow in just over twenty minutes. I spotted Nick's patrol car in front of a small, tan-colored house bracketed by two big lilac bushes. In the back yard, there was a white Dodge pickup with a white camper on its back. An ambulance was also parked outside the front door of the house. Nick stepped out onto the porch as I turned the motor off. "That was fast," he remarked.

"From the sound of your call, I thought it was important."

"Not so important as weird," Nick replied. "The house is owned by Mabel McInnis. She lives here with her grandson Danny Ross, his wife and their two children."

"The ambulance?"

"It's for Mabel. She passed away a few minutes ago."

"And you found the harp here?" I was having a hard time buying it.

"Got a call from one of the hospice volunteers who have been coming in to help with Mrs. McInnis," answered Nick, stifling a yawn. "She's been sick for a long time. Come inside."

As I cleared the jamb of the front door I could hear soft harp music. Nick led me into the living room which had been converted into a bedroom for Mrs. McInnis. A hospital bed sat alongside the far wall facing the front bay window so she could look out into the street. White sheets were draped from the walls and a white gauze-like material, similar to the cloth used for wedding veils, covered the furniture. It looked as if I had stepped into a cloud. Near the foot of the bed stood Philomena's harp, but no one was playing it. Through the kitchen doorway I could see two little children dressed as angels. The harp music was coming softly from a CD player while the two ambulance attendants and the hospice volunteer prepped Mrs. McInnnis' body.

"Pete, this is Danny Ross," said Nick, introducing me to a young man in his twenties. "Danny works for the Triple T Ranch Company." Danny Ross was all cowboy: well-worn cowboy boots with mud stains on the sides, tight-fitting Wranglers, a western shirt, and a deeply tanned face.

"Sheriff, hello." He extended his hand to me in greeting. "I guess you're here about the harp."

"Yes, son," I replied. "This is kind of an interesting set-up. Mind telling me what's going on?"

Ross shook his head in acknowledgement and said, "We did it for Grandma. She's been sleeping all the time, kind of like a coma, and going to die."

"I understand that much."

Ross continued, "We wanted to wake her up one last time so we could tell her we loved her and say goodbye."

"Yeah, that's understandable. And the harp?"

"Well, Sheriff, we wanted to make her think she was in heaven."

CHAPTER SIX

The Curious Case of the Rubber Gloves

BENSON About 3:30 P.M. Friday before the start of the three-day Memorial Day weekend, Darryl Hurley bludgeoned Adam Wainright to death with a piece of pipe. No one witnessed the crime and, aside from the murder weapon, there was little physical evidence. Nevertheless, by Monday, Darryl had confessed and was in custody. It was a most interesting, and some might say, bizarre case.

Customarily, when I describe these vignettes from my life as a police officer, I do so largely from my perspective. Now that Darryl has confessed and accepted the judgment of the District Court, he consented to tell his side of the story as well.

HURLEY

If there was ever an individual who deserved to die, it was Adam Wainright. He moved to Rodgersburg about eighteen months ago after he bought out his cousin's half-interest in United American Title. We met at a Christmas party and hit it off immediately. I invited him into my home and steered him to a couple of small but profitable business deals, and he repaid my friendship by taking up with my wife and cheating me out of a land acquisition I had been working on for several years. After my wife filed for divorce four months ago and moved in with Wainright, she tipped him off about my plans to purchase a hundred and twenty acres of land, prime for development, at Boulder Lake. Adam stepped into the picture, offered slightly more to the seller and left me holding the bag.

In retrospect, I probably should have killed my wife instead of Wainright, or maybe both of them. Jill was really the treacherous one. Adam was merely an opportunist. Jill's desertion hurt me more than I can describe. I thought we had a good marriage. When I learned otherwise, it really scrambled my brain. I became completely obsessed by what had happened to me. I couldn't sleep. I couldn't work. I wanted revenge, but I didn't plan to kill him. That sort of... just happened.

BENSON

I was in the office Friday afternoon going over some supply requisitions for the jail with my chief deputy, Johnny Titan. A titan he's not, at five feet six inches and a hundred thirty-five pounds, but he makes up for his lack of size with tenacity and consistently good police work. Like me, he got into police work while in the military. We met one Christmas when Johnny was back in Rodgersburg on leave. He was discharged four months later, came back home, and I offered him a deputy spot. It wasn't long before he was chief deputy.

Johnny was spending far more time explaining the requisitions than I wanted to listen to. His management of the jail is meticulous and, frankly, I trust him. If he tells me we need plumbing repairs costing $6,252, then we need them. Johnny, however, wants to make sure I am fully informed and for that I should be thankful, but it was a gorgeous day outside. I wanted to head home and get a little jump on the weekend.

The sound of the telephone startled us both. Agnes Cutter, a retiree, was crossing Tower Park near the duck pond and spotted a pair of shoes near some bushes. She looked closer and discovered that the shoes were attached to a pair of legs. She called us on her cell phone thinking she'd just discovered some drunk sleeping it off.

The duck pond is located on the southern end of Tower Park, right below the Tower, a rectangular piece of limestone reaching about a hundred sixty feet into the sky. Immediately adjacent the tower is a narrow gap in the cliff through which flows Tower Creek. The Tower was once part of a waterfall. The creek meanders through the center of Rodgersburg, past softball fields, horseshoe pits, a basketball court, a bandstand, and picnic area, on its way to the Pacific Ocean. The entrance to the duck pond is a metal gate suspended between two large stone pillars.

After arriving on the scene, I went over to thank Agnes for her report while Johnny went into the brambles to help the afflicted. He wasn't in there but a few seconds before I saw him backing out, carefully placing his feet where he had stepped before. My puzzlement didn't last long.

"Pete, we've got a problem here," said Johnny.

I told Agnes we would take care of everything and stepped over to Johnny. "What's up?"

"Homicide. Generally that's the case when the head has been beaten to a pulp."

"Do you recognize the victim?"

"Yeah. It's Adam Wainright."

"Oh, my God...Darryl, you think?" I asked.

"No one's got more motive. I'll get the place taped off so we can work it."

A couple of minutes later, Charlie Roper showed up with the ambulance, followed by Fred Early, the county coroner. The four of us worked the crime scene for more than an hour before I released the body to the morgue. There was some blood spatter on the sidewalk on the opposite side of the bush from where the body was found. Fred found a bloody, four-foot-long piece of heavy galvanized pipe inside a clump of aspen trees next to the duck pond. Attached to a burr on the pipe thread was a triangular piece of latex about an inch across. The killer had worn rubber gloves. As evidence goes, that was a fair start. I've been on lots of cases with much less to go on. The victim was dressed in a sweat suit. Fred confirmed that Wainright was a runner.

"Looks like Adam was out for his afternoon jog," observed Fred.

"Was it something he did regularly?" I asked.

"Yup. Like clockwork," answered Fred. "I usually see him when I go over for coffee. He'd leave the office right around three, take two laps around the park, and I mean big laps—down past the swimming pool and back. Then, he'd return to the office, shower and work until six, sometimes later."

"Someone knew his schedule and lay here in wait."

"Works for me, Pete. It's pretty clear from the blood spatter on the sidewalk that he was clubbed right in front of the entrance to the duck pond. I'd say the killer hid on

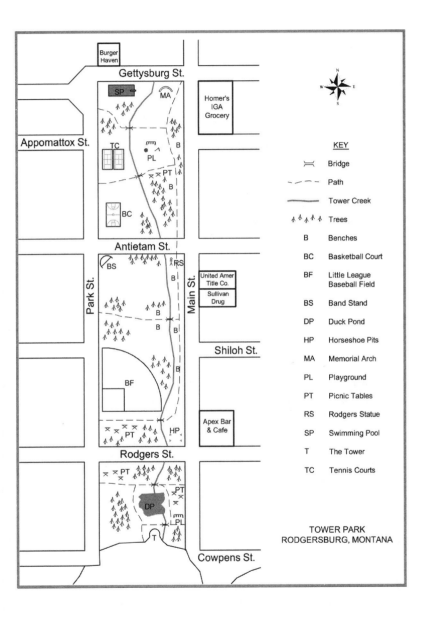

KEY

⋈ Bridge

- - - - Path

——— Tower Creek

⋏⋏⋏⋏⋏ Trees

B Benches

BC Basketball Court

BF Little League
Baseball Field

BS Band Stand

DP Duck Pond

HP Horseshoe Pits

MA Memorial Arch

PL Playground

PT Picnic Tables

RS Rodgers Statue

SP Swimming Pool

T The Tower

TC Tennis Courts

TOWER PARK
RODGERSBURG, MONTANA

the west side of the gate pillar and came out swinging. A lefty for sure."

"Why do you say that?" I asked.

"Adam was hit on the front and right side of his head," replied Fred. "The killer swung the pipe while he was still hidden behind the pillar. A right-handed guy couldn't do that. Either he would have been facing Adam and likely been seen, or, if he stayed hidden, the blows would have landed on the left side or back of Adam's skull. You're looking for a lefty."

"Is Darryl Hurley left-handed?"

"Darryl?...Oh, yeah...Sorry, Pete. I don't know but surely that won't be too difficult to discover."

"I suppose it's time to pay him a visit," I said with a tinge of regret. I didn't know Darryl well, but he seemed like a genuinely nice guy. I also knew that seemingly nice guys commit murder.

HURLEY

Fred Early's analysis of what happened Friday afternoon was an interesting theory, but that's not what happened.

My brother Dan and sister-in-law Carol are both dentists. I'm their business manager. Dan and Carol went to Scottsdale on Tuesday to attend a conference and decided to spend the weekend down there. The two dental techs also cut the week short so I was the only one in the clinic on Friday. I took a late lunch. It was a beautiful day so I decided to walk back to the office through Tower Park. I stopped to feed the ducks at the pond. I was enjoying the sun and time seemed to slip away. I looked at my watch and saw it was 2:45 P.M. so I got up from the bench I was sitting on and made my way back to the entrance to the duck pond. Who should I meet there, but none other than Adam Wainright. Initially, I thought he'd jog right by me, but no, he stopped and stared at me with this big smirk on his face. I took it for about five seconds and then said to him, "Leave me alone. You've taken the best part of my life—enjoy it," and I started to walk away. Then, he laughed and said, 'Darryl, you're such a loser.' And he laughed some more."

"Loser," I thought to myself. I lost my wife, my land, my dream. Yeah, I lost. To a thief, a cheater. I felt myself go white hot.

The next thing I knew I was standing over Adam's body with a bloody pipe in my hands. I must have pulled it from the broken fence near the gate. There was blood all over my clothes. Then I panicked. Given what had happened between the two of us, I knew no one would ever believe me so I decided to hide the body in the brush. Then I went back to the clinic, pitched my clothes into the incinerator, took a shower and swallowed a sedative to calm my nerves, and went into my office. Fortunately, I always keep a clean shirt and trousers at my office in case I spill something on my clothes. I was sure that no one had seen me, but I also knew that Sheriff Benson would be looking for me the minute Adam's body was discovered. I thought about getting out of town but that would prove my guilt. I waited at the office. Just before five the front door opened.

BENSON
"Sheriff Benson!" Darryl seemed genuinely surprised by my visit. "I am sorry, but we're closed today."

"Darryl, this is a professional visit," I replied. Darryl's

about forty, medium build, with light brown hair with just a hint of gray around the temples and above the ears. He and his older brother Dan look so much alike people frequently mistake them for twins. Today he was dressed casually, with dark blue trousers and a light yellow sport shirt. Every time I've seen Darryl in the office he was wearing a sport coat and tie.

"Sounds serious," answered Darryl pleasantly. "Please come in. I am not nearly as proficient as Dan or Carol, but if you'll give me the X-ray, I..."

"No thanks, Darryl, I don't need you to identify any corpse from the dental records. While I am thinking of it, could you give me a couple of sets of rubber gloves? Connie's going to have me working in the garden all weekend, and I like latex gloves for that type of work."

"Certainly, said Darryl graciously. "Do you take a medium or large?"

"Large."

Darryl got up from his desk and walked across the hall to a small supply room. He pulled a box off the shelf, pressed it open, and pulled out four gloves with his left hand.

"Here you go," Darryl said.

The gloves caught me by surprise. "They're purple. I've never seen latex gloves like these before."

"They're not actually latex—the new stuff is made from nitrile, Sheriff. A lot of people seem to be allergic to latex these days."

"Oh, I didn't know that," I replied. Actually I did because one of my nephews is allergic to it. What I didn't know was that the Hurley Dental Clinic had switched over to nitrile. I was in there a month ago to have a crown repaired and they were still using white latex gloves. Obviously, Darryl had put more thought into his crime than I expected.

"Glad I could be of help, Sheriff. Was there anything else? I've got..."

"Bear with me a minute more, Darryl. I said this was a professional visit." I gave Darryl a stern look in the eye.

"But you said you didn't need me to identify any dental records," he replied with a confused look.

"Yes, that's right. We know the name of the deceased. What I want to know is your whereabouts today," I said.

"Me? Whatever for?" asked Darryl calmly.

"Because the dead man is Adam Wainright." I looked him right in the eye, expecting him to wither before me.

"Adam!" shouted Darryl. "Surely there is a God!" His glee was evident.

"God's got nothing to do with it," I said. "He was killed by a fellow human being swinging a pipe."

"And you think I did it?" Darryl's voice had an incredulous sound to it.

"Well, given your history with Adam, you top the suspect list, Darryl." I said it coldly, but Darryl completely ignored my efforts to pressure him.

"Yes, certainly, but I am not the only one Adam has cheated." Darryl's speech had become quite rapid, almost exuberant in tone. I've been a law enforcement officer a long time and I've never had that happen, not once. Either Darryl was innocent and truly enjoying the news I had given him, or he was a first-class actor.

"You can give me that list in a minute, Darryl, but for now, I want a complete description of your day."

"Certainly, Sheriff. I got up at my usual time, around

seven, got ready for work, ate breakfast and left the house just after eight. I stopped by the library and dropped off two books in the overnight return slot. Then I went to Homer's IGA and bought coffee for the office. I got here about 8:45."

"Who was working the till at Homer's?" I asked.

"Annette."

"What did you do after you got to the office?"

"I stayed here until 12:45 when I went over to Burger Haven and got lunch."

"Who was with you in the office?"

"No one. Dan and Carol are at a conference in Scottsdale. They'll be back Monday. Mary Lou doesn't work Friday and Judy took the day off, some kind of long-standing appointment."

"Who's Judy?" I asked. There was no Judy employed at the clinic a month ago.

"Judy Ryan. She's only been with us about two weeks, originally from Copperton."

"So no one can verify that you were here," I said seriously.

"Not every minute," replied Darryl matter-of-factly. "Bob Tate dropped the mail off around 10:30 and the UPS guy came by maybe an hour later."

"And you ate lunch at the Haven?"

"Yeah, and then I took a short walk through the park, down by the basketball court."

"See anybody in the park?"

"No, not that I can recall, why?"

"That's where Adam was killed," I answered.

"What?"

"Yes, today, not long ago."

"In broad daylight?" Darryl asked. "Who would do that?"

"When did you get back here?"

"I got back about 1:30 and have been here ever since."

"Can anybody verify that?"

"Not after I got back. You're my first visitor, Sheriff."

"Talk to anybody on the phone?"

"I called the bank this morning. All incoming calls are being handled by the answering service. I'm paying the bills and closing the books for the month. I didn't want to be disturbed."

"No alibi witness. That's not a good thing," I answered.

Darryl shrugged his shoulders. "It's a circumstantial thing, Sheriff. I haven't been near Adam Wainright in several months and if he's dead, I can assure you I had nothing to do with it."

"I hope not, because we found a piece of a latex glove on the murder weapon. A lot of people don't understand that we can pull finger and hand prints off the inside of these gloves. Sometimes we can get DNA. We can also analyze the rubber and match it to specific shipments."

"Well, best of luck, Sheriff," Darryl said, his face flushing. "And now, if you don't have anything further, I have a couple of things I need to do before closing up."

The interview with Darryl Hurley was short but most informative. On the one hand, his answers were composed and his voice disturbingly happy. He also kept patting the left pocket of his trousers, an interesting nervous tic to say the least. When I mentioned that we had found a piece of latex glove, Darryl's face visibly flushed. He's left-handed as well. Score one for Fred Early. I was ninety-nine percent certain that Darryl was the perp, notwithstanding his behavior. Unfortunately, I also knew that finding something really useful on that piece of latex was a long shot. Without an eyewitness or more physical evidence, the chance of successfully tagging Hurley for Wainright's murder was nil. I needed a plan.

Normally, I don't like to rush to judgment and focus exclusively on one suspect. Having been in the law enforcement game for half my life, I've seen plenty of situations where the most likely suspect was innocent and another party, frequently one who never made the suspect list at all, emerges as the villain.

But, in this case I felt it appropriate to apply Occam's Razor, as derived by William Ockham, a medieval English logician who posited that when two competing theories make the same predictions, the simpler one is preferred. "Just keep it simple," I said to myself out loud. The likelihood that anyone else did in Adam Wainright was minimal. So focus on Darryl.

HURLEY

I went home a little after six, cooked dinner, watched a little TV, and had just stepped out of the shower when the telephone rang. "Hello...Hello...Hello. Who's there? Son-of-a-bitch." I slammed the receiver on the cradle and turned toward my bedroom to finish getting ready for bed. It was about 9:45 P.M.

Then the phone went off again. "Hello...who's there?" The silence on the other end disturbed me and I felt myself getting angry. I wished I hadn't been so cheap and had gotten caller ID.

Then, a woman's voice pierced my ears. "Just me, Darryl," she said, "and I'm not going to let you get away with it."

"Go to hell, Jill," I replied and pounded the receiver down for the second time. I could feel my face flush with heat. Anger, no, rage was growing within me. Stop! Stop! Stop! I started telling myself. You can't afford to get angry. You successfully fended off Sheriff Benson this afternoon by keeping your cool. Get angry and you'll make a mistake, Darryl. Keep a cool head.

I went downstairs and poured myself a big shot of Jack Daniels and continued to talk to myself until I calmed down. Then I went to bed and quickly fell asleep. It was quiet for almost an hour and a half, then the telephone rang again. Fearful it was that voice again, I refused to answer it. But the ringing never stopped. I disconnected the phone in my bedroom but the one downstairs rang all night. I never got back to sleep and by the time daybreak rolled around, I was exhausted and a nervous wreck.

I needed to do some yard work and decided the exercise and fresh air would do me some good. After breakfast, I got dressed. I was putting my keys into my left front pants pocket when I felt it. I didn't recognize the texture, so I pulled it out, a white latex glove with a triangular piece ripped out of the palm, just like the one I burned yesterday! I felt a surge of panic rush through my body. How could this be! I burned that glove along with the rest of my clothes! Those calls last night—it's someone trying to drive me crazy. It was Jill. Oh my God—No! Jill's in Japan with that tour group. She might not even know about Adam. Even if she does, she wouldn't call me all night long from over there!

I felt my body shudder again. What was going on? No one was in this house last night but me. Someone or something put that glove in my pants pocket. One thing was for sure. I had to get rid of it—quickly.

BENSON

I had a great night's rest, which is unusual for me when I am working a big case. My mind gets to running rapid fire as I examine and re-examine the evidence over and over in my mind, and I frequently wake up thinking about the case. But not last night. I knew who the killer was. It was just a matter of time before he tripped up. My job was to push it along if possible, or if not, sit back and wait patiently. He'd come.

Darryl Hurley is a man full of rage but he's not a criminal in the customary sense of the word. To the contrary, his life is very regular and ordinary. His ex-wife, Jill, told my wife the main reason she left Darryl was that she couldn't stand the boredom any longer. Darryl meticulously planned every detail of his day, starting with setting out the clothes he intended to wear the next day, to scheduling how many chapters of which books he wanted to read in the evening, often days in advance. There was nothing spontaneous about Darryl, and that was going to be his undoing.

There's no such thing as a perfect crime. No one can plan for all the incidents and contingencies that pop up in a murder investigation, and Darryl didn't have the temperament to roll with the punches and improvise along the way.

HURLEY

I couldn't put the rubber glove in the trash or try to hide it around the house. Sheriff Benson would get a search warrant sooner or later and they'd go through my house with a microscope. I needed a place close by and yet undiscoverable...ah hah! The perfect place. My neighbor across the alley is building a concrete block wall to fence his lot off from the alley. I'll shove the glove down one of the cavities in the wall, cover it with some sand, and when the contractor finishes the job the glove will be gone forever.

I picked up a bag of trash and started for the alley. Dumping the trash would give me a plausible reason for being out by my neighbor's wall. I was walking along the side of my garage to the trash receptacle when I spotted the Sheriff's Department squad car backed into my neighbor's driveway and Deputy Titan watching the back of my house.

My heart started to race but I tried to appear casual. I waved at Deputy Titan. He waved back and I proceeded with my task. Back inside the house, my legs became rubbery and I started to shake as I leaned against the back door. That was close. I needed a new plan for getting rid of the rubber glove.

Oh, my God! There on my workbench was a box of latex gloves. I wear them when I am painting. Now I've got twenty-five or thirty gloves to get rid of. What am I going to do!

BENSON

I got to the Law Enforcement Center about 8:30 and was pleased to see that the judge had approved a search warrant for Darryl Hurley's home. It would be best to do that when it would cause maximum disruption, all the more to upset Darryl.

After checking on things with the dispatcher I decided to take a ride over to Darryl's home to talk with Johnny

Titan. Last night we'd parked a squad car down the street from the Hurley home. There was no one in it. The Department is too small to affect round-the-clock surveillance, but I figured if Darryl saw the car he'd think it was occupied and it might heighten his nervousness. Johnny had taken up his post behind Darryl's home around 6:30 A.M.

HURLEY

It took me a little while to regain my composure once I realized I had a whole box of rubber gloves to dispose of. I decided to cut them into small pieces and flush them down the toilet. That task was about finished when I heard a car drive into the alley. It was Sheriff Benson. He'd come to visit his deputy.

BENSON

Deputy Titan told me about Darryl's trip to the trash bin in the alley but otherwise it had been quiet. I decided to ramp things up a bit so I walked through his yard to the front entrance. There I pounded on the screen door and shouted, "Open up, Darryl. I know you're in there."

The door squeaked open slowly, only to be followed by a squeaky Darryl Hurley. "Sorry about that, Sheriff," he said. "I was back in the kitchen. As you can see, I don't have a doorbell."

All the animation that had driven Darryl's conversation with me yesterday had disappeared. He also looked pale. I guessed he hadn't slept too well, a surmise he confirmed by yawning several times.

"We need to talk some more, Darryl. May I come in?" I asked in a robust tone.

"I think not, Sheriff," answered Darryl in a monotonic voice. "You've indicated that I am a suspect in Wainright's death and I ..."

I interrupted. "Then let's just sit down out here on your porch."

"I've got some yard work to do," came Darryl's hesitant reply.

"Well, I'll help. I'll get Johnny too. He's parked in the alley watching the back of your house. With three of us, it won't take long."

"Thank you no, Sheriff. I prefer to work by myself," Darryl said loudly.

"You seem a little edgy, Darryl."

"You'd be edgy too, if you were a suspect in a man's death and you were innocent."

"No. I wouldn't, Darryl, not if I was innocent."

"Good day, Sheriff," Darryl said and closed the door.

Well, I found what I wanted. Darryl was as nervous as a cat at a rocking chair convention. Now, if we could only find some hard evidence.

I called Johnny Titan on the cell phone right after I left Darryl's front porch and pulled him from surveillance duty. It was Saturday and he was entitled to a day off. I figured Darryl's mind was probably racing 1,000 miles an hour and, if left to its own devices, would mess him up. We'd search his house tomorrow.

HURLEY

I closed the door on Sheriff Benson and headed for the bathroom for some aspirin. My head was pounding. When I got there I saw the floor flooded with water and tiny pieces of latex. My toilet had plugged. I grabbed hold of the door to steady myself. Good Lord, what else can go wrong?

I ran downstairs to my wood shop, found my toilet snake, and opened the clean-out tee. Flushing latex gloves down the crapper was a new experience, but unclogging the drains in this old house was not. Everything was back to normal in fifteen minutes and all of the latex flushed away.

I was putting back my plumbing tools when I spotted a box of latex gloves sitting right where the other box, which I'd just destroyed, had been resting. Am I losing my mind? The back door is locked, the deadbolt is in place. I wasn't twenty feet away working on that drain. Nobody came in, of that I was certain.

By that time the pounding in my head, which I'd momentarily forgotten while I unplugged the drain, came roaring back to match a similar throb in my chest. I could feel the sweat pouring off my forehead and trickling down my cheeks.

I realized I needed a new plan. I couldn't risk plugging the toilet again and chances are the more latex I flush down the drain, the more likely it will show up at the sewage treatment plant and someone will start asking questions. I should take the new box of gloves up to the office and incinerate it, but what if Benson or one of his deputies stops me? No, I need to get rid of it here at home.

BENSON

I took a drive over to Sullivan Drug and talked with our local pharmacist "Doc" Sullivan about Darryl Hurley. I was hoping he'd tell me that Darryl had purchased some latex gloves recently, but I came away empty handed.

I was just paying for a candy bar, something to carry me for the next couple of hours until I met Connie for lunch, when my assistant Kay and her younger daughter Erin entered the establishment.

After a quick but pleasant hello, Erin headed to the corner of the store that harbors the women's cosmetics. When Erin was out of ear shot, Kay offered, "She's got a big date tonight and she absolutely had to have new lipstick and nail polish. You know how it is at that age."

Actually, I didn't. I am the father of two boys and I would have been delighted if they had shown any interest in boosting their personal appearance up a notch before calling on a lady friend. So, I nodded in agreement to at least appear sympathetic and said, "Who's the lucky guy?" Erin takes after her mother by being bright and beautiful but inherited her father's shyness gene, and she hasn't attracted a lot of male attention around the high school.

"Kyle Berquist," replied Kay. She paused as if she were searching for her words. "He seems like a nice boy."

"I think he is. Phil says he's a good guy but that generally means the guy's a dweeb."

"A dweeb. What mother can't like that for her daughter's first boyfriend? You've made my day." Kay smiled, a sense of ease crossing her face. "How's the Wainright case going?"

Kay had been out of the office yesterday shepherding a female prisoner to the Montana Women's Prison in Billings. Now she wanted details about the murder.

"I think we know who did it but there's not much physical evidence and no witnesses."

"Darryl?" Kay replied, making it sound more like a pronouncement than a question.

"Who else?"

"Are you looking for other suspects?" Kay asked.

"Johnny and Fred had a couple of ideas but they both concede they're real long shots. I am going to keep this one simple."

"Oh, yes," Kay said with a big smile. "Keep it simple. Remember the Old Man's Razor."

"Old Man's Razor?" I thought to myself. Oh, Occam's Razor. Either it's another Kayism or she's putting me on, and given the grin on her face, I am voting for the second option. But, I let it slide. Never correct a woman in public— that's always trouble later. The sad thing is that I learned that little "lesson of life" the hard way, rather than reading it in a book.

"Yeah," I finally answered, "but Darryl's the only logical choice and I think we'll get him. Actually, I think Darryl will get himself. He's just too much of a plodder. He can't think on his feet, and eventually he'll trip up."

"Oh," answered Kay. She paused and I could see that she was analyzing what I had to say. She brushed her bangs off her forehead, one of her tell-tale tics when she's trying to figure out what to say. "Pete, I don't know. Maybe you're looking at Darryl too simplistically."

"Speak up," I answered. "I always appreciate your perspective, even if I don't always agree."

"Okay, you're right about Darryl. He's a plodder, very detailed about everything he does."

"Yeah, we agree on that point," I replied.

"So consider this," said Kay. "Darryl's been planning this murder for a long time. Maybe he's got a script and it's going along just fine. He's smart enough to know that if anything happens to Adam, he'll be suspect number one. So maybe Darryl's playing it that way."

"Interesting theory," I replied. Just then, Erin rushed back to her mother. "C'mon Mom, I want you to check out these colors. I think they'll be great with my skirt and sweater."

"Bye," I quickly interjected. "I'll think about what you said and give you a call if we get any movement on the case."

I found Kay's observations a bit disquieting. She's got excellent insight into people's motive and behavior and she just suggested that perhaps Darryl has scripted the whole thing. That piece of rubber glove fits a planned scenario. After all, who waltzes through everyday life with latex gloves in their pockets? If it weren't for the fact that Darryl looked like a man who hadn't slept, a condition I know something about given my periodic insomnia, I'd give Kay's observations more credence. Then again, maybe that's part of Darryl's script. One thing is certain. I don't know what's going on in Darryl's head. I can only react to what I see. If he does have a script, I need to force him to cut to the chase.

I went home to pick up Connie and take her to lunch at the Huggy Bear. When I walked through the back door, I could see that the dining table had been set and the boys were ambling in its direction from the living room. Apparently, plans had changed. Tom had come home from college a few days ago. He was working at Rukoff's Lumber Yard for the summer and I had expected him to be at work today. Phil is almost never home on Saturday. I think he's afraid that I'll put him to work mowing the lawn or some such. His fear is well placed. It's exactly what I'd do, if I could find him.

Connie greeted me with a peck on the cheek as she paused midway through filling up four bowls with beef stew. I took my place and enjoyed a convivial hour with the family. I think the last time we were all together for a meal was back during the Christmas holidays.

Phil broke things up by announcing that he was going over to the Earlys. He and his friend Jimmy were rebuilding the engine in Fred's old Toyota. Then Tom said to me, "How about a quick game of one on one?"

"On a full stomach," I protested.

"It'll help you digest the food," he replied.

"Go ahead, Pete," injected Connie. "Tom's been home a week and you two haven't played once."

"I'm in the middle of a case..."

"It can wait fifteen minutes, pa. It won't take me long to put you down."

"Nah, I've got..."

My comment was cut off by Connie, once again injecting herself into the conversation. "Pete Benson! There was a time when you couldn't stand a taunt about your basketball ability and now, you just roll over. I can't believe it." She shook her head and walked away, pretending to be irritated with me. It was just a show, her way of telling me family first, the job can wait.

"Okay," I said. "Give me a minute to change." Tom and I have been playing basketball together since he was six. When we play "one on one" we play to ten, each basket counting as one, but the winner must win by two baskets.

I got the ball first and as I started the game, I expected it to be over quick. The kid plays Division One college ball and I was almost thirty years older. But, it didn't go down that way. I tied it up at 10 and we were into overtime. Ten minutes later it was 18-17 in Tom's favor. Suddenly it hit me. Tom's messing with me. He's sagging off on defense so I can take my shot and dogging it on offense. There's no trash talking the old man. Instead, he's being subtle. Just toying with me, letting me think that I can still play with him.

I decided to prove him wrong, my resolve hardening my confidence. I said nothing, simply stepped up my own game. Another fifteen minutes passed. I was up by one, 33-32, and went up with a jumper for the win. Tom closed in on me and went up late, but not late enough. He swatted the ball right back at me, picked up the loose ball and scored. I hung in there.

At 2:00 he was up 45-44. We'd been playing just shy of an hour. I was drenched in sweat, my legs two appendages of pain propping up an old, tired torso, and he says to me, "Let's pack in till up tomorrow, Pa. I've got to get over to Kirsten's."

He's out here beating me into the concrete and he wants to quit so he can go see his girl, I thought to myself. The subtle taunting I could handle, but not the quitting, not now, not after I gave it my all. "Like hell you're quitting," the irritation in my voice quite clear. "You asked for this game. Now we finish it," I commanded.

Tom shrugged his shoulders and nodded his head. He brought the ball in from out of bounds, feinted right, dodged left, and was by me in an instant. Two steps followed by a hard, one-handed jam so powerful it nearly tore the net off the rim, and it was over. Tom pitched the ball back to me with a soft underhand toss, smiled, and said, "See ya. Tell Mom I'll be back for dinner," and then he jogged down the driveway, off to see his lady love. I staggered over to a lawn chair and sat down, breathing hard, and wondered why he had kept us playing so long.

HURLEY

It took a while, but I finally calmed down courtesy of a smidgeon of Valium I keep around the medicine cabinet for such purposes. I should have taken the Valium last night instead of the whiskey. It might have helped me sleep. Now, I need to think. Think, damn it, think.

You need to get rid of a bunch of latex gloves. They need to vaporize without leaving any telltale odors or residues behind.

I got on the Internet and looked for compounds that dissolve latex. Oils and greases will do the job over time, but time was something I didn't have a lot of. Then it hit me, rubber bands dry out over time, get brittle, and break. Maybe I could accelerate the process.

Soon I had two sheet cake pans in the oven roasting a couple dozen rubber gloves. Just in case, I mixed up two big bowls of cake batter. If Benson or his team showed up, I'd pour the batter over the gloves and hope for the best. I tried to keep my mind occupied but I found myself looking at the clock and checking the oven every few minutes. After an hour of roasting, I could see this process was working but was likely to take some time. Well, I had all day so I went into the living room, lied down on the couch, and promptly fell asleep. I had no sooner drifted off into neverland than the telephone in the dining room began to scream. Groggily, I staggered over to it on the edge of the buffet and answered it. I said hello several times and was about to put it back down when a female voice said, "You're not going to get away with it, Darryl."

"Jill?" I shouted. "This isn't Jill. Who is this?" I demanded. "You're going to hang, Darryl." The voice had a sweet, playful sound to it. It could not be Jill—not that voice. "Damn you!" I yelled and hung up the phone. It hadn't been back on the cradle ten seconds when it rang again. I decided that I was not going to listen to that crap all day. So I pulled the wire out of the phone jack. Instantly, solitude returned.

BENSON

After my game with Tom, I needed to relax. Fifteen minutes in the hot tub and a cool shower gave me time to think. As the old proverb goes, "Anger is the wind that blows out the lamp of the mind."[1] I needed to get Darryl riled up, but not so much that he might go off the deep end and hurt himself or someone else, or try to run. When a guy gets desperate, he gets dangerous. I needed to break up his control over the routine aspects of his day. This is something I understand well. At times my work life can be incredibly chaotic, having to respond to a number of challenges or problems simultaneously, many of which are not under my control. To keep from collapsing under the stress, one needs stability and routine in the other aspects of their life. Darryl is very much a creature of habit. He craves regularity in his life and now, he needs it more than ever.

So, I called Charlie Roper, Chief of both the Sheriff's Reserve Corps and the Rodgersburg Volunteer Ambulance, and asked him to have his members stop by Darryl's house every hour or so to see how he was doing. And I didn't want anybody wearing a uniform.

HURLEY

Those latex gloves in the oven seemed to be cooking up nicely but it was more time consuming than I hoped. I heard the doorbell ring and was certain it was Sheriff Benson, but I didn't want to act prematurely and mess up my latex cooking project if I didn't have to. I peeked out the windows on both sides of the house. No police vehicles were in sight so I pulled the curtain back on the front door. I was greeted by the sight of a young man in his mid-twenties. He looked familiar but I couldn't place him.

"May I help you?" I asked.

"Sorry to bother you, sir," said the young man politely. "I am from the ambulance service. Sheriff Benson said you were feeling poorly and asked me to stop by. Are you okay?"

"Oh, how thoughtful of the sheriff," I replied. "I'm fine, just fine. Thanks for your concern."

That young man was the first of a series of visitors from the ambulance service who called to inquire about my health, courtesy of Sheriff Benson. Any plans that I had for taking a nap went to the wayside. I was exhausted and could feel my nerves becoming more brittle by the minute.

Around four o'clock I checked on the rubber gloves drying in my oven. They weren't drying out as quickly as I'd hoped, so I moved on to Plan B. I put the gloves in an empty milk carton, filled it with water, and put it in the quick freeze section of my freezer. Within an hour or two I would have a solid block of ice that I could grind down using my electric grinder turning all those latex gloves into a small pile of white powder.

BENSON

Each of the members of the ambulance service called me after their visit with Hurley. Without exception, they reported him to be courteous but jittery and pale. One commented that Hurley had said he slept poorly the previous night and "just needed a little rest." Because of his behavior, I had pretty well eliminated any lingering doubt about his guilt. Any normal person would have gone ballistic if he'd been pestered every hour by someone knocking at his door and asking how he felt, but Hurley was working overtime at not calling attention to himself.

HURLEY

In between visits from the Rodgersburg Ambulance corps, I went down to my shop and used the grinder to turn the frozen rubber gloves into latex dust. Then, I mixed the powder with the contents of a big bag of potting soil, fairly certain that Sheriff Benson would never be the wiser.

BENSON

About 9:00 Saturday evening Hurley finally lost control and told the ambulance attendant to "Get the hell out of here. I'm fine and I don't want anybody bothering me any more and make sure Benson understands that."

Now I was really concerned. Darryl sounded suicidal. It was imperative we get someone in that house to look after him so I asked Dr. Paul Coombs, our local general practitioner, to stop over and see Darryl.

HURLEY

I heard the doorbell sound off for the umpteenth time and I could feel myself grow into a red rage. I jerked the door open and shouted. "I told the last one..." My voice faltered when I realized it was Dr. Coombs standing there. "Oh, Dr. Coombs, I'm sorry. I thought it was someone else."

"I heard you were having a rough time, Darryl," Dr. Coombs replied quietly. "I thought I should stop by."

"Thank you, but I'm fine, I really am," I said in reply, not believing a word I had said.

"You don't look too good, Darryl. Your eyes are completely bloodshot and you're shaking. Have you eaten?"

"Come to think of it, no. I was doing some work in my wood shop and completely lost track of the time. But, I'm fine Doctor, I really am."

"Let's get you some food and I'll give you a quick once-over," Coombs answered as he stepped past me and walked through the living room toward the kitchen.

"Thank you, Doctor, that would be good," I replied, almost as an afterthought as I followed him into the kitchen, taking a seat at the dinette table next to the window.

Dr. Coombs scrambled some eggs and fixed a salad. We talked mostly about baseball and fishing. I told him that I'd been having more trouble than usual getting a good night's rest. He wanted to take me to the hospital but I wouldn't hear of it. In the end, he gave me an injection and promised me a restful sleep. The doctor left my home about 10:30 P.M. and I climbed into bed immediately thereafter. I could feel myself plunging into the darkness of sleep when the telephone went off, its noise shattering both my sleep and sensibilities. Full of rage, I grabbed the telephone and tossed it into the hallway. Then I remembered. I had disconnected the phone last night. How could it ring? I could see the phone lying on the hallway floor in a rectangle of light from the street light outside my home. I felt my body tense and when I turned to lie down in bed, the phone started to ring again. That couldn't be. It wasn't connected to the line! A surge of fear shuddered through my torso. I went to the hall closet and took out my hunting rifle and, using the stock, beat the telephone over and over again. Finally, the ringing stopped.

Then the telephone downstairs started to ring but I had unplugged that one too. I couldn't help it. I started to cry and fell down on the carpet in the hallway, each ring pounding at my brain like a hammer on an anvil. At any moment I expected Satan to appear and gather me into his arms.

BENSON

I watched the late night news. It had a short piece on the Wainright killing with my photograph and a voice-over quoting me as saying the matter was still under investigation. Truly, I wasn't sure where we were in the investigation but I was sure we were doing better than Darryl Hurley. On that optimistic thought, I climbed into bed beside my sleeping wife and wondered what the next day would bring.

HURLEY

Lying in the hallway, I completely lost track of time. I only knew two things for sure. First, the shot Dr. Coombs gave me didn't work; I stayed awake the whole night through. Second, it was the sound of a flock of cedar wax-wings greeting the morning sun from their perch in the ash tree outside the hallway window which broke my trance and told me I had survived the night.

As I climbed to my feet, my body completely drained of any energy from two sleepless nights, it finally hit me: Benson's doing it. That son-of-a-bitch is the one calling me. I took a shower and returned to my bedroom to dress. Benson was harassing me. He had no right to do that. I needed to go on offense. Better call my lawyer. He'll know what to do. I should have called him Friday when Benson made it clear I was his prime suspect. Damn. It's only 6:10. His office won't open for two more hours. No. Wait, it's Sunday. Rod won't care. I'll call him at home.

As my mind raced through my plan to stop the sheriff's harassment, I pulled on my clothes. After cinching my belt, I unconsciously patted my front pants pocket. Something felt funny. There was a little bulge like the pocket had knotted up. I was pushing my hand inside when my middle finger encountered something soft. I knew instinctively what it was. My pulse started to race while I gingerly pulled it out of the pocket, my mind hoping against hope. And there it was, a latex glove with a triangular piece ripped off. Benson, that son-of-a-bitch! No, wait. It couldn't be. No one's been in this house but me and Dr. Coombs, and Coombs was never out of my sight. Suddenly I was freezing.

BENSON
Again, I slept well. There was little of interest in the newspaper. Connie reminded me that her sister and family were coming over for dinner around 4:00 p.m. and I was expected to do the barbecuing. With that reminder, I rescheduled my plan for the day—we'd search Darryl's house after I got back

from church. After notifying my deputies of the change in schedule, Connie and I went to services. I wondered if Darryl Hurley was a man of faith.

When Connie and I returned from church we were greeted by the voice of Rod Bain, attorney-atlLaw, who had taken up residence on a chaise lounge on my back deck with a newspaper and cup of coffee at hand, obviously waiting for our return.

"Good morning Pete, Connie. Beautiful day."

"Yes, it is Rod, and it's my day off as well, but seeing you here, I think I've got to go to work."

"Not for too long, Pete."

"What's up?" I asked.

"Darryl Hurley. He called me this morning, claims that you've fingered him for the Wainright killing and have been harassing him ever since."

"Sorry Rod, but Darryl's not telling it like it is. Everybody in town knows that Darryl has a helluva lot of motivation for wasting Wainright so, yes, he's a suspect, and right now the best suspect I have. But since the investigation started on Friday night, I've only talked with Darryl twice, once at the office and again at his home yesterday morning. That doesn't sound like harassment to me."

"Darryl's claiming that for the past two nights his telephone has rung all night long and he hasn't been able to sleep. He also said there has been a steady stream of visitors from the ambulance service banging on his door at all hours of the day."

Rod was matter-of-fact without any hint of aggressiveness, which is not the usual Rod. He typically is a pain in the butt. I was puzzled by his behavior so I decided to give it to him straight up. "When I saw Darryl yesterday he looked terrible and seemed kind of manic, so I asked Charlie Roper to have his folks keep an eye on him. Paul Coombs told me this morning that he visited Darryl last night and gave him a sedative. No one has seen Darryl since, except possibly for you."

"I haven't actually seen him, Pete. He called me earlier this morning."

"Well," I conceded, "maybe the ambulance crew was a little over-attentive in their concern for Darryl, but harassment is a real stretch."

"Not when combined with the phone calls," answered Rod quickly.

"I can't help you there. I haven't called Darryl nor has anyone with my department, and that is a statement that both my men and I can make under oath and on a polygraph."

"Who then?"

"If I had to pick a name, I'd say either his ex-wife or her sister."

"Darryl said it sounded like a female voice, at least, at first."

"We can speculate all day but that's not going to stop either you or Darryl from believing it was me. So, I am going to give you a name at the telephone company and an authorization form. You fax it to them and they'll tell you who called Darryl's house."

"Really?" Bain was truly surprised by my offer.

"Yeah. I've got nothing to hide."

HURLEY

After discovering the rubber glove in my pants pocket, I checked several other pairs of trousers in my closet, but none of them contained gloves. I then ran downstairs to my wood shop fully expecting to find another box of latex gloves sitting on my workbench, but nothing was there. I breathed a sigh of relief and went upstairs to have breakfast but before eating I burned the glove I had found that morning and ran the residue through my garbage disposal.

BENSON

I gave Rod the necessary paperwork and we engaged in a little fraternal chat before he went on his way. A little past noon, I knocked on Darryl's door and served him with a search warrant. The man looked as if he had aged twenty years during the past twenty-four hours. His face was pallid and drawn and his speech painfully slow.

Darryl called Rod Bain to let him know that we were searching his house and my men got busy. About ten minutes later Johnny Titan asked Darryl if he could get a drink of water. Darryl responded by offering coffee or a soft drink and Johnny asked for a Coke. Darryl went downstairs to get it from a storage refrigerator while I went back out to my squad car to radio the office.

HURLEY

I had just pulled a can of Coke out of my refrigerator when I saw it out of the corner of my eye. It couldn't be! I started to tremble. There was a box of latex gloves sitting on my workbench again! It wasn't there this morning! I had to get rid of it! I opened the back door with the intention of tossing them over the fence into my neighbor's back yard but one of Benson's deputies might see or hear me.

Back inside I scanned the wood shop. I couldn't hide

anything there. The deputies are upstairs going through everything with a fine-toothed comb. It won't be any different down here. What can I do?

It was a long shot, but maybe I'd get lucky. I opened the freezer door. There was a big box of frozen pork chops inside. I opened it, pulled out several chops, stuffed the rubber gloves inside, covered them with chops and pushed the box back inside. Then I took the empty glove box and shoved it inside another box and folded its flaps inside. It looked like a single empty box if one didn't look too closely. I was pushing the box to the back of my workbench when Sheriff Benson yelled downstairs, "Darryl, what are you doing down there? Hiding evidence? It doesn't take five minutes to get a can of Coke."

"Not hardly, Sheriff. I got distracted by a strange sound coming out of my furnace. I'll be right up."

BENSON

My team searched the house for three hours. The only thing we found out of the ordinary was a telephone that had been beaten to death by a rifle stock. We took both items into evidence. I had decided to call off the search for the day and return on Monday. The men were packing up to leave when Rod Bain came through the front door.

"Sheriff, could I visit with you and Darryl for a moment?" asked Bain. "The phone company just sent me the list of numbers which had called Darryl's telephone since Friday."

"You bet," I replied.

"Why don't we sit down," offered Darryl.

"What did the phone company tell you?" My curiosity was well engaged and I wanted to know what Bain had found out.

"They have records of Darryl receiving six calls. Three Friday night," answered Bain.

Then Darryl injected himself into the middle of Bain's talk. "The first call was some woman. The second sounded like Jill and I hung up on her."

Bain continued. "The third call was never answered, but the caller persisted until 6:00 A.M. Then Darryl got two calls Saturday afternoon."

"I disconnected the line that time," Darryl explained.

"The last call was placed Saturday night and only lasted eight seconds," Bain continued.

"But the phone rang all night, just like Friday," Darryl said, clearly surprised by Bain's explanation. "I didn't imagine it."

"Let's cut to the chase," I said. "Who made the calls?"

"The calls originated right here in Rodgersburg," answered Bain.

That brought Darryl right out of his chair. "I knew it!" he exclaimed.

"From a cell phone registered to Darryl Hurley," answered Bain.

Darryl's expression was priceless, and he exploded. "What! I don't have a cell phone. Jill has a cell phone and she's in Japan. And, why would I call myself?"

"You don't have a cell?" I asked. "These days everyone has a cell, particularly businessmen like you."

"No, never. I hate the things," answered Darryl.

"There's a cell phone in your desk," I replied.

Darryl was incredulous. "There couldn't be."

"Counselor," I said, "why don't you do the honors? It's in the desk; one of the side drawers near the window."

"Surely." Bain got up, crossed the room, and started opening drawers. He reached in and slowly withdrew his hand holding up a cell phone. "This was in the bottom drawer."

Darryl gasped. "That's Jill's phone, but I am sure she took it when she left."

"Turn it on, Rod," I instructed. "Let's see whose name pops up."

"I already have," answered Bain. "It's registered to Darryl and the number matches the one which called Darryl's home."

"No!" Darryl screamed. "I'm telling you the truth. I never made any calls to myself and my phone rang all night long."

I stood up and walked over to Bain. "Rod, would you put that phone in this evidence bag. We're going to need to take it into custody." Then I turned to Darryl and said, "Darryl, I've got to tell you that this looks real bad. Either you're trying to fabricate evidence to obstruct justice or your mind has slipped a gear. Right now I'm not sure which."

The deputies concluded the search for the day, leaving me alone with Darryl and Rod Bain. Our conversation ran another forty-five minutes but, frankly, it was a waste of time. Darryl continued to insist that he had nothing to do with the phone calls and, to tell the truth, I half believed him but it was clear that his lawyer did not. Bain repeatedly asked Darryl to check into the hospital and get some rest. The strain he was experiencing was obvious to all, but Darryl was equally adamant in his refusal. Together Rod and I left the house about mid-afternoon.

"So what are you going to do, Pete?" Bain asked.

"Work the case. I don't have any other option." I replied.

"Are there any other suspects?"

"None within a country mile of Darryl, counselor. Johnny checked out two potential leads Friday. One was out of town and the other was in a three-hour meeting with a slew of witnesses."

"So Darryl's the focus," concluded Bain.

"It's pretty simple, Rod. Darryl has motive in abundance. He was three blocks from the scene of the crime, and he doesn't have a verifiable alibi for his whereabouts at the time of the murder. And, I might add, his behavior during the past three days has become very bizarre. I'd say it all adds up to one very big hint."

HURLEY

Bain was right. I needed to go to the hospital, but I had to get rid of those rubber gloves I had stashed in the freezer. After Benson and Bain left my house I went downstairs to retrieve them. The room looked exactly like I left it. I had stayed in the kitchen monitoring the search and no one went downstairs. They'd search here tomorrow. I opened the freezer. The box with the pork chops was there but as I started to remove the chops I knew something was wrong. I got frantic and spilled its contents on the floor. No latex gloves!

To be honest I really don't know what I did next. In retrospect my mind plays a tape showing me moving at breakneck speed searching every nook and cranny of my basement. All I know for sure is that when I heard a sound of some type outside the house, I seemed to wake up, like I'd been in a trance or something. I was sitting on the basement steps, my wood shop completely torn apart, every shelf and drawer dumped onto the floor. And I didn't care.

I went upstairs to the bathroom, found my sleeping tablets, popped every last one into my mouth and lay down on the bed. It was 8:20 p.m.

BENSON

I was very worried about Darryl. So was his attorney, and I finally convinced him that Darryl shouldn't be left alone in the house. He consented to let someone from the ambulance crew stay over and Charlie Roper agreed to go.

Charlie got to Darryl's just before 9:00 p.m., found the door open, and let himself in when Darryl didn't answer the bell. He found Hurley lying on his bed talking to himself. Charlie reported that Darryl turned to him and said,

"Charlie. I just took every damn sleeping pill I had, trying to kill myself, and look at me. I am wide awake. I can't even do myself in, how could I have ever thought I could kill that bastard Wainright and get away with it?"

We took Darryl into custody that night, where, in the presence of his attorney, he made a full confession. Later, after he'd explained his actions to the Court, Darryl's conscience still wouldn't let him rest. "That about right, Darryl?" I asked.

"I guess so, Sheriff."

"You've pled and been sentenced. How would you like to set the record straight and tell the truth?"

"What do you mean?" Darryl asked.

"Your opening statement about meeting Wainright in the park and killing him in a rage after he insulted you was pure fiction. No one goes to the duck pond in the park wearing rubber gloves. You lay in wait for Adam with malice aforethought."

"What difference does it make how it happened?" answered Darryl. "My mind is so scrambled I'm not sure what's real anymore."

"Okay, Darryl. Thanks for your cooperation. The deputy will return you to your cell."

"Bye, Sheriff."

After Darryl was gone, Dr. Coombs, who had come over to the jail to check on him, observed, "Most bizarre, Pete. A man descends to the brink of insanity, pushed there by rubber gloves which inexplicably appear in his home and by telephones ringing in the night. It's amazing what the mind can conjure up when racked with guilt."

"What do you make of it, Doc?"

"Not being a trained psychiatrist, I hesitate to offer a diagnosis, but it would appear that Darryl is suffering from a very severe case of dissociative disorder."

"Heard of it. How does it work?" I asked.

"It comes in several forms—amnesia, fugue, multiple personality disorder. The mind compartmentalizes its actions, completely separating what it does in one setting from what it does elsewhere. I am sure you've had contact with suspects involved in violent crimes and they describe the event as if they were watching a third person doing it, not consciously aware that they are the ones actually undertaking the act."

"Like watching it in a movie."

"Exactly."

"Sounds like a defense attorney's ploy."

"There's some of that for sure," answered Coombs, "but it's also a legitimate, but comparatively rare, psychiatric condition."

"But Darryl didn't describe what happened like someone else had done it. He denied doing it, until he finally confessed."

"True," answered Coombs. "Darryl seems to have something more pronounced. He's doing two things which, in this case, are the complete opposite from one another—proclaiming his innocence and torturing himself with remorse. His conscious brain has no recollection of what he's been doing."

"So, let me get this right. On the one hand, Darryl's remorseful over killing Adam and subconsciously he wants to get caught, so he drives himself crazy by making telephone calls to himself using his ex-wife's cell phone and then can't remember doing it."

"Yeah, that's what I think happened. I also think he kept planting and replanting the rubber gloves around the house while he was consciously trying to destroy the evidence of his crime."

"Sounds pretty bizarre to me, Doc, but it's either that or poor Darryl just spent three days in the twilight zone. I am also puzzled about another thing too."

"What's that, Pete?

"How could Darryl take a whole bottle of sleeping pills and not just survive, but stay awake through the whole ordeal?"

"Oh, that I can answer. I had Darryl on placebos."

"Fake pills?"

"Indeed," answered the Doctor. "After Jill walked out on

Darryl, he came to me and complained about insomnia so I gave him a prescription to help him through a rough patch. He was back to see me two weeks later wanting a refill and I figured Darryl was on a path toward drug abuse. I switched his medication and told him that he might have a sleepless night or two as his body adjusted to the new prescription, but afterward he'd be fine."

"So, he's been taking sugar pills or some such?" I offered.

"Some such. Bicarbonate of soda mixed with quinine to give it a medicinal bite. It's a little concoction I worked up with "Doc" Sullivan down at the drugstore."

"And it works?" I was unconvinced.

"Like a charm in most cases," replied the good Doctor. "For Darryl, it was perfect. For most people, insomnia is really nothing more than fear or worry about whether they will be able to sleep. The more they worry about getting to sleep, the worse it gets and the less they sleep. If they take a pill which they think is going to knock them out, chances are it will."

"Fascinating," I replied.

"I thought you'd find it interesting," the doctor said. "Want me to fix something up for you when you're having one of your late nights?"

"A placebo or the real deal?"

"Maybe a little of both?"

"No thanks, Doc. In my job it's already hard enough separating fact from fiction."

CHAPTER SEVEN

The Death Watch

I was late getting to the office. Not fashionably late, but a full hour behind schedule. Over breakfast I had a little dust up with my bride of nearly twenty-five years over the dead fir tree in our back yard. Back in May its needles started turning red. By June, its epitaph had been written. I announced a plan to cut down the tree but, one thing after another had intervened and now, weeks later, it was still standing sentry over the house and yard. It's a huge tree, over three feet in diameter, and probably a hundred feet high. No doubt it's been standing there for more than a hundred fifty years. On more than one occasion Connie has inquired when I was going to remove it. I believe the proper term for that form of serial discussion between spouses is "nagging." This morning I was feeling well nagged and it didn't help that she was right and I wrong.

When I opened the front door of the Law Enforcement Center my mind clicked back into work mode. We were shorthanded again this week. Kay Best, the department's chief dispatcher, office manager, and general "go to" person was in Butte for medical tests, and my chief deputy, Johnny Titan, was at the State Police Academy for a few days. Nick

Colusa, the deputy based in Winslow, was back in Rodgersburg covering for both of them. Fortunately, it had been very quiet for the past several days and I had actually found time to go fishing over the weekend, which beats cutting down a massive fir any day.

"How was coffee?" greeted Nick as I cleared the front door of the office and picked up the mail neatly piled on the corner of Kay's desk.

"Anything happen while I was gone?" I replied, fully expecting that the answer would be no.

"Lady by the name of Paula Davis and her son Shawn came by just after you left. Said they wanted to talk with you," Nick answered to my great surprise.

"They say what about?"

"No, I asked a couple of times but she said they'd be back to see you. I took a chance and told them I thought you'd be here between 10:00 and 10:30."

"Fine. I'll have a chance to look at the mail."

With that I went to my office and was just starting to sit down when I heard the front door open followed by a woman's voice saying "Hello again, deputy. Has Sheriff Benson arrived?"

"He has, Mrs. Davis, and is expecting you."

After a greeting and a few minutes of small talk about family and happenings around town, which is the customary way of transacting business in Montana, Paula Davis asked her son to "show the sheriff what you found on the road last night."

Shawn, who was about twelve years old and as shy as he was blond, pulled a silver watch from his pants pocket and placed it on my desk. I picked it up by the edge of the wristband to examine it. It looked expensive but I am no expert, and it could have been just an expensive looking knockoff. There was an inscription on the back which I read, "M.T. Love A.T.," and then thoughtfully repeated to myself, "M.T. Love A.T."

At that point, Paula Davis injected herself into my thought pattern by noting, "I thought about it all last night, Sheriff. The only M.T. and A.T. that I can think of are Micky and Anna Thompson."

"Plausible," I replied, "very plausible."

"Look," Paula continued, "the gunk next to the face looks like blood to me."

"You're doing my job very well, Paula," I said lightly. "I suspect you're right. Where did Shawn find the watch?"

"You tell him, Shawn," directed his mother, but Shawn shook his head no and then whispered that she do so.

"Shawn and a couple of his friends were fishing up above Clearwater Campground last night. He said he found the watch in the middle of the road just outside the campground entrance."

"What time was that?" I asked.

"He was home just before nine so it must have been around 8:30. Is that right, Shawn?"

Shawn nodded yes in reply to his mother.

"Well, Paula, thanks for bringing this in. I can't think of anything more that I need from either you or Shawn right now, but if I do I'll give you a call."

Nick and I tried repeatedly to reach the Thompsons by phone to determine whether Micky was missing a watch but our calls went unanswered. In the early afternoon I drove over to the house, a poorly maintained doublewide in Kidston's Trailer Court, and had the same result—no one home. About 3:30 the Department received a call from the Forest Service reporting that their campground clean-up crew had found an abandoned truck in the Clearwater Campground, license number 57T-1406. A quick check with the Montana Motor Vehicle Division revealed that it was registered to Michael (Micky) Thompson. Now I was real interested. Nick and I went off to find the rig.

"Nick, given that bloody watch the Davis boy found, let's treat this as a crime scene, at least for now," I directed.

"Okay, boss. Micky was probably up here fishing. It's one of his favorite haunts."

"How do you know that?" I asked.

"I ran around some with him when we were kids. We did a lot of fishing together. When we got into high school we went our separate ways. Micky got into partying and the trouble that went with it."

"And nothing has changed," I added.

"Oh, no. Micky's a lot calmer, ever since he married Anna. You've never seen the real Micky Thompson, particularly when he's got a full load on."

"Nice truck," I observed. Micky had a late model Ford F-250, chrome wheels and likely every factory option available. Micky wasn't the only one in town living in a dump not befitting a pauper and driving around like he was a king, but he was certainly the most notorious. "I'll try the driver's side...locked."

"Same here, Pete," Nick replied, "and there's no fishing gear either."

"Let's check along the creek."

Our scouting trip along the stream didn't yield any-

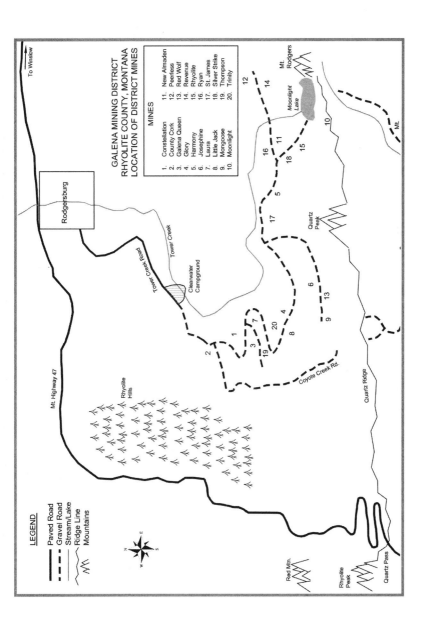

LEGEND

Paved Road
Gravel Road
Stream/Lake
Ridge Line
Mountains

GALENA MINING DISTRICT
RHYOLITE COUNTY, MONTANA
LOCATION OF DISTRICT MINES

MINES

1. Constellation
2. County Cork
3. Galena Queen
4. Glory
5. Harmony
6. Josephine
7. Laura
8. Little Jack
9. Mongoose
10. Moonlight
11. New Almaden
12. Peerless
13. Red Wolf
14. Revenue
15. Rhyolite
16. Ryan
17. St. James
18. Silver Strike
19. Thompson
20. Trinity

thing of value. Tower Creek starts in the mountains about ten miles from Rodgersburg at Moonlight Lake, named after an adjacent, now abandoned mine. The stream tumbles down to Rodgersburg through a series of rapids and pools. Just above the campground the stream plunges over a twelve-foot waterfall and then meanders through a series of beaver dams that flank the campground on the south. Tower Creek is a decent, but not spectacular fishery, hosting eight to twelve-inch rainbow trout. It's primarily fished by youngsters and retirees who appreciate convenience and easy access to a fishing hole. The more serious fishermen go elsewhere, particularly to Rock Creek.

As Nick and I tramped along a fisherman's trail following the waterway, we found one spot where the grass had been trampled down, but it could have been done by anyone. I made arrangements with Goodyear Ford to tow Micky's truck back to their garage where we could check it more carefully. That done, I went home to dinner with my wife Connie and our two sons, Phil and Tom. It was a warm evening and we ate on the deck behind our house, after which I took a quick drive to the Thompson residence and, again, no one was home. This time I left a note on the front door asking that I be called as soon as someone returned.

That was a mistake. I was rewarded for my diligence by the blare of the telephone at 1:30 A.M. Anna Thompson was on the other end and I quickly explained the reason for the note. Anna didn't seem terribly interested or concerned but I continued to press the issue until she agreed to see me.

I reached the Thompsons' front door fifteen minutes later. Anna let me in and introduced me to her mother, Jane Fischer. Both women had cigarettes in their hands and the smell of stale cigarette smoke was overwhelming. It momentarily brought me back to my youth in Butte. My spinster aunt Mary was a heavy smoker and the smell of stale cigarettes hung over the inside of her home like a pungent quilt, numbing my nostrils and suffocating my lungs. Mary was a dear woman and very good to me, but I never wanted to stay in her house very long.

"Sorry about disturbing you, but we can't seem to locate Micky," I explained as I tried in vain to shut down my olfactory nerve.

"Micky's not here, Sheriff," answered Anna. "He's probably fishing up at the headwaters of Madison Creek or over at Bulldog Lake. He said he was going up there Sunday."

"I don't think so," I said in reply. "We found his truck in the Clearwater Campground."

"That don't mean nothing, Sheriff. Micky probably went off with one of his friends. Micky's always trying to get someone else to drive and front the gas."

"Is he also in the habit of leaving his watch in the middle of the road?" I questioned.

"What?" Now there was a little excitement in Anna's voice.

"One of the kids from town found a watch outside the campground Sunday night. The inscription said 'M.T. Love A.T.'"

"That's Micky's watch. He must have dropped it."

"Well, he might be hurt, Anna. There was blood on it."

"Oh, my God, where is he?"

"That's what I came here to find out, Anna. Now tell me, aside from fishing on Madison Creek, what were his plans for the weekend?"

Anna Thompson was now clearly befuddled. Her mother put an arm on Anna's shoulder as a comforting gesture. I waited.

"I don't really know," began Anna. "I left Friday morning to go to Salt Lake. I met Ma there. She lives in Arizona. We spent the weekend with my sister and her family and came home on the late flight to Butte, which was late itself. All Micky said to me about the weekend was that he'd likely go fishing up Madison Creek, if the weather wasn't bad."

"Nothing else?" I probed.

"Oh...he said he might haul in a load of wood. Micky, Vern Overstreet, and a couple of other guys have been sawing up slash in those clearcuts below Bulldog Lake. Micky usually cuts a truck load and then goes fishing for a couple of hours."

"Micky been having trouble with anybody, Anna?"

"You know Micky, Sheriff. He has trouble with lots of people."

"Enough to want to hurt him?" I continued.

"Hmm...yeah. To be honest about it, there might be a dozen or more, but recently Micky's had some issues with both Walt Zander and Doug Raymond."

"Why?"

"Walt had his swather stolen last year."

"I remember, Anna. Fact is, I talked with Micky about it."

"Yeah, well Micky didn't do it but there's no convincing Walt otherwise."

"He's not the only one who feels that way." I looked Anna straight in the eye so that there was no mistaking my position on the matter. "What about Doug Raymond?"

"Micky had a contract to cut poles on Harding's land. Doug's got some property nearby. Someone went onto Doug's and cut a bunch of timber."

"And Doug blames Micky, imagine that."

"But Micky didn't do it," came Anna's repetitive retort.

Micky didn't do it, I thought to myself. I wish I had a dollar for every time I heard that line—I'd be able to buy a new car. Admittedly, Micky didn't do it all the time, but he did it often enough. The problem was getting the evidence. Micky was smart, and most of his alleged transgressions, usually a question of his fingers sticking to someone else's property, were small matters, misdemeanors if he'd been caught. Walt Zander's missing swather, a class one felony, was really a step up for Micky, assuming that he did it. I believed it, but I hadn't found a real piece of evidence to implicate Micky. "Okay, Anna, that's enough for tonight. If you hear from Micky, call me. Nice to meet you, Mrs. Fischer. I'll be in touch."

I left the Thompson residence, mentally checking off the people I wanted to see. First, would be Vern Overstreet, one of the bartenders at the Shamrock Bar, the roughest saloon in town. Vern's a tough guy and I mean that in the pugilist sense, but he's straight as an arrow and would give me the straight scoop about Micky. Then, I'd need to see both Walt Zander and Doug Raymond. Walt wasn't terribly happy about the fact that I never found either his swather or the party that stole it.

I went back home, slept in, and got to the office about 8:30 A.M. I had Charlie Roper, Chief of the Sheriff's Reserve, organize a search of the Tower Creek area where we had found Micky's truck. Then I headed over to Vern

Overstreet's home where I found him mowing his front lawn. Alongside the house was an old Chevy half-ton stacked high with firewood. He cut the machine off as I came through the front gate and pointed me toward the front steps where we could sit a spell.

"What brings you around here, Sheriff?" Vern asked as he pulled out a can of Copenhagen.

"I am looking into something involving Micky Thompson," I replied while watching Vern get a pinch of snuff ready for his lower lip. It looked mighty inviting, but I'd given up the habit years ago so it wasn't much of a struggle to say no when Vern offered me the can.

"Ole Mick never seems to be too far away from the law. What's he supposed to have done now?"

"Nothing that I know of for sure, Vern. We found his truck up at Clearwater yesterday but nobody, including Anna, has seen him for several days."

"I ain't seen him either," Vern answered quickly.

"Anna said Micky's been cutting firewood with you and a few other fellows up near Bulldog."

"That's true, Sheriff. We started about five weeks ago after the loggers left. Lots of good wood in the slash piles. It's a little green, but it'll be real good late winter and next year," explained Vern, who then paused to shoot a stream of tobacco juice into the adjacent flowerbed, knocking a big grasshopper to the ground.

"Was Micky there this past weekend?" I asked.

"Nope," came Vern's quick reply.

"He say anything about why he wouldn't be there?"

"The wood cutting isn't an organized thing, Pete. We ain't working together. Fellows that want to cut usually show up between eight and ten in the morning and start cutting. About noon we get together to have lunch, maybe a beer or two, and chew the fat. Afterwards, everybody goes their own way. Micky usually goes fishing. When he didn't show up Saturday nobody thought anything about it."

"Micky give you any indication that anything was wrong?" I asked.

"Well, now that you mention it, his behavior was a little odd week before last."

"How so?"

"Hmm...," answered Vern as he spat another big wallop of tobacco juice onto his wife's roses, this time hitting a butterfly. "It was just about noon and I was tying off my load. Micky was down the road about fifty yards doing the same thing. Doug Raymond came down the road in that red three-ton he drives and stops next to Micky. I couldn't hear anything, but it looked like they exchanged a word or two. Then Micky backed up a step or two with his hands up like this," and Vern held up his hands like someone was threatening him. "Doug started to drive again and Micky just watched him drive away."

"Did you talk to Doug?"

"No. He didn't stop, just gave me a big wave. He had his son with him, the kid with all the pimples. They had some fence stuff in the truck so I assumed they had a job somewhere up the hill."

"Did Micky say anything about the encounter?"

"No, he didn't, Pete, and that's why I said he was acting odd. Normally, Micky is full of b.s., talking a mile a minute. When we quit for lunch Micky started over toward us, then

changed his mind, went back to his rig and drove back to town.
"He passed up a chance to fish? Now that is odd, for
Micky," I added.

"Don'tcha know," answered Vern in reply.

I visited with Vern for a few more minutes. He didn't
have anything more to add about Micky, so I returned to
the office, and saw my number one assistant at her desk. "I
didn't think you'd be in today."

"Neither did I," Kay said with a smile, "but I hit it just
perfectly and got all of the tests done yesterday."

"Results?" I inquired.

"Not until Thursday, but the doctor didn't seem overly
concerned."

"Great. Nick around?"

"In the kitchen."

"Well, c'mon back and join us for a cup. We've got our-
selves a missing Micky Thompson."

After filling in Nick and Kay on the results of my visits
with Anna Thompson and Vern Overstreet, eating a slice of
banana bread and downing a large cup of coffee, Nick and I
headed over to Walt Zander's ranch, about three miles east
of town. Walt was standing next to the door of his shop
building when we drove up.

After getting out of the patrol car I greeted him. "Mornin', Walt."

"Sheriff, Nick, how have you been?"

"Good, Walt," answered Nick.

"We're looking for a missing person—Micky Thompson," I said.

Walt was slow to reply. "I hate to say this about any man,
but I hope you don't find him."

"We know you're not too fond of him, Walt," answered Nick. "That's why we're here."

"You think I might have something to do with it?" Walt queried.

"We don't think anything just yet," I injected, "but it would help us if you could tell us where you were over the weekend."

"Sheriff, I'll go you one better," Walt answered, "and tell you where Thompson was as well."

"Okay. That'll help."

Walt paused temporarily and looked off toward the horizon as if he were lost in thought.

"Saturday, I was in Butte all day with my wife and son. We were shopping for a car for him. We had dinner at the Silver Bow Café and got home after dark."

"And Thompson?" asked Nick.

"Saturday night," Walt replied a little less thoughtfully. "When we drove past, his truck was outside the Pot O'Gold."

I followed up by asking, "You stay home all night?"

"Yes," Walt quickly responded. "We had breakfast with the hired man before we went to church."

"Then where?" I asked.

"To Winslow for Beth Bender's wedding. We got home late, close to eleven."

Nick concluded the interview by observing, "That's good, Walt."

Rather than head straight over to Doug Raymond's for another interview, Nick and I decided that we should follow up on the lead Walt Zander had provided. We made a stop at the casino and confirmed that Micky Thompson had, in fact, been there Saturday night until after midnight. We also checked with Thompson's neighbors. A lady two doors down the street said that she had seen Micky's truck in front of the house late Sunday morning, but no one had seen Micky.

"It looks as if Micky vanished sometime between Sunday in the A. M. and when the Davis boy found the watch that evening," Nick offered after we'd both climbed into the patrol car.

"I'm inclined to believe that Micky drank too much Saturday night and slept in. Then, instead of going fishing up Madison Creek, he went up Tower Creek to the campground, sometime in the afternoon," I answered in return.

"So you think Micky drove the truck up to where we found it?" asked Nick.

"What's the alternative?" I said, answering Nick's question with one of my own.

"Someone else could have driven the truck up to the campground, maybe as a diversion," replied Nick.

"I think you're watching too many detective stories on TV, Nick. Yeah, that could have happened, but here in Rodgersburg, what's the likelihood of it happening?"

"About as likely as a hound dog singing opera," answered Nick with a shrug, quickly adding, "I didn't mean your singing, Pete."

"Good thing," I said.

"We're acting on the theory that Micky is the victim of a crime. Charlie and the search party may quickly prove that theory wrong," I added.

"True, Pete, but it's the only thing we've got right now. Why don't we pay a visit to Doug Raymond?"

"I don't want to bother him when he's at work. He's working on that power line relocation near Ajax. Should be home around six tonight. We can catch him then."

Nick and I decided to split up, with him spending some more time in Thompson's neighborhood while I went downtown to canvass Micky's usual haunts; principally the town's saloons. No one reported seeing Micky on Sunday. Several reported that he was alive and well on Saturday night.

Nick came over to the house and had a bite to eat with the family. Nick gets along well with my two sons. Phil, the younger one, considers himself Mr. Cool, God's gift to the ladies, and Nick loves to badger him about his love life. Afterward, we paid Doug Raymond a visit. Nick took a walk around to the back of the house and I went to the front door.

Doug Raymond was a bit surprised to see me standing on his front stoop. "Sheriff! If it's about that fine I still owe on, I..."

"It's not. Can I come in?"

"Honey," yelled Doug as he turned back into the house. "Sheriff's here." He then opened the screen door and asked if I "would like some ice tea or, maybe, a beer."

"No thanks, Doug," I replied. "I'm here to talk with you about Micky Thompson."

Doug replied, "I heard a rumor that he's missing. For good, I hope."

"And you two were such good friends."

"Micky's a damned crook and he stole from me, but I didn't do nothing to him. Hell, I ain't even seen the man in a month."

"That's not what Vern Overstreet told me this morning," I countered. "He said you two had words about a week ago up in the clearcuts by Bulldog."

"Sorry," answered Doug. "I spoke too fast. I did see him up there, but we never talked. Micky saw me coming down the road and yelled at me to stop. I did. Then he acted like he was drunk, saying some gibberish and waving his arms around.

"I heard that he backed up funny with his hands in the air like a man would if another was holding a pistol on him," I offered.

"I didn't hold no gun on him. Never done that to any man. Besides, I had my boy with me."

Our chat was briefly interrupted by Mrs. Raymond bringing Doug a glass of iced tea. She asked whether she could get me anything but I declined and went back to questioning her husband. "Where were you on Sunday?"

"Around the house till around three in the afternoon," Doug answered. "Then I went up Tower Creek fishing until seven or so."

"Who was with you?"

"No one, Sheriff, I went by myself." Doug's face went ashen. No doubt he'd heard that Micky's truck had been found abandoned in the Clearwater Campground. He'd just implicated himself in Micky's disappearance.

Nick stuck his face in the front door and asked me to step outside. Once outside Doug's hearing range I asked, "What's up?"

"I found some blood and hair in the back of Doug's pickup. The hair is light brown, like Micky's."

"Looks like we'd better bring both the truck and Doug in," I concluded.

I went back and broke the news to Doug. He started to say something but stopped to shake his head, and then shut up. I handcuffed him and read him his rights. He stayed calm, which is more than I could say for his wife. For a moment there, I thought I was going to have to cuff her as well and bring her in for obstruction of justice. We impounded Doug's truck, collected several blood and hair samples, and found a couple of fingerprints. We've collected specimens of various types from Micky before, given his frequent "suspect" status in crimes around the county. It didn't take long before we had a match between the blood and fingerprints found in Doug's truck and the records in Micky's file. All the while, Doug maintained his innocence.

"Doug, your claims of innocence aren't good enough," I admonished. "We have you admitting to being at a location very near where we found Micky Thompson's truck. Then we find his hair and blood in the back of your pickup."

Doug responded vigorously. "I don't know what's going on here! I didn't touch Micky. Hell, I didn't even see Micky on Sunday!"

"You have to agree, Doug, it's a little curious that you were in the same spot as Micky, especially given all the places there are to fish around here."

"Not really, Sheriff. Anyone who knows me will tell you my favorite fishing spots are the beaver dams along Tower Creek. I go there all the time."

"So what are you trying to tell me?" I asked.

"I was doing what I always do. I fish Tower Creek. It's my place. Close to home. Micky only goes there once in a while."

"And?"

"Don't you see it, Sheriff? Someone knew I'd be there. They set me up."

"A frame-up!" I replied. "This isn't the movies, Doug. So far as I know, there were only two people with motive enough to go after Micky—you and Walt Zander, and Walt's got an alibi. You don't, and there's the little matter of Micky's blood and hair in the back of your truck."

"I didn't know it was in there!" Doug said. "God Almighty, don't you think I would've washed my truck if I had a body back there? I'm being framed, I tell you."

It was late by the time I got home and into bed but the confrontation with Doug Raymond left me in no mood to sleep and, I didn't. After tossing and turning for about an hour, I rose, went down to the basement and picked up my copy of *The Desert Generals*, an account of the North African Campaign during World War II, and put Micky Thompson out of my mind for an hour or so. Sleep finally came but when the alarm went off, my weariness seemed magnified. I've never been able to figure out why I am more tired after sleeping two or three hours than I am if I stay awake continuously.

The Sheriff's Reserve search team combed the Tower Creek drainage all day Tuesday and half of Wednesday but found no sign of Micky. Doug Raymond was arraigned late Wednesday morning and he posted bail. I was in the office talking with Nick around 4:00 P.M. when I received a call. After listening to my half of the call, Nick wanted me to fill him in.

"That was a guy named Art Mozer with Trans-Global Insurance out of Helena," I said.

"What did he want?"

"Seems that he got a call this morning from Anna Thompson. She said her husband had been killed and she wanted to file a claim for his death benefit—$500,000.

What Mozer found so interesting was her claim that Micky had been killed, not died. That made him a little edgy and he called us for verification of the circumstances of Micky's death, which I couldn't do, of course."

"Any chance Anna might be involved?" Nick asked.

"She was in Salt Lake with her mother and sister when Micky disappeared. That's a helluva good alibi and I am not aware of any connection between her and Doug Raymond."

"We should check with Kay, Pete. She always knows all the gossip. If Anna had a thing going on with Doug, Kay'd know."

"Where is she?" I asked, and just then we heard the front door open and close.

"I'd say she just returned."

"Kay!" I yelled, something I almost never dare to do to her.

"Yeeess!" came her elongated response.

"Nick and I need some help with the gossip side of law enforcement."

We could hear the escalating tap of her cowboy boots as she crossed the anteroom toward my office, followed by "And you think I know who Micky's been messing around with?" as she stepped through the door.

"Or Anna, maybe," added Nick meekly.

"That's a dead end, boys," added Kay confidently. "Micky has his share of bad habits, but I've never heard of him playing the field. He's strictly a one-woman man, and the same with Anna."

"Well," said Nick. "Another good theory gone to waste."

"What theory was that?" asked Kay. She looked at me, then to Nick, and back to me.

"My God," she said and then started to laugh. "You two had Anna with Doug Raymond?"

Nick and I knew enough to keep our mouths shut.

Kay's laughter continued. "Pete, you're so lucky Connie found you, cause given what you know about women...well, let's just say you'd likely be as single as Nick." Then she left, granting us time to quietly muse about our ignorance of things female.

"Back to Mozer, Nick. He said Anna seemed real anxious about collecting the death benefit. When he told her that the company wouldn't pay off until there was an official ruling of death, she seemed confused, and kept saying Micky had been killed."

"The lack of a body tends to slow the process of determining if a death has taken place," Nick observed factually. Nick was so serious he was beginning to sound like a TV detective.

"Mozer made that observation as well, and one other, and I quote, 'This smells. I can't give you facts, Sheriff, but when you've been in the insurance game awhile, you develop a sense for when things aren't quite right. I'm smelling insurance fraud.' Unquote."

Several times that evening I thought through my conversation with Art Mozer. Next morning, I discussed the situation with Nick again.

"It sounds pretty farfetched to me, Pete. Maybe you're the one watching too many movies."

"Touché," I confessed.

Nick continued. "Except for maybe swiping Walt

Zander's swather, Micky has always been a small-time hustler and sticky finger artist. I can't see him coming up with a complicated fraud scheme. But, if you're going to pull an insurance scam, what better way to pull it off than to frame Doug Raymond for murder."

"Anna is the beneficiary of a big policy, far larger than they could ever afford. That suggests that if Anna and Micky are involved in fraud, they probably have a partner, someone who could come up with the cash to pay the premium, probably for a cut of the action."

"I hear you, Pete," Nick replied, "but I'm inclined to think it's just Micky and Anna. Anybody with money for a big premium would know that an insurance company isn't going to hand over a big check just because someone is allegedly dead."

"Good point," I added.

Nick and I resumed our discussion of how we might investigate the fraud angle the next day, but our efforts were derailed by two calls received mid-morning. Nick went to Ajax to investigate a cabin break-in and I went up to Boulder Lake on a vehicle accident. It was early afternoon by the time I was finished at the accident site. I headed over to the Evergreen Saloon for lunch.

The Evergreen menu is pretty short but the burgers are without peer. I was just sinking my teeth into one when my cell phone went off. It was Nick reporting that Micky Thompson was alive, in the Rodgersburg hospital. A couple of high school kids out riding their four-wheelers found Micky in one of the old buildings at the abandoned Ryan Mine. He was injured, but they managed to get him aboard one of their vehicles and took him to the hospital.

I took the time to finish my lunch. I figured Doc Coombs would take a while to examine Micky and I wouldn't be able to talk with him right away. I got to the hospital about 2:10 P.M. Nick was there talking with Anna Thompson outside Micky's room as I walked down the hall.

"Anna, how's Micky?" I asked.

"He's resting now, Sheriff, but Doctor assured me he'd be all right."

"Did Micky say where he had been?" Just a little probe to see what Anna knew.

"I was just so glad to see him, I didn't ask." Serious business, I thought to myself. This is the first time I think I've ever talked with Anna when she wasn't smoking a cigarette or chewing gum. She must be really worried. "Could you guys please excuse me?" Anna continued while nodding first toward Nick and then me, "Micky asked me to get him a few things from home."

"Sure, go ahead," said Nick. "We can talk to you later."

I waited for Anna to disappear around the corner and then asked Nick, "How badly is Micky hurt?"

"Doc said Micky's not hurt bad at all. He's got some contusions and a couple of small cuts, nothing very serious. I share the Doc's opinion. After seeing Micky, I think he's acting more hurt than he really is."

"Did you see any cuts on his head, something which would fit with the blood and hair we found in Doug Raymond's truck?" I asked.

"There's a little nick in front of his left ear. Might have bled a fair piece. The big cut is on his left wrist. Looks like someone tore his watch band off."

"How is he mentally?"

"The Doc said that Micky claimed to be woozy. The kids who found him said that he was asleep and it was hard to wake him up. Micky said he didn't know it was Thursday."

"Was he drugged?"

"The doc took a blood test. We'll know tomorrow."

"Did you get a chance to question Micky?"

"No, Pete, sorry about that. I was about to question him when Anna came into the room. I deferred to her. They talked a little while, and then Micky drifted off to sleep."

"How about the kids that found him? What else did they say?"

"They spotted him lying down on a couple of old planks. The kids said once they saw him they were going to leave but one of the boys, Frank Harper's son, said he'd heard about Micky being missing so they went in to find out if that was who it was. Then they brought him here."

Nick and I parted company. He headed back to the office while I went in search of Dr. Paul Coombs, our all-purpose physician here in Rodgersburg. He gave me a quick once-over on Micky's condition and invited me to come back the next morning if I wanted to chat with Micky. I was there promptly at 8:30 A.M. "So Micky, how are you?"

"Huh...oh, it's you, Sheriff. I must have dozed off." Micky's speech was slow and quiet, not the usual Micky.

"So, how are you feeling?" I tried again.

"Sore, pretty sore. It feels like someone beat me with a stick." Micky reached to the table next to his bed and took a sip of water from a plastic cup.

"Can you tell me what happened, Micky?"

"Some of it. I can't seem to remember things," came Micky's halting reply.

"Well, tell me what you do remember," I quickly added.

"I went up to Tower Creek to fish a little...I was standing there just getting ready to drop my line in the water, when whack...something hit me on the back of the head...then everything went black."

"Did you see who it was?"

"Not then, but later."

"Who was it?"

"Doug Raymond." With that Micky's tone was both definite and forceful.

"What happened next, Mick?"

"Don't know for sure, but he must have drug me to his truck. He dumped me in the back, that's when I saw him."

"Oh?" I replied, with the echo of disbelief in my voice.

"Yeah, I kind of came to for a second or two. That's when I saw him."

Micky seemed to be getting stronger. He was almost talking normally. The slow, halting gait of his first sentences had disappeared. I pressed on. "How were you lying in the truck?"

"What?"

"How were you lying, Mick? On your back or stomach?"

"On my back."

"Where was your body positioned?"

"Hmm...I'm not sure. I think my head was toward the cab."

"Okay, Mick. How about the wrist? How did it get hurt?"

"I don't know."

"Did you scuffle with Doug?"

"Not that I can remember. He bushwhacked me from behind. A god-damned sucker punch!"

"How about your watch? Where is it?"

Micky had been speaking normally and he must have realized what he was doing because with his next answer the slow speech began anew. "I don't know."

"After you were loaded into the truck, what happened next?" I pressed.

"We must...we must...we must have started up the Tower Creek road." Now he was acting confused, but I wasn't buying it.

"And then?"

"I don't know...how long we'd been driving," said Micky, almost in a whisper, "but I came to and I saw the old railroad trestle above the road."

"What happened next?"

"My head cleared just a little and I pulled myself together and I jumped out of the truck just before it crossed the bridge on the creek. Then I crawled into the brush." Micky's voice was completely without inflexion. He had just escaped his alleged captor, but he sounded like he was reciting his phone number. I pressed him again.

"What did Doug do?"

"Nothing. He must not have seen me."

"What side of the truck did you go over?"

"Passenger side. Sheriff, could we do this another time? I'm tired."

"Just a couple more, Mick, and then I'll let you get some sleep. What happened next?"

The slow gait of Micky's speech returned. "I went up the creek, crossed it below the falls and hid out in that telephone line shack below the Ryan Mine.

"Why didn't you come back to town?"

"I was afraid Doug would find me...that he had a gun."

"What do you think he was going to do to you?"

"Dump me down one of those old mine shafts so I'd never be found."

I never kept my word to Micky to let him get some sleep. Instead, I interviewed him for close to an hour. He stuck to his story, but I doubted its veracity. More importantly, it created a quandary for me. Micky had accused Doug Raymond of attacking him. Much as I now doubted Raymond's involvement, I felt I was going to have to arrest Doug once more. I went back to the office, talked the whole thing over with Nick, and then we went out and picked up Doug at his home. This time he wasn't so cooperative and we ended up cuffing him right there in front of his kids.

After locking Doug in his cell, I wandered back to the office wondering what my next move was likely to be when Connie called. "Pete, about the tree ..."

"Look," I interrupted, "I am sorry about not getting that done, but the Micky Thompson thing has kind of occupied my mind this week. I'll call Kevin right now."

"You don't have to," Connie answered. "I already took care of it. He'll be here around 4:30 but he wants to talk with you about the project."

"I might not be able to get there. Tell him what you want," I said in reply.

"I did," Connie answered. "Kevin said he wants to talk with you. Sounds like one of those guy things, he wants to 'talk with the man of the house.'" Then she sniggered.

"Okay, I'll try," I promised. "Tell Tom to hang around the house. We might need his help."

"Roger," said Connie. "Base 1 to Car 1, over and out."

"Please," I added. My wife dislikes imperative statements from me. She is, after all, my wife, not a member of the staff. "If Kevin gets there before me, please offer him a beer." With that I rang off.

It was about 4:40 when I drove my pickup into the driveway and parked in front of the garage. Kevin was sitting in a deck chair, beer in hand talking with Connie and Mary Cahill. Mary teaches in the elementary school with Connie. They've been friends for nearly thirty years. Kevin's been seeing Mary for the past couple of years.

"Pete," called Connie, "come see what Kev made for Mary." At that point she held a needlepoint pillowcase aloft.

I moved in for a closer look. There was an intricate pattern of rose blossoms in red, white, and pink interspersed with marigolds and purple larkspur.

"Isn't it just exquisite!" chirped Mary. "Look at the tight weave of the stitches."

I guess a tight weave was a good thing. I looked from the pillowcase over to my old buddy Kevin, the logger, football freak, and arguably the toughest guy in the county. "So, it's true?"

Kevin nodded.

"And you knit and crochet too? At least that's what I've heard." I'd been hearing these stories about Kevin for years but he never said anything to me about his textile skills and I never asked. But, here it was right before me. The cop came out in me. "How? Why? It doesn't..."

"Remember when I fell off the log loader and broke my pelvis?" answered Kevin, completely unbothered by my inquiry.

"Yeah."

"My Aunt Sarah came down from Augusta to visit. She's my mother's sister. Last one of the family alive, except for me. At any rate, she pulls out her knitting and starts it while she talks with me. After a while, I just got curious about it and asked her if I could try. She showed me what to do and it kind of relaxed me. I had her go buy me a set of needles and some yarn and that's how I whiled away the hours in the hospital and at home till I could go back to work."

"And the needlepoint?" I asked.

"That came later, after I met Mary. She loves needlepoint so I tried it to make her a birthday present."

"I do love it," Mary chimed in. "And it's extra special because I know Mr. Macho made it. He's soooo sweet." She leaned over and gave Kev a peck on the cheek.

That topic exhausted, the girls paraded into the kitchen so that Kevin and I could get after the tree. He wandered out to his truck to get his chainsaw and falling wedges, while I went into the garage to pull on a pair of coveralls over my uniform.

When Kevin returned he said to me, "Pete, how do you want to do this?"

"What are my options?" At that point, no doubt prompted by his mother, Tom came out the back door, pulling on a pair of work gloves.

"We can take it down from the top in small sections, say four to six feet," said Kevin. "The problem is, since the pelvis thing, I can't climb anymore, so the cutting is going to have to be done by you and Tom."

"Or?" I asked, already knowing what option I was going to select.

"Or, I drop it in that gap between the house and the garage," Kevin answered.

"Is there room?" asked Tom, joining the conversation.

"Plenty of room," replied Kevin nonchalantly, "But you're gonna have to move your pickup. The top's gonna fall just short of the fence over there."

"Did you measure that?" Tom asked.

"Just with my eyes," Kevin answered.

I shifted my eyes back and forth between the tree, the garage, house, and fence. It looked pretty tight to me and I was about to get a tape measure when I thought, Relax, Pete. Kev knows what he's doing. You'll insult him if you doubt his competence by measuring the clearance.

I simply said, "Okay, you're the pro." Then, I asked, "Kev, I'm a little curious. How come you wouldn't decide on a cutting plan with Connie?"

"Easy. Most women kind of overreact to logging. They don't like the mess. And," Kevin paused momentarily while he cranked up the chainsaw, a Stihl 880 with a 41-inch blade, "we are gonna have a helluva mess. It's kind of unfair."

"What's unfair?" I asked over the firing of the chainsaw.

"It's gonna take me fifteen to twenty seconds to cut the tree and the fun's over. Then we spend the next hour or two clearing up the mess." Kev paused again. "And since you made the decision, Pete, the mess is your responsibility." With that Kevin walked around the tree looking at it from several different angles. Tom and I went behind the tree as Kev stepped into position and began the initial cut for the front notch. That completed, he stepped behind the tree and crosscut the trunk toward the notch, leaving about two inches between the two cuts. He quickly grabbed a steel wedge and hammered it into place with a short three-pound sledge hammer. The tree started to move, gaining speed as it tipped toward the ground. A sharp crack sounded as the felling hinge, that is, the uncut section of the trunk, snapped in two. The movement of the branches created a whooshing sound which was followed by a heavy thump as almost five tons of wood kissed mother earth.

Kevin's execution was flawless. The tree cleared the garage by four inches, the house by eleven, and its tip sliced right through the fence rails like a hot knife through butter. My decision, my responsibility. Kevin shrugged his shoulders and got ready to cut the limbs off the tree.

Connie then appeared on the back step, ready to announce that dinner was ready but instead said, "My lord, what a mess." Turning to the backyard, her hands went up to her cheeks and she uttered, "Oh no! Look how empty it looks!"

"That's your fault too, pard," Kevin said with a laugh as he sent the saw tearing into one of the limbs.

Saturday morning I went to the office for a few minutes to finish writing up the accident report from the wreck on Thursday. I'd been there about twenty minutes when Micky Thompson came through the door.

"Morning, Sheriff."

"You're looking pretty fit for a man who experienced a close brush with death."

"The doctor just held me for observation. Said I could go home. I came to get my truck. I heard you impounded it."

"True, Mick, we've got it down at Goodyear's, but with you alive and well, there's no sense in keeping it. I'll call Billy and tell him it's okay to give you the truck. The dispatcher has the form. Just sign it." The paperwork completed, Micky departed to get his truck and I forgot about him until Monday afternoon coffee.

Sunday morning was born with strong gusts of wind and an advance guard of clouds moving into the valley over the western mountains. The forecast was for isolated thunderstorms.

After months of entreaties from Abby Strong, choir director at our church, I had agreed to sing a solo after the sermon. Abby had been at the theater the night I had belted out a couple of stanzas of "Old Man River," and she's been on me like a hound dog following a quail through the brush, trying to induce me to join the choir. My work schedule and responsibilities don't allow me to keep commitments like choir practice, and I told her so repeatedly. But she insisted that I had to "use my God given talent, for the glory of God." That was taking faith a little further than I would go, but I finally acceded to her request with the hope that it might quell the nagging.

When the hour approached I stepped up the microphone, but before I could utter a note, the mic started to screech and whoop like microphones do from time to time. The preacher fiddled with the controls and finally got it to settle down, and I stepped back in place to try again. The organist started into the introduction of the song when, suddenly, there was this immense flash of light outside the building, followed by the lights going out in the sanctuary, and the roar of thunder.

After a few moments of silence, Lucky Jack Carter, a banker in town, piped up, "Pete. I think it's God's way of telling you to take voice lessons first." The congregation roared, Abby blushed, her mortification total, and I went back to the pew with my family, my mission completed, even if it was not fulfilled. The power came back on just as we left church.

On Monday, Micky Thompson's ordeal was the talk of the day, but I told the fellows at coffee that I couldn't speak about any investigation in progress so they'd just have to speculate on their own. I got back to the office around 4:00. Nick had returned to his duty station down in Winslow and Johnny Titan was on duty. He was just hanging up the phone.

Johnny turned to me and said, "That was Gil. Walt Zander is in there having a drink with two of his boys. Micky T. just came through the front door and the two of them are sizing up one another. Gil would like us to get down there before it gets out of hand."

"Let's do it," I replied. "You drive and let's use the siren. Maybe it'll prevent someone from getting tagged with assault."

We reached the Apex in about two minutes. I went in the back door while Johnny moved around the side of the building to the front entrance. It took a second for my eyes to get used to the dim light, but I didn't see either Walt Zander or Micky Thompson.

"Where are the boys?" I shouted to Gil Stewart, the owner and day shift bartender.

"The minute they heard the siren they must've known it was for them because the whole bunch—Micky, Walt, and Walt's kids hightailed it out the front door."

"Yeah, I saw Micky's truck make the corner onto Shiloh. Looks like he was heading home," added Johnny.

"What happened?" I asked, turning back to Gil.

"Micky came through the front door and spotted Walt and the kids right away. One of Walt's kids must have seen Micky in the mirror about the same time because he turned to Walt and said something. Then Walt turned around on the stool and was eyeing Micky the same as Micky was eyeing the three of them."

"Micky or Walt say anything?" I continued.

"Not then," answered Gil as he shook a filtered Camel out of a pack and stuck it in the corner of his mouth. "Then, Micky kind of shrugged his shoulder and started walking up to the bar acting nonchalant. He goes up to Walt and says, 'Afternoon boys, Walt.' Then Walt responded by saying, 'Thompson, you damned thief.'"

"That had to provoke a reaction from Micky," Johnny observed.

"It did," Gil said. "Micky turned back to Walt and just laughed. Then he gave Walt that sneer, like he does, and Walt came unglued. He jumped off the bar stool and yelled, 'I'll kill you yet, you son-of-a-bitch.' Then Micky laughed again and Walt took a swing at him but missed. Walt's two boys got off their stools, one on each side of their father, and Micky started edging toward the door. About that time, we could hear your siren and they all went sailing out the door, Micky in the lead."

"You want to file a complaint, Gil?" I asked.

"No," he replied, exhaling a long plume of smoke.

"Fine. All's well that ends well. But, I'd better have a little talk with Walt. His anger may be justified, but I don't want him to become his own victim."

Johnny and I took a ride out to Walt Zander's ranch, but his wife reported that he had not come back from town.

I asked her to have him give me a call when he returned.

That wrapped up the day as far as I was concerned. Johnny dropped me off at the Law Enforcement Center where I picked up my truck and headed home for dinner. My evening meal completed, I was repairing the lock on the back storm door when Connie called me to the phone. I recognized the number. It was District Judge Cliff Pollard calling from his home over in Cottonwood.

"Pete, I got a call from Steve Fenton around four this afternoon. He said you jailed that Raymond fellow again." Fenton is an attorney in Rodgersburg and was representing Doug Raymond.

"I did, Judge. Micky Thompson, the guy whose blood and hair was in the back of Raymond's truck, turned up alive Thursday. Some kids found him up at one of the old mines. He was hurt, and when I interviewed him at the hospital the next morning, Thompson fingered Raymond. He said Raymond slugged him from behind, tossed him into the back of the truck and was hauling him up into the mountains when he escaped and hid out until the kids found him."

"So you like Raymond for the crime?" asked the Judge rhetorically.

"No, no I don't, Judge. I hauled him in simply because I was legally obliged to do so given the victim's statement, but I think it's a lie."

"Well then, what's going on?"

"We're thinking insurance fraud," I replied.

"How's that?" asked the Judge with a puzzled tone to his voice.

"The day after Thompson went missing, his wife Anna called the insurance company and asked how to file for his death benefit because he'd been killed. As it turns out, they had purchased a $500,000 policy on Micky a few months ago with Anna as the beneficiary."

"That's a helluva policy for a working stiff," answered the Judge. "Sounds like you are thinking through all the angles, Pete."

"Well, I can't take credit for the insurance fraud idea. The adjuster, a guy out of Helena, called and said it smelled like a scam."

"Well, okay, but Fenton still wants me to do something about Raymond. He claims that he's a solid citizen and is not a flight risk. What say you?"

"Normally, I'd agree with Steve, Judge, but Doug Raymond is full of hate right now. When we went back to get him, he got abusive and I charged him with resisting arrest as well."

"Do you think he'll run?"

"No, but he's convinced that Micky Thompson has tried to frame him, a theory I am pretty partial to myself, so I am a little concerned that Doug might go after Micky."

"I understand your concern, Pete, but I don't like the idea of an innocent man, and that's what you're telling me he is, being locked up in jail. So how about this. You've held him over the weekend so he should be calmed down. I'll call Fenton and tell him here's the deal. Raymond will be released with the same bail for the assault but he pleads guilty to resisting arrest and I'll sentence him to three days in jail with credit for the time served. Will that work for you?"

"Judge, you're the boss. Make sure that Fenton wises Doug up and keeps him away from Thompson. He doesn't need to be making his situation worse."

"Okay, Pete. We've got a plan."

I called down to the office and had Doug Raymond released. He had calmed down considerably and called me to apologize for his behavior toward me on Friday. I accepted it readily and advised him to keep his counsel and stay away from Micky Thompson.

Tuesday was quiet so I took the afternoon off. I managed to polish off a full slate of household chores that I never got to over the weekend. Then, Connie and I met her sister Melinda and her family at Boulder Lake Campground for a picnic. It finally dawned on me as we drove home that night that Walt Zander had never called me as I had requested. When I got home, I called his house. Mrs. Zander told me that Walt had come home Monday night around ten, packed a bag and said that he had an idea about his missing swather and "was going to put that S.O.B. Thompson away for good." She said she had not heard from him since. Her voice had a hesitant quality about it and I sensed that she was worried.

Wednesday started uneventfully. I was in the office reviewing bids to replace two of the department's patrol cars when I heard Johnny Titan answer the phone in the anteroom where the deputies' desks were located.

"Pete, that was the Forest Service. Micky's truck is back up at the campground and they need you right away."

"They say why?"

"Yeah. Micky's in the truck—dead."

"Get the jailer to cover the phones and meet me in the car."

We found Micky with two bullet holes in the right side of his chest. He died quickly, shot at close range, most likely by someone in the truck with him. The Forest Service campground crew had found the truck and the body.

There were no witnesses. After we'd finished the crime scene investigation, Johnny had the vehicle taken back to Goodyear's for further examination. I went over to Micky's house and broke the news to his wife and her mother.

Anna burst into tears and said, "It can't be. We talked this morning. He was going out to get a load of wood." Mrs. Fischer put her arms around Anna to console her but said nothing other than to excuse the two of them from my presence while she guided Anna toward the living room couch. Anna promptly reached for her cigarettes, lit up and took a long drag, her sobbing paused for a few seconds.

I hesitated, my mind running a quick compare and contrast analysis from the last time I had talked with Anna about Micky being "gone." Admittedly, he was only missing the first time and now, he was dead. Having just watched the scene that had played out before me, it was clear that last week Anna was acting upset; this time her emotions were genuine. The insurance fraud angle has been confirmed, at least to my satisfaction, although there probably isn't enough evidence to make it stick in court. More problematically, who committed the murder, their partner?

Perhaps I should press the issue with Anna right now, while she's emotionally vulnerable. No. I'll wait. If this shapes up the way it seems to be heading, Anna will talk.

"Anna," I said across the room, "get some rest. We'll need to talk some more, later."

She meekly nodded in reply. In contrast, her mother gave me a cold stare as if to say, "Have you no heart, Sheriff?"

After exiting the house, thankful for a breath of fresh air, I went in search of both Doug Raymond and Walt Zander but found neither. I had this terrible feeling in my gut—

both of those guys were full of anger and I felt like I was hoping against hope.

Johnny called me at the house that evening about 8:30. After hearing what he had to say, I decided to pay another visit to the grieving widow.

"Sheriff, why...what brings you here tonight?"

"Your husband's murder, Anna."

"I expected that, it's just that I'm so tired, can't it wait until tomorrow?"

"It could, but I can't. I have some questions."

"All right, come in....Sheriff, you remember my mother?"

"Yes, ma'am, how are you this evening, Mrs. Fischer?"

"Exhausted, upset, what you would imagine, Sheriff, after everything we've been through. This has been such a trial for Anna."

"Sure. I won't be long. Anna, Micky tried to feed me some cock-and-bull story about Doug Raymond attacking him."

"Micky told me that at the hospital. Can't you see Doug came back to finish the job?"

"No, he didn't. Doug decided to avoid any possible chance of a confrontation with Micky. He's been out at the McCallum Ranch since he got out of jail Monday. There are witnesses."

"There are? Then it must have been Walt Zander."

"No, Anna. Walt thought he had a lead on his stolen swather. It's probably a wild goose chase, but it's kept Walt out of town for the past few days too."

"Then who, Sheriff, who?" asked Anna emphatically.

"That's why I am here. It was a good plan. Commit insurance fraud, disappear, and tag Doug Raymond, a guy known to have it in for Micky."

"Sheriff, I don't understand. Insurance fraud!" Anna's voice had risen in pitch. She was trying to sound incredulous. "How could Micky do that? The only insurance we have is life insurance."

"True, which would pay his wife $500,000 upon Micky's death."

"But, I've lost Micky...wait, you think I killed..."

"I didn't say that, Anna. I think the plan was for Micky to fake his death, hide out at the old mine for a few days, and then disappear until you showed up with the money."

"Sheriff, I know nothing about..." Anna's eyes were starting to tear up, but I couldn't ease off.

"Hold it, Anna," I said forcefully. "I know about your call to the insurance company, and it's real clear to me from the way you're acting that you're as much a part of the fraud scheme as Micky. You want to tell me about it?"

Anna broke down sobbing. "We needed the money. We were going to get out of here, start a new life. Nobody was supposed to get hurt."

"Except maybe Doug Raymond," I added, "who could have been sent to prison for a crime he didn't commit."

"Micky said they'd never convict him, not without a body."

"What went wrong, Anna?"

"Those kids found Micky's hiding place," replied Anna through a veil of tears.

"I'd already figured as much. I meant about Micky getting killed."

"I don't know what you mean. I didn't hurt Micky. I loved him."

"Well, maybe you don't know anything, Anna, but your mother does."

"Mother does? What?" Anna turned from me toward her mother with a puzzled look.

"Why did you kill him, Mrs. Fischer?" I asked.

"Stop being ridiculous, Sheriff," came Jane Fischer's sharp retort. "We're under too much strain without you making silly jokes."

"It's no joke, Mrs. Fischer," I replied quietly. "You see, a week ago Monday when we discovered that Micky was missing, we went over his truck with a fine-toothed comb looking for any and every clue possible. We checked his truck a second time after we found his body, and this time we found two pieces of evidence that weren't there the first time we checked. Three fingerprints on the dashboard—prints about the size that would be made by a small woman. I think you'd agree that 'small' would accurately describe you."

"It also describes Anna and any number of other women."

"True, Mrs. Fischer, but Anna isn't a peroxide blonde... you are. We also found your hair on the seat."

"Mother? Mother?" Anna's voice had turned to a growl.

"Give it up, Mrs. Fischer. A DNA test and a set of fingerprints are going to put you at the scene of a murder. Now, why?" I pressed.

"Sheriff, I..."

Then Anna loudly interrupted, her face turning red, a mask of hate. "Mother, how could you? My own husband, how could..."

"Oh, shut up," Mrs. Fisher said sharply. "I killed that crooked, worthless excuse of a man you were married to. It was easy. I was here last fall, remember? I heard the two of you hatch this plot to bilk the insurance company out of its money. I saw him drag you down to his level—in the gutter. And you, once so sweet, such a willing partner."

"You killed Micky to protect me from his influence on me?"

"Hardly," Mrs. Fischer answered. "You're beyond redemption now."

"Then why?" Anna was truly confused.

"To protect my investment," Mrs. Fischer calmly answered.

"What investment? What are you talking about?"

"My investment in Micky. After I found out what you two were going to do, I posed as Micky's mother and took out my own insurance policy on his life with me as sole beneficiary. After that moron husband of yours couldn't fake his own death, I had to take matters into my hands because I sure couldn't collect my quarter-million benefit if Micky was still alive."

CHAPTER EIGHT

Bootsey's Mine

It had been a quiet week in Rodgersburg and, truth be told, the office had become a little boring. I headed over to the Burger Haven Café to grab lunch and hoped that I might see someone who had something to talk about other than the weather. It had been a long winter; everyone wanted to see some sign of spring but it had been slow coming and people's moods were foul.

I was about halfway through my coleslaw, chili, hard roll, and coffee when I heard a voice behind me say, "Bootsey, whatcha gonna have?"

"Just coffee, Doris, ahh...why don't you give me a piece of cherry pie too, if you got it. I am gonna visit with my friend Sheriff Pete for a minute."

My luncheon companion was Sylvester Gorman, age eighty-one, known by young and old alike simply as Bootsey, a nickname, I am told, that he acquired about seventy-five years ago when he went to school wearing galoshes several sizes too big for him. Bootsey, his brother-in-law "Pal" Blankenship, now deceased, and my father-in-law, Art, also deceased, were fast friends. They worked together in the mines around Rodgersburg for more than forty years starting in the early 1940s. Bootsey has been a family friend, practically a family member, forever. "You've certainly got a big smile on that mug of yours for such a foul day," I said after Bootsey had pulled off his coat and gloves and plopped his frame into the chair across the table from me.

His weathered hand encircled the steaming cup of coffee the waitress had just delivered and he took a light sip before answering me. "Pete. It's Montana and it's April. It might be spring somewhere else, but here it's still winter. You know that. Gawd, you grew up in Butte. It's colder there."

"I do, Boots, but thanks for reminding me. The snow, which never seems to stop, has everybody in a bad mood, except you for some reason. So, what gives?"

"It looks like my ship is about to come in, Pete; I'm gonna get my mine." Bootsey's face lit up like a kid in a candy store.

"I've heard that before. The whole town has. How many times now, fifteen, twenty?"

"I know, Pete, I've been a little exuberant in the past, but this one looks real. I'm convinced."

"Okay, tell me the good news." This is almost an annual rite of passage with Bootsey. Every spring he seems to have a new prospect that's on the verge of being a bonanza.

"You remember last year I leased my claims to that company from Canada, Star Western Exploration?"

"Yeah, and they did some drilling last summer, if I remember correctly."

"You do," Bootsey replied, almost giddy. "I ain't seen no results yet, but it must have been good. I got a letter today from their president, Aaron Fletcher. They're planning to do some more work this spring and he wants to talk with me about doing some work for them."

"Well, that is good news, Boots. Congratulations!"

"And it might be good for you and Connie too," answered Bootsey quickly. "Aaron's coming down to Rodgersburg next week and he wants to meet with you folks about your claims." He then pushed back in the chair, took a long drink from his coffee mug, and looked at me over the top of his glasses.

I shook my head. "Connie will be gone next week. Some kind of EMT training in Helena."

"That's okay, Pete. Probably be better if he just met with you first anyways. Fletcher's kind of a guy's guy and he might come on too strong for Connie and piss her off. You talk to him first, then bring her up to speed. That would work better."

"Fine," I replied. "Just let me know when he gets to town. I'll be around."

"You'll like 'im, Pete. He's an old time mining guy— willing to take a chance and get something done. Most of today's miners are either stock promoters or lawyers— lots of talk but not much dirt gets moved. Ya know what I mean?"

"I do, Boots, I do."

South of Rodgersburg, extending from just above the Clearwater Campground up to Moonlight Lake, flanked by Mount Rodgers to the east and Quartz Peak on the south and west, lays the Galena Mining District. If you saw a map of the district, one unfamiliar with hard rock mining might think it was some type of massive subdivision with a slew of little rectangles laid out next to one another like lots in a planned housing development. Upon closer inspection, you would see that there weren't any streets or roads and that some rectangles were laid out over the top of other rectangles.

The rectangles are mining claims. A standard lode claim measures 1,500 feet long by 600 feet wide and contains 20.6 acres of land. Claims can be smaller but never bigger, and if it should happen that one prospector lays out a claim over the top of another, the party who staked and recorded the claim first is the one whose claim is valid.

About a third of the way up the Tower Creek Road, call it four miles, lie the remnants of an old mine called the Galena Queen. It is situated on a block of twenty-three mining claims that form the leg of a large block of claims in the shape of a "Y" tipped over on its side. Starting in 1900 and for the next eighty-three years, the Galena Queen was a high-grade silver and lead producer and the largest mine in the Rodgersburg area.

Just west of the Galena Queen on the lower fork of the "Y" is a block of thirteen claims owned by Bootsey Gorman. Immediately adjacent Bootsey's ground lies still another block of nine claims owned by Bootsey's sister Myra Blankenship. My wife Connie and her sister Melinda own three claims to the west of Bootsey's land, uphill from Myra's claims. The upper fork of the "Y" is a block of fifteen claims that were part of the old Thompson Mine, which play no part in this story.

A few days later I met Aaron Fletcher, President of Star Western Exploration. He reminded me of a lawyer, full head of white hair, dark blue sport coat, with a tan shirt and matching trousers. My wife would say that he looked distinguished. There was the slightest hint of an accent but

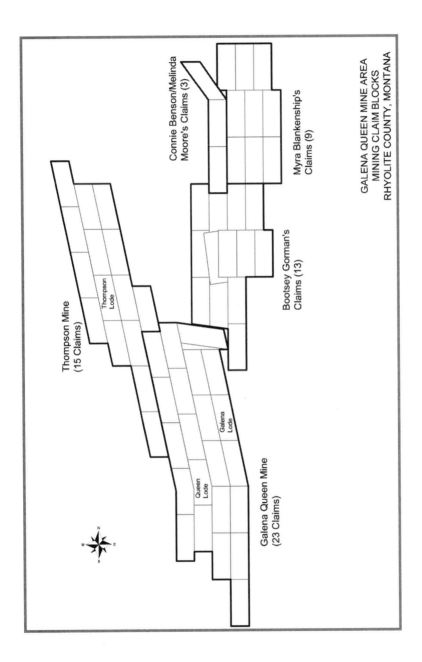

Connie Benson/Melinda
Moore's Claims (3)

Myra Blankenship's
Claims (9)

Bootsey Gorman's
Claims (13)

Thompson Mine
(15 Claims)

Thompson
Lode

Galena
Lode

Queen
Lode

Galena Queen Mine
(23 Claims)

GALENA QUEEN MINE AREA
MINING CLAIM BLOCKS
RHYOLITE COUNTY, MONTANA

N
W   E
S

I couldn't type it. He didn't sound like a Canadian to me, and he didn't really look like a "guy's guy" as Bootsey had said. "Have a chair, Mr. Fletcher. Would you like a cup of coffee or a beer?"

"Thank you, Sheriff, but no. I had dinner with Mr. Gorman and had a couple of glasses of your local beer. It was quite good, but I don't recall it from my trips to Rodgersburg last year."

"No. It's new. Been open a few months now. Microbreweries have become quite the rage in Montana during the past several years. Two guys from Bozeman put up the money. Rodgersburg is being recreated as a tourist town."

"I am sure the view out your front window must be quite spectacular, when it's not snowing." Fletcher had turned his back to me as I sat down at the dining room table. A few minutes ago, it had been partly cloudy, and now, there was a blizzard, the flakes falling so furiously that it wasn't possible to see more than about a half block.

"You don't need to remind me about the snow, Mr. Fletcher. It's been on the ground since October 3rd. I would like to experience some of that global warming I keep hearing about."

"Mr. Gorman said much the same thing," replied Fletcher with a light laugh. He turned back toward me and sat down in the chair to my immediate left. "There's still a lot of it up in the hills. Bootsey, I mean Mr. Gorman, and I went up to look at the property but we really couldn't get off the main road. Snow, and if it wasn't snow—mud. I was hoping to get this year's drilling program started next week but it looks like it won't get going until May. Maybe that will turn out for the better. There are a couple of claim groups which I'd like to lease before we get too far into this year's drilling program."

"Which accounts for why you've come to see me," I injected. "As I told Bootsey, my wife is in Helena all week for EMT training."

"According to the title report, the claims are owned by your wife and her sister Melinda Moore. You're not an owner?"

"That's right. The land belonged to their father. The girls each have an undivided half interest. Melinda has given over management of the claims exclusively to Connie, and Connie will make the decision to accept or reject your proposal, after she consults with me."

"Is there an interest in leasing?" One thing was for sure, Fletcher wasn't the least bit tentative.

"If the terms are right," I replied. "We had an operator in here a few years ago..."

"CanMont?" interrupted Fletcher before I could finish my sentence.

"Yeah, and they treated us real good, so you're not starting out trying to overcome a bad taste in everyone's mouth."

"Did you happen to get a copy of their drill data and assays?"

"Not to my knowledge. Connie would know."

"If she has it, we'd like to see it. It could help with our offer."

"And that is..."

"Right now, we don't have any information that points to the presence of a mineralized structure on the property, Sheriff, so we're looking at it primarily as a strip of buffer zone. We'd go $2,000 for a signing bonus, $1,000 per claim per year as an annual rent, and a five-year option to buy the property for $60,000."

I didn't respond right away, hoping that my hesitation signaled little to no enthusiasm for what I had just heard. Finally, "That's a bit less than a thousand an acre," I said.

"To buy? Oh...yes," replied Fletcher quietly.

I paused again, played with my ink pen for a few moments then asked, "No royalty?"

"Oh, I'm sorry. Yes, certainly, Sheriff, five percent net profits."

"And, what if Connie has some data?"

"It's going to have to show ore grade intercepts—at least two of them—over eight feet of true vein width."

"What are you calling ore?"

"Quarter ounce, .25 opt, gold equivalent."

I paused to mull that over and ran a quick calculation in my head. I knew exactly what Fletcher meant but decided to play dumb. "This is a silver district, not gold."

"No question, Sheriff, but we convert all metals into a gold equivalent basis. With gold at $350 per ounce and silver at $5.00, a quarter ounce of gold is worth $87.50. That's equal to seventeen and a half ounces of silver."

"Gotcha. Sorry, Mr. Fletcher. I am just a country sheriff. The nuances of the precious metals business escape me."

"No problem. The terminology's a little tricky if you're not involved in mining. We do the same thing with other payable metals—copper, lead, zinc. And, we take a deduction for detrimental elements such as arsenic and mercury."

"Yeah, I've heard Bootsey talking about payable metals and deductions but, frankly, it all went in one ear and out the other. What metal price are you going to use?"

Fletcher gave me a long look. I quickly realized I shouldn't have said that. Here I am trying to play dumb cop with a mining executive, and I drop an "insiders" line like that.

Finally he said, "We prefer London. Do you have a preference?"

"Probably whatever Bootsey would recommend," I replied, trying to schlep back into the cop character. "He follows that stuff all the time. And, the deductions. When Bootsey and Connie's dad were leasing the Red Wolf, I heard about smelter deductions."

"Ah, yes. The bane of every miner—the smelting penalties. Smelters have a great way of wringing out every last bit of profit from the miner's ore."

"Bootsey gets red in the face on the subject," I replied.

"We all do, Sheriff. But back to your question, we'll use the smelter schedules from Teck's smelter up at Trail now that East Helena is closed."

"Fair enough. So if we have the CanMont data and it shows a couple of ore grade intercepts, then what's the deal?"

"Everything doubles," responded Fletcher.

"Okay, I'll talk to my wife and she'll talk to her sister. It'll take a couple of days."

"Thank you. I'll be in Rodgersburg through next Wednesday."

I watched Fletcher walk down my sidewalk to a white, four-wheel-drive, Ford F-150 pickup, well splattered with gray mud, characteristic of the soils south of town where Fletcher's project was located. At least that part of our conversation was on the square.

I am no expert in mining leases, but I've heard a lot about them and I recognize a low ball offer when I see one. I am even less of an expert when it comes to understanding ore grades and mineral economics, but Fletcher's explanation of converting a silver assay into a gold equivalent basis to determine if it was ore grade material didn't make sense. Gold equivalency is most commonly used with polymetallic ore bodies in which the principal mineral being mined, in terms of value, is gold. I'd never heard of anyone using such a calculation for a silver-lead-zinc ore body, and it put me on edge. It struck me as a ploy for a sharp operator to devalue the mineral potential of a mining claim as a way of reducing the lease payments to the owner.

Fletcher was also offering a five-percent net-profits royalty on the value of production. Only a fool agrees to a percentage of the net profit. I know Bootsey would never agree to it, so why would Fletcher offer that to us? He knows we'll talk to Bootsey. It didn't add up. I felt a growing sense of uneasiness about Star Western Exploration and Mr. Aaron Fletcher.

Connie called me about 8:00 P.M. and gave me a rundown on her day. She was a little frustrated over how the course was organized and took several minutes to explain it all to me. I listened and offered the perfunctory, supportive comments on cue. It's taken a while, but I have finally learned to recognize when a woman is venting and to just listen without offering advice.

That task taken care of, I told Connie about Fletcher's visit and the offer he made. She listened to my concerns about Fletcher and then suggested that we simply not respond to him at all. Instead, we'd wait for a few days to see if he'd come back with something a little more exciting.

The next morning I found Bootsey waiting for me at the office. "Mornin', Boots. To what do I owe the pleasure?"

"I was just curious to see how it worked out with Fletcher."

"Nothing's done, at least for now. I told Connie about his offer and she'll think about it some. You know Connie. Then she'll talk to Melinda and think about it some more."

"Well, I sure hope you can get something worked out. I think Fletcher is on to somethin' big. It'd be nice if you folks could get in on it too."

By this point, the two of us had wandered through the outer office, stopped at the office kitchen for coffee, and entered my personal sanctum. "Hope springs eternal, Boots. If it's not Fletcher, it'll be someone else."

"Not this time, Pete," answered Bootsey forcefully. "I'm telling you, it's there."

"You sound so definite. What makes Fletcher different from all the rest of the guys who've leased from you before?"

"Two things. First, he offered me one hundred thousand shares of Star Western if I could get Myra to sign with him. That's twenty-five thousand bucks today, and it'll be worth a lot more after the mine gets going."

"Why doesn't he just sign up Myra himself?"

"He tried. Didn't get anywhere. In fact, he said Myra got downright pissed."

"Imagine that." My voice carried just a hint of cynicism.

"Yeah, you know Myra, Pete."

"Not as well as you. She's your sister, although given the geniality of your disposition and the irritability of hers, it's hard to believe. So it's worth a few shares to Fletcher to have you get the lease. Good luck."

"I told Fletcher I didn't think it would work, but he insisted I try. It's too bad Pal died. He's the only one who could reason with her."

"Like I said, good luck. Anybody you want special for pallbearers?"

"C'mon, Pete. She ain't that bad."

"That ain't my line, Boots. I heard it from you the time Myra fell behind in her car payments to the bank and Lucky Jack had to go collect."

"Yeah, yer right. Anybody without Jack's luck would've been dead. He got off with a little cut on the side of his head when she threw a candy dish at him."

At that point Bootsey started to laugh. After he'd had his chuckle, I asked, "So what's the other reason?"

"Other reason?" Bootsey seemed confused.

"You said there were two reasons why Fletcher was the real deal this time. The first was Myra."

"Oh, yeah. Sorry." Then Bootsey leaned over my desk and whispered, "I seen the assays, Pete."

"C'mon, the guy isn't that much of a fool. The only thing more secret than a mining company's assays is the location of the Navy's nuclear submarines."

Bootsey continued his whisper. "I didn't say he showed me. I said I seen them."

"I don't think I want to hear anymore, Boots. You might have done something criminal."

"I'm tellin' ya anyways, Pete. Like that sign over the stage in the high school auditorium says—'knowledge is power'."

"All right. I might as well be a co-conspirator."

"Fletcher asked me to meet him over at that little office

they have in the building they rent for core storage. They got an assay lab in there too."

"What building is that?" I asked.

"Myra's warehouse, down by the tracks."

"Okay, I'm with you."

"Well, I get there and the door's open but no one's around. I figure Fletcher must still be with you so I sit down and wait. Pretty soon my back starts to kink up so I stand up and start pacing around. Then I sees 'em. There's a file on the desk titled 'Assay Results.' So, I take me a little peek."

"Looked pretty good, did they?" Now, my interest was piqued.

"Not all of 'em, Pete, they never do. But there is a string of intercepts on the vein down deep with the silver running from eighteen to forty-six ounces per ton and the lead almost thirty percent. I think it's an extension of the West Galena vein."

"Just like you old timers used to mine years ago."

"You know it, but that isn't the half of it. Last year they drilled three holes way out on the far west side of my claim block where it butts up against Myra's ground. They told me they was just drilling for structure."

"Huh?" Now I was confused.

"Drilling to look at the geological layering."

"Oh."

Bootsey was trying to whisper again but his excitement wouldn't allow him to keep his voice low. "They found structure awright. A vein, probably a continuation of the West Galena, but maybe an extension of the Queen. There's a fault angling through my property so it's hard to say for sure. Anyways, the assays started at thirty-three and went over sixty ounces per ton. Pete, it's a bonanza, a damned bonanza. Only problem is, it runs into Myra's ground."

I took a sip of coffee and wondered why my cop antenna was going off. "So, if I've got this figured, Fletcher shows up a few minutes later, never mentions the assays, but tells you he needs a little help getting Myra's cooperation."

"That's about the size of it."

"And, surprise me now. The offer he wants you to sell to Myra is just a tad bit on the low side."

"That too." Bootsey adopted a look of resignation on his face.

"And, there is the moral dilemma of knowing that you can only profit if Myra gets less than a fair deal. You've got your work cut out for you, Boots."

"Don'tcha know," answered Bootsey, completely ignoring my comment about his moral dilemma. "Maybe I can throw her an even lower offer to see if she counters with something that Fletcher will accept. It's all I can do."

I didn't see Bootsey for several days. I figured he wasn't making much progress with Myra. She's a pretty astute old gal who knows how to wring every nickel out of every asset she owns.

Aaron Fletcher stopped by my office early in the morning to follow up on our conversation. After the preliminary small talk and my offer of refreshment, which he once again refused, Fletcher asked, "Did your wife and her sister have a chance to review my offer?"

"They did and decided it was much too early to make any commitment."

"Too early? I don't understand." Fletcher actually looked confused and I believe that he was.

"The ladies have decided that they are going to wait until after you sign with Myra Blankenship, and then they'll want to pattern their deal after the one you sign with Myra."

Fletcher wasn't confused any longer but I credit him with a good rebound. "Oh! Well, they may be waiting a long time. Mrs. Blankenship is proving a bit problematic, which has come as a great surprise. She was most accommodating and reasonable when we rented her warehouse, even threw in janitorial services with the rent."

"Myra's got her own chemistry and, predictably, it isn't one of her virtues," I replied.

"All I can say, Sheriff, is that we're talking and it's not going well."

"Getting Bootsey to help was a good idea."

"I hope so. I thought I had a pretty good relationship with Myra, but when I raised the prospect of leasing her claims, she wouldn't hear of it. But, Sheriff, I didn't come here to talk with you about my problems with other landowners. I am interested in you folks' reaction to my proposal."

"It's not good."

"No?" This time Fletcher's confusion was feigned.

"Connie and Melinda talked it over. They thought you were a little light with the cash and any talk of a royalty on net profits is a non-starter. They're of the mind they'll divide the acreage between the kids and give each of the four of them a lot."

"I see," replied Fletcher, but I am not sure that he fully comprehended what I had to say.

"So, Mr. Fletcher, if you want them to reconsider your offer, it's going to have to be sweetened substantially."

"How much?"

"I don't know for sure. It depends on what you get done with Myra."

"What if I don't sign with Myra?"

"Then you don't sign with the girls. But, don't worry. Myra Blankenship is a good businesswoman. She didn't get wealthy being mule-headed."

"So, you're telling me it's about the money."

"When is it not about the money? I don't know if I should say this..."

"Speak up, Sheriff. I'll take all the advice I can get."

"Okay, here it is, straight up. Folks around here aren't stupid. You're not the first guy to come through here leasing mining claims. You're probably not the hundredth. Your offers are low and they know it, so quit trying to play them for suckers."

Fletcher turned away from me, momentarily pursed his lips and scratched his chin. Either he had thought folks around here were stupid and didn't understand mineral leases, or he hasn't got enough money behind him and is trying to do everything on the cheap. My money was on the second.

"Okay Sheriff, fair enough and thanks. I'll think about it, and I appreciate the talk."

Later that day I headed down to Winslow and met Nick Colusa, my deputy who covers the eastern portion of the county. A couple of the local ranchers were missing some cattle and wanted us to look into the possibility of cattle rustling. Even in this day and age, it still happens from time to time but I doubted we had a case. Nevertheless, I visited with the two stockmen, got the brand information and tracking numbers for the cattle and told them we'd do what we could. I totally forgot about Aaron Fletcher. But Bootsey didn't let me forget for long. He spotted me outside the Apex Bar and Café getting back into my squad car following a late lunch.

"Pete! Pete! Over here."

"Boots. Sorry, I didn't see you."

"You wasn't lookin'. Too much on your mind."

"That too. How are things going with Fletcher and Myra?"

The way Bootsey pursed his lips told me what I wanted to know. "With Fletcher, fine. With Myra, not so good as I'd hoped, but she finally put a proposal on the table. Just talked to her, in fact. Fletcher ain't gonna like it."

"Oh?" I really didn't want to pry but he knew full well that I was going to find out anyway.

"It's okay, Pete, if you want to know. You're family, and I know you ain't gonna take it down the street."

"I didn't want to put you on the spot by sticking my nose in."

"I won't give you all the details, just the concept. Myra says she won't lease, but she'll sell the land."

"Sell? Well, for big money, no doubt?"

"Yup, just as you'd expect. Myra's smart. She's put Fletcher in a box. He's got to buy the place on faith alone and hope that vein he found on my land continues on to hers. If he spends the money buying her land, he said he won't have enough to do a good drilling campaign. I don't know what to advise Fletcher."

"Yeah, you're in a quandary, Boots."

"If Fletcher could just drill a hole or two, it would probably be fine." Bootsey adopted a thoughtful look which wasn't terribly characteristic of my friend.

"Good luck getting Myra to agree to that. If the drilling doesn't confirm the presence of the vein on Myra's ground or, if the grade drops, Myra's got nothing. She won't let him drill."

"Yeah, I know. What am I gonna do?"

"See if Fletcher will try to be a little more flexible."

"How so?" asked Bootsey earnestly.

"I'm not sure. You're the miner, not me. Think about some of the leases you've seen over the years. I am sure Myra isn't the first landowner who's driven a hard bargain."

"I've got an idea, but it's a long shot. I don't think Fletcher would be interested."

"What's that?" I asked, curious to know what kind of scheme Bootsey had thought up.

"Pretty simple, Pete. Get Fletcher to pay her a decent price to do some drilling. If he hits it, he pays Myra a lot more than what she asked to buy the land."

"What are we talking about for money, Boots?"

"Myra asked Fletcher for a million."

"So, under your plan, she could get what, one-point-five or more?"

"Yeah, something like that," replied Bootsey.

I paused for a couple of seconds to digest what Bootsey had just said. "Well, if the vein is as good as you say it is, that shouldn't be a problem. If the vein's not there, Fletcher's just out a few thousand. Have you talked to Myra about it?"

"Yeah," answered Bootsey sheepishly. "It was kind of her idea. Actually, she gave me an either/or offer. Fletcher could pay the million and take his chances or she'd let him on the property to drill three holes. Then, if he wanted the property it was going to cost $2 million."

"Wow." I always knew Myra was a shrewd businesswoman, but the size of her demand was truly amazing. I continued, "You've got the basis of a deal, Boots, and Myra's on board."

"On board with the approach, Pete, not the money. And, three holes ain't enough."

"It may be all that you're going to get, Boots. The ball's in Fletcher's court. You'd better find him before he leaves town."

The next day Bootsey called. I was in a meeting with Bill Harkness from the State Drug Task Force but I took the call anyway.

"Sheriff Benson speaking. May I help you?"

"It worked, Pete! It worked!" Bootsey's excitement was evident, but I was still thinking about meth and I was confused.

"What are you talking about?" I asked.

"The deal with Myra. I told Fletcher what you said. He bought it and so did Myra."

"What I said? Boots, you told me it was Myra's idea."

"Well, technically it was Myra's idea, but I didn't think Fletcher would go for it if he thought it was from her, so I kind of told Fletcher you thought it up. He liked it."

"So the deal is done?" I replied. At this point, Bill got up from his chair and left the room to give me some privacy.

"The principles are agreed to, Pete, but it'll take a few days to get the paperwork done."

"So, Myra's going to get two million?" I asked.

"Not quite. About 1.3 million, call it 1.4 if you count the

100 K for the drilling program. I didn't think it was gonna happen, Pete. We stayed up till past midnight. Fletcher put his last and final offer on the table and Myra, she don't say nothing, just gets up from the table and starts for the door. I felt like I was going to pass out, and then Myra turns around, looks at me, and busts her gut laughing. She says, 'Sylvester, I am taking a lot less than those claims are worth, but I know how important this is to you. So yes, Mr. Fletcher, I'll take your offer.' Then she just walked out the door, still laughing. I wanted to kill her and kiss her at the same time. You know what I mean?"

"I do Boots, and good job."

"There's still some downside, Pete."

"What's that?"

"Fletcher said he's not going to do anything with that ground Connie and Melinda have."

"Easy come, easy go, Boots. I don't think the girls are going to care too much. If the vein proves up, someone's gonna come looking to lease their land."

Over the next several days Fletcher papered his deal with Myra, a drill rig appeared, and several exploration holes were punched in the center of Myra's claim block. Then Myra bought a new pickup. I saw little of Bootsey and was told he was spending every waking moment up at the property which was about to become "his mine," at least in the emotional sense. I finally caught up with him on the street outside of the bank and, surprisingly, he didn't look all that happy.

"Howdy, Pete."

"Boots, I've been hearing that you're about to go mining again, you and Fletcher. Looks like it's been a successful partnership."

"It didn't last long, Pete. Less than two weeks, actually. Fletcher's gone. Sold the property to a new outfit. It's called Flying Horse Minerals."

"But, you've still got your deal, don't you?" I asked, curious about Bootsey's melancholy.

"Yeah, but Flying Horse is a bigger company. I don't know the players and up until now, everything they've done has been in Canada. They don't know their way around Montana. Things could get slowed down."

"Shouldn't be any different than with Fletcher. Star Western was a Canadian company," I observed.

"Just incorporated up there, Pete. Fletcher's an American, from West Virginia originally. He used to be with Frank Davidson and Hobart Thomas. Had a piece of both the Landusky Mine and Beal Mountain. Fletcher knew how to get things done. I ain't so sure of these new guys."

I could see that Bootsey was worried but there wasn't anything I could do or say that was going to make things better. "Well, Bootsey, good luck."

"Thanks, Pete. I'm going to need it."

A few days later I ran into Bootsey again. He reported that he had met with Lyle Boscomb, the Vice President of Exploration for Flying Horse Minerals, two days earlier and they seemed to hit it off, at least according to Bootsey. He said Flying Horse was bringing in three drill rigs with a plan to drill 30,000 linear feet. That was a decent commitment of dollars.

The next afternoon, after coffee and another episode of Wisdom Time, Apex Saloon style, I got up from the table and started toward the side door when Gil Stewart, owner of the Apex, came out of the kitchen and waved me over. "I probably shouldn't tell you this now since there are a few days left, but you're the Wisdom Time winner this month."

"Aren't you jumping the gun?" I asked, quite surprised by Gil's announcement. To my knowledge he'd never declared a winner early beforehand because "Some good quotes might be submitted yet."

"I am not saying anything to anybody but you. As you know, I've got some pull with the judges and the matter has been decided."

"Well, thanks, I guess. Connie will be pleased that she can park the range for a night. What did you like? The quote from Johnny Wooden?" I asked.

Gil favors "words of wisdom" from famous coaches and athletes. He firmly believes that the great lessons of life are not learned on the battlefields of adult life, but rather on the playing fields of youth. It's why he's such a consummate supporter of all forms of youth athletics. The Apex must sponsor a half dozen teams for boys and girls alike.

Gil stunned me when he said, "No, it was the quote about parenting. I think it's the best one we've ever had since the contest began. Is that a Benson original?"

"Not hardly," I answered. "I heard it at church in Arizona when Connie and I went down to watch Tom play in that tournament at Arizona State."

"It really hit the nail on the head."

"Maybe I shouldn't tell you, but the original quote was written by a guy talking about church sermons, not parenting. I just tweaked it a bit and gave it a title."

"I don't care where it came from," answered Gil. "I like it so much I am thinking about having copies printed up

and mailed to every house in the county, or maybe put it up on that billboard down by Carmichaels for a couple of months. I can see it now:
The Essence of Parenting

I might misunderstand the lectures that you give, but there's no misunderstanding how you act or how you live.[1]

"Be careful, my friend," I cautioned. "Don't get too preachy. It's a small town. And, thanks for dinner, Connie will be thrilled. Gotta go."

May faded into June. Flying Horse's drilling program was designed to confirm the accuracy of Star Western's geological information and assay results. Bootsey explained that it was all part of Flying Horse's due diligence program and the deal between Star Western and Flying Horse wouldn't be final until the test results were completed. Bootsey was on pins and needles most of the month.

I had just returned to Rodgersburg from Helena following a meeting of the State Drug Task Force and stopped at Jack's Exxon to replenish the vehicle's tank. Ronnie Hale, one of the owners, gave me the news. "Pete, maybe you better head up to the Apex. Bootsey's buying drinks for one and all. Nobody's money is any good but his."

"I guess that outfit, Flying Horse, completed their deal. Maybe Bootsey's getting his mine after all."

"Be good for the town if he did, Pete. It wouldn't hurt to get a few jobs, and the taxes would be great."

"Don'tcha know." I was trying to be supportive but not terribly committal. Like most of the people in Rodgersburg, Ronnie doesn't have much good to say about environmentalists. Before Bootsey would be able to actually see a mine in operation, Flying Horse would have to obtain an operating permit from the State Department of Environmental Quality, and the state's environmentalists, which are generally vociferously anti-mining, would likely intervene in the permit process.

I walked to the station door on my way back to my patrol car, turned back to Ronnie and simply said, "Keep your fingers crossed."

"I will Pete, be seeing ya," answered Ronnie as he tucked a filtered Camel into the corner of his mouth.

I had to stop by the Apex and see Bootsey. Judging by the number of cars and trucks parked in the back lot and along the street, the place must be packed. It took me five minutes to get from the side door, across the restaurant and out to near the front door where I found Bootsey, his arm around his sister Myra, the two of them talking with my wife Connie. Boots was talking a mile a minute and swinging a bottle of beer around to punctuate his speech. As I approached I heard Bootsey say, "The only thing I am sorry about is that Pal and Art didn't live to see this day. We worked our guts out, the three of us, we made a living, but we never made it big and now I do, at eighty-one and too old to do much with it. It just don't seem right."

"Don't worry about Pal and Art, old timer," I injected, "They're still with you, enjoying every minute."

Bootsey turned to me and gave me an immense bear hug. As he stepped back he said, "Pete, I owe it all to you. Your idea cooked the deal. I owe you man, I owe you."

I started to object to Bootsey's statement but he wasn't having it, so I grabbed a Coke and joined the party. It was a dandy. Connie and I left around 7:00 in the evening. Son Phil would be home expecting a home-cooked meal from his mother, notwithstanding the fact that he'd probably already raided the refrigerator in a pre-meal meal that would keep me filled for two days. Phil has been working at Best's ranch for the summer and when he comes home, he chows down for three.

The following Monday the drill rigs returned as Flying Horse Minerals expanded the mineral exploration. Bootsey explained that this effort was to further delineate and expand the known ore reserve on the property. The larger the ore reserve, the easier it would be for the company to borrow the funds necessary to finance the mine. Suffice it to say, Bootsey was on cloud nine.

After his party I saw Bootsey only once in June, running into him on the street outside First American Title. He was carrying a small package which had been gift wrapped in yellow paper with a blue bow. I asked about it.

"Oh, this," he replied. "It's for Myra. Earrings. I always buy her earrings for her birthday and Christmas. The woman's forever losing them."

"I understand," I said in response, and I did. "Connie too. She quit wearing them to work for the same reason."

"It's not all bad, Pete. It makes it easy for us guys to shop for the ladies in our life. I tried buying clothes for my wife a couple of times, bless her soul, and all I ever did was buy the wrong size and wrong color."

I nodded in agreement. I've got the same problem. Gift certificates have become the solution to my wifely shopping woes.

"Besides," said Boots with a grin, "it's good for the mining business." He pulled open the door on his '64 Dodge pickup, cranked the engine to life and waved goodbye as he pulled out into the street.

I went back to the office to pick up garnishment papers that needed to be served on Mark and Taryn Nyland. After grabbing my briefcase I started toward the door when Kay reminded me, "Here's your cell phone. I put in a new battery."

"Oh, thanks, I would have completely forgotten." I turned toward the door again.

"Oh, Pete, if it's all right with you..." I turned back to face Kay. "I would like to leave early today. There's a bunch of stuff I need to pick up for the ranch."

"Fine. See ya," I said as I headed back out the door.

It was a nice day for a ride, partly cloudy but warm. Mark and Taryn Nyland lived west of town about fifteen miles. Nice people but they seem to have a problem paying their bills in a timely manner and both have had their paychecks garnisheed several times previously.

With my singing ability "outed" as a result of Kay playing a practical joke on me (described in the case *A Real Pretty Picture),* I had become more casual about playing my pipes. A couple of months ago at lunch, Kay casually asked if I were practicing my voice. I admitted that I was and, further, it was a bit of a problem around the house since I didn't want to disturb Connie or Phil with my crooning. I told her the garage and car had become my favorite practice sites.

So driving west through the valley I entertained myself by singing "They Call the Wind Mariah,"[2] "Some Enchanted Evening,"[3] "Cabaret,"[4] and several other melodies from operettas or Broadway shows. It's my favorite kind of music but it seems to me that the best songs written for the male voice are for tenors, not us bass-baritones.

When I returned to town about forty-five minutes later, I went to the County Treasurer's office in the courthouse where Barbara Buck, one of the clerks, said to me, "That was mighty good singing, Pete."

Dumbfounded, I asked, "What do you mean?"

"All those songs you just sung. Kay put them through to all of the offices. All we had to do was turn on our speaker phones. I heard you had a great voice but I never heard you sing before."

"Speaker phones? Kay did that?" I could feel myself getting angry, mostly from embarrassment. Another one of Kay's pranks.

"Uh," Barb answered slowly. "She said you were practicing for a concert you were gonna give later, but we could all listen. Ya know, I really like the way you sang "Time to Say Goodbye."[5] Most of the time it's a duet or sung by a woman, but it's really nice with a deep voice like yours."

I thanked Barbara for her compliment, promptly forgot why I had come to the Treasurer's office, and turned to go find my practical joker. It took me fifteen minutes to get out of the courthouse. After Barbara, I saw Paige in the hall by the Clerk's office. Then Janae, Michelle, and Sara called to me from the Commissioners' office, and Kathy came over from the Extension Service. They were all very curious, praised my singing, and laughingly said I should be on Broadway.

"Best!" I bellowed when I opened the front door of the Law Enforcement Center.

"Not here, Pete," Johnny Titan answered quietly. "After

she arranged your concert, she thought it best to get out of Dodge until you could calm down and relax." Then Johnny started to laugh and was quickly joined by Laura, the afternoon shift dispatcher.

I could feel my blood rise again, after being somewhat mollified by the admiring audience in the courthouse.

"Ya came in over the phone from the car," Titan said. "Good signal, very good, in fact. A cappella, no less."

I gave Johnny a hard stare. He's the department's electronics specialist and I suspected had a hand in the affair. "Now, how would Kay know how to rig my cell phone so that she could catch me singing?"

"Well, Kay handed you the cell phone just before you left the office. It must have been dialed to her desk phone and put on hold."

"Very clever," I said flatly, staring at Johnny.

"Yep," he said, trying to hold back a grin.

I sat down next to Johnny's desk, shaking my head in disbelief. Then I started to laugh. "Man, did she get me good this time. She must have been planning this thing for a couple of months. Back in April she asked me where I practice and I told her, the car and garage."

"She gets you good every time, Pete. You don't have the guile necessary to keep up with Kay and her tricks. None of us do, actually," answered Johnny.

Kay's prank was a complete success and brought a measure of calm to the office. She'd give it a rest for a while which, hopefully, would allow me to come up with a suitable plan for revenge.

On July 16th, a Thursday, about three weeks after I had last seen Bootsey and serenaded the courthouse gang from my patrol car, I heard a knock on the door. "C'mon in," I shouted.

A tall, thin, partially bald man dressed in brown chinos and a tan shirt pushed open the door and entered my office. He paused momentarily and said, "You must be Sheriff Benson."

"I am...and you are?"

"Sorry, I am Lyle Boscomb with Flying Horse Minerals. We're..."

My manners temporarily escaped me and I interrupted. "I know about your company and some about you as well, Mr. Boscomb. Bootsey Gorman is a bit of a family friend."

"Is there anyone who's not Bootsey's friend?"

I sensed frustration in his question. "Not many, but say, if you're here about my wife's family's mining claims, they aren't much interested in leasing."

"No. I am not here about the claims. Right now, I've got plenty. I'm here on police business."

"Oh!" This was a surprise. My mind started to race—vandalism, theft...What kind of problem could Boscomb have?

"Sheriff, I believe my company has been defrauded by Star Western Exploration, led by Aaron Fletcher." Boscomb flashed a look of disgust across his face. "Fletch is...was...an old friend. Do you mind if I sit?"

I nodded toward the arm chair next to my desk. "Defrauded? How?"

"By salting the mine or, more accurately, by creating a series of bogus assays reporting a lot more mineral in the ground than is really the case. And..."

"And selling you a bunch of worthless or nearly worthless claims," I said.

"That's it in a nutshell," Boscomb agreed.

"Pardon me if I seem a little puzzled by this. If memory serves me correctly, you folks did a lot of due diligence on the property before signing on the dotted line."

"We did. Twinned every hole except for those on Ms. Blankenship's property. Star Western didn't actually control that property until after we'd done the deal."

"Twinned every hole? I'm sorry, Mr. Boscomb, what does that mean?"

"We drilled a second hole right next to the one drilled by Star Western, usually within three feet, and assayed the rock. All the holes we tested on Bootsey's ground matched up fine."

"So what's the problem?"

"We started in-fill drilling to test the areas in between the holes Star Western had drilled. The first couple of holes were fine. Then, all of a sudden, the assay results dropped like a rock. Instead of twenty-three ounces per ton of silver, we started getting three."

"Maybe you just hit a spot of low grade. It happens," I observed.

"I don't think so. Overall, of the nine holes we drilled after confirming Star Western's results, seven of them were a disaster. So, I had the assayers redo the first two holes, the ones which were consistent with Star Western's results, and they came back bad on the second analysis, too. Our assays are an average of twenty ounces lower than those drilled by Star Western."

"Did you test their holes again?"

"We did, not by drilling another set of holes but by re-assaying the sample pulps Star Western left behind for each hole. They were all dogs too." Boscomb flashed another look of disgust. "I can't figure out what happened, but I know I've been had."

"I just saw Bootsey two days ago. He didn't act as if anything was wrong. In fact, if anything he was absolutely joyous."

"Mr. Gorman doesn't know. I gave the assayers strict instructions that the only person who was to know the assay results was me. As much as I like Boots, I don't want my business all over the street."

"Smart. But this problem is beyond my expertise. We need an expert, and around here, that's Bootsey. He has to be told."

Boscomb gave me a long look. "I'll trust your judgment, Sheriff." Then he rose from the chair and turned to leave.

"One more question," I said. "How much did you pay Fletcher?"

"$17.5 million," answered Boscomb. "If we don't get that money back soon, we'll go bankrupt."

Boscomb and I met Bootsey at Myra Blankenship's warehouse where Star Western had installed an assay laboratory. The warehouse had been Steve Galt's Auto Repair. Steve died unexpectedly from a massive coronary about eight years ago and the business failed soon thereafter. Myra bought the building from Steve's widow for a song, cleaned it out, and began renting it to whoever needed some temporary storage space, principally town folk wanting a place to park a boat or RV away from the winter weather.

The main door is on the east side of the building and, entering it now for the first time in several years, I was startled by the transformation. To the left, just inside the door, was a large room used as an office first by Fletcher and currently by Boscomb. Next to it was a smaller room used by the assayers. The first office had a stark, empty appearance reflecting the small amount of time anyone actually used the room. In contrast, the assayer's office had two computers and other equipment, a refrigerator, coffee maker, calendars and photographs on the walls, and waste baskets filled to the brim with paper and empty food containers from the town's various restaurants.

Along the opposite wall of the building were two larger rooms—one where the assay equipment was housed, and next to it the preparation room where the rock samples were pulverized into a fine dust in preparation for assaying.

Next to the prep room was a utility sink with shelves containing cleaning supplies. In the far corner where the south wall meets its peer on the west side was another small storage room made of concrete block walls and a heavy metal door. The door was secured by a metal bar that folded down across the door into a bracket welded on the door frame. When Steve Galt had the building, he stored oxygen and acetylene tanks there.

The balance of the building was given over to racks of shelving constructed from rough-cut two-by-fours and three-quarter-inch plywood. Here the core samples were stored. Core is nothing more than a rock cylinder carved out of the earth by a drill bit shaped like a doughnut. The geologist monitoring the drill rig keeps a log of the type of rock encountered—limestone, dolomite, granite, or whatever. The geologist breaks the core into two-and-a-half-foot lengths and places the pieces into core storage boxes, each box holding ten feet of core and weighing anywhere from ten to forty pounds. There were several hundred, maybe a thousand, core boxes on the warehouse shelves.

Notwithstanding the ninety degree temperature outside, the warehouse was cool. Myra had converted the garage's ventilation system into an air conditioning system. It was an ideal place for what was likely to be a hot-tempered meeting on an already hot day.

We explained the problem to Bootsey. His reaction was predictably extreme: a burst of anger over the apparent fraud coupled with utter and complete disappointment that he wouldn't realize his dream of having a mine of his own. But he pulled himself together and got down to work. First, he reviewed all the sample preparation and assay procedures used by Star Western and Flying Horse. Then, he interviewed the two assayers, Frank Carney and Art Ferkin, at length. Finally, he had the assayers cook up several different sets of assays verifying the quantity of materials used in the procedure.

It was too complicated for me. I found a cold can of 7-Up, wandered over to Boscomb's office, pulled a chair up close to the desk, raised my feet, and waited for Bootsey to enlighten me. A couple of hours passed. I checked in with Kay at the office but nothing was going on. Boscomb and I whiled away the time in conversation on a number of topics. He was good company.

Finally, Bootsey joined Boscomb and me. He looked dispirited and said, "I think I have it figured out."

"I knew you knew the mining business, but I didn't know you were an assayer," I replied.

"Learned it back in '64. I was working up at the Galena Queen when I broke my leg bad. After I got out of the hospital, old John Schrader, he was superintendent then, gave me a job in the lab. He knew I couldn't afford to be without work, not with the family and all."

"Well, I'll be. Didn't know that."

"Yeah, Myra taught me," answered Bootsey as he pulled the tab on a can of Coke.

"Myra?" I asked. "I thought she was a med tech."

"She is, but back then, assaying at the mine paid better than working at the hospital."

"Gentlemen," Boscomb injected, "could you reminisce some other time? What happened with the assays?"

"They're crooked, no doubt about it," Bootsey answered. "I think my old pal Aaron Fletcher salted the litharge."

"Litharge?" I asked.

"Lead oxide," replied Bootsey. "You use it along with soda ash and borax when you melt the sample in the oven. The soda ash and borax form a crude glass and carry away the waste rock. The gold and silver melt down with the lead and you separate them out later. So, I tested different amounts of each of the soda ash and borax to see if I could change the assay."

"And you couldn't?" Boscomb asked.

"That's right. And that's with a new can of litharge. Frank said they opened it a few days ago," Bootsey said just prior to drawing a large swig from his soda.

Boscomb got to his feet and started to pace. "Let me guess, we started using the fresh can of litharge about the same time the assays started to go bad. Right?"

"That's about the size of it, Lyle," Bootsey said. "We'd know for sure if that old litharge can was around, but the boys tossed it in the dumpster and it's long gone to the landfill."

"Okay, Boots," I directed. "In layman's terms, explain what you think Fletcher did."

"Pretty simple, Pete. He got some powdered silver and mixed it into the litharge. Every time Frank or Howard put the litharge into the assay crucible they were adding silver without knowing it."

"Wouldn't they have seen it?" I asked.

"Maybe if they were looking for it, but in assaying they measure things in terms of milligrams and grams. It doesn't take much silver to get the desired result and it would be hard to notice, particularly in the dim light over by the prep table."

"But Fletcher had to know he was going to get caught," I said.

"Discovered, yeah, but caught?" Bootsey said. "I wouldn't be surprised if he's on some beach somewhere drinkin' a tall cool one, livin' under an assumed name."

"Laughing himself silly about the screwing he gave me!" Boscomb added harshly.

At that point the conversation abruptly stopped. The three of us looked at one another. Bootsey shrugged. Boscomb looked at me with a look that said—what are you going to do about it, Sheriff?

I pulled my feet off the desk and got ready to stand when the exterior door of the building opened and Myra Blankenship walked in. She was wearing dark pants, a maroon and silver University of Montana t-shirt, and white running shoes. It doesn't make any difference what type of weather we're having—sun, rain, or two feet of snow—Myra will be wearing her running shoes. She gave us the quick once over and asked, "Sylvester, what are you doing here so late?" Before Bootsey could answer, Myra turned to me and added, "Sheriff Pete! That old fool haul you down here so he could crow about the ore on his land?"

"Not quite, Myra. What brings you down here? Checking up on the tenant?" I answered.

"I wish," she responded while pushing her glasses back up on the bridge of her nose. "I made the mistake of tossing in janitorial service when I leased the space. Now, I've got to do the work."

"I thought you hired Jason Smith's kid?" asked Bootsey.

"I did," answered Myra with a tone that reflected irritation. "He's like a lot of kids these days. Just thinks a job is about getting paid, not actually working. So, I let him go."

"Sister, you're too old to be doing this work," Bootsey said.

"Oh, shove it, Sylvester. I've been doing the job for the past year just fine. Besides, I ain't as old as you." Myra turned to walk away, caught herself and turned back to Bootsey. "Sylvester, you ain't acting right. Something wrong?" Nothing like a woman's intuition.

"No, nothin'," answered Bootsey much too quickly and totally without any conviction in his voice.

Myra looked toward me. "Is that right, Sheriff?"

I didn't reply, but Bootsey shot a glance toward Boscomb and me and said, "We might as well tell her, boys. If she knows, she'll keep her mouth shut tighter than she holds a nickel, but if she thinks I am trying to hide something from her she'll badger me about it until I am plumb crazy."

I looked to Boscomb. "Lyle, it's your call. It's your business."

"Okay, Bootsey. You've never given me a bum steer yet, so if you say she's okay, it's good enough for me."

"Okay," Bootsey said quietly. Then to Myra he added, "There's a problem with the assays. It looks like Fletcher salted the samples to make the assays look a lot better than they really are. Then he sold the property to Mr. Boscomb here."

I expected tough old Myra to give Bootsey the "I told you so" lecture. Instead, she walked over to him, put her hands on his shoulders and pulled him toward her. "I am really sorry, Sylvester," she said. "I know how much this meant to you. If I can help just ask."

"Thanks, Myra," replied Bootsey, getting choked up. "Sheriff Pete may want to talk with you, find out what you know about Fletcher, that kind of stuff."

Myra released Bootsey and turned toward Boscomb and me. "That's fine. I never saw much of Fletcher, just enough to know that with him, the only business I was going to do was cash business. Just as I told you to do, Sylvester, but no, you had to have a mine."

Ah, the real Myra has returned, I thought to myself. "Sheriff Pete, you know where to find me," Myra said as she padded out of the office.

Myra's departure ended the meeting. I headed over to the Law Enforcement Center and tried to call County Attorney Tom Wilson, but his wife said that he wasn't expected home until after midnight. We needed a warrant for Fletcher's arrest but it could wait until tomorrow. First we had to find him.

The next day I contacted the Denver police. Star Western might have been incorporated in Canada but its corporate office was in Denver. After explaining the situation to the folks in Denver, I faxed them the warrant, but I wasn't terribly optimistic they would find him. Bootsey had told me that his comment about Fletcher "sitting on a beach somewhere" wasn't a joke. He said Fletcher had made several comments about retiring and moving south. Bootsey never asked Fletcher if he had a specific place in mind and, unfortunately, when you're in Montana, "some place south" is a lot of territory.

The next day the Denver police called to say they'd come up empty-handed. His home in Littleton, a Denver suburb, had been sold almost three months beforehand. Star Western's corporate office had closed about a month ago, and neither the landlord nor other tenants knew where the company's two other employees had gone. The post office had no forwarding address, and Fletcher's bank account had been closed. Fletcher must have been planning this venture for months; he'd done a great job of covering his tracks. I reluctantly called Lyle Boscomb and gave him the news. He took it a lot better than I would have, if I'd just been ripped off for $17.5 million and knew that my company was about to collapse.

I waited another day hoping I'd hear something positive from Denver, but it never happened. Then I went looking for Bootsey. There were a couple of aspects about the case and Aaron Fletcher in particular that didn't add up. I found Bootsey sitting on the porch of his house, looking dejected.

"C'mon Boots, jump in and I'll buy you a beer," I said through the rolled down window of my patrol car.

"Sure, Pete, never could turn down a tall cool one, especially if it's free."

A few minutes later we took up residence at a table in the far corner of the Apex, bordered by a wall of video poker and keno machines which, fortunately, were not being played.

Mandy Lynn brought out our beers, flirted with Bootsey for a few seconds, and gave me a wink when she pocketed the two dollar tip I gave her after delivering our beers and left us alone.

"Any luck finding Fletcher, Pete?" asked Bootsey with a tone of resignation.

"No, and that's part of what's bothering me. It doesn't fit."

"What doesn't fit?"

"Fletcher disappearing, Boots. It doesn't fit."

"Why not? He clipped Boscomb for seventeen million. He's not going to hang around and try to explain how it's all just a big misunderstanding."

"Yeah, but stealing that amount of money and disappearing is completely inconsistent with who Aaron Fletcher is."

"Huh?" answered Bootsey with a confused cast to his eyes.

"Think about it this way. Aaron Fletcher had a successful career in the mining industry for what, twenty-five to thirty years?"

"Probably," answered Bootsey, not sure where I was going with this conversation.

"I've checked with the FBI and the Mounted Police, and Fletcher has no criminal record. Far as I can tell, he's never done anything the least bit unbecoming."

"So?" came Bootsey's terse reply. He didn't like the idea that Fletcher might not be the villain who destroyed his life.

"So why does a guy like that suddenly become a swindler?" I asked.

"For the money, Pete. Big money. Never have to work again money. Fletcher may not have a record but he's spent his entire career doing mining stock promotions, which many people consider scams. He's got the mind for exactly this kind of thing."

"Boots, I don't buy it. There's a big difference between behavior which may be considered unethical and that which is illegal. You're the guy who repeatedly told me that Fletcher was on the square."

"I did, Pete...which just goes to show you how good of a con man the guy was. He had me fooled and I can spot 'em a mile away."

I wasn't getting anywhere with this line of questioning so I decided to change focus. "Okay, Boots, have it your way. Tell me something though. How well did you know Fletcher?"

"I thought I knew him real good. I took him fishing a couple of times. We went out to dinner when he was in town. But as things turned out..."

"No, that's not what I mean. How long have you known Fletcher?"

"About two years," answered Bootsey. "Met him for the first time in September. He called and expressed an interest in leasing my claims and he came over a couple of weeks later and we put the deal together."

"How much did you see him after that?"

"I didn't see him until the next spring when he came over, leased the building from Myra, started the lab, and began the drilling campaign. After that, he was in town about every other week for two to three days. He usually came up on a Sunday, checked things over, and then went back to Denver mid-week."

"Another thing that bothers me, Boots, is how did

Fletcher juice the litharge with the powdered silver? He wasn't here all that much."

"It's not that tough." Bootsey pulled down a long swallow from his beer bottle. "Fletcher ordered the supplies. Most of the stuff came UPS. At night when the staff was gone, it wouldn't be any problem for him to go in and mix in the silver. Probably wouldn't take fifteen minutes."

I talked with Bootsey for another half hour and bought him two more beers, but never learned anything more of value, nor did I shake his belief that Fletcher was the culprit. The next day I stopped by Myra's house and talked with her about Fletcher. I learned several things: Fletcher was divorced and had been so for a long time, he had a daughter who was married in Las Vegas the previous summer, and Myra made a great peach pie. I had two pieces and coffee, and waddled back to work.

Myra also told me she had a prospective renter for the warehouse and had hired Bootsey to tear down the assay laboratory and clean out the place. Myra figured Bootsey needed the money. She had heard that Gil Stewart, owner of the Apex, hadn't been fully paid for the party Bootsey threw that Friday evening when he thought he was in the chips.

Myra's mention of the assay laboratory triggered something in my brain, and for the balance of the day my mind kept flashing back to the inside of the warehouse. I would pan every aspect of the structure, then rewind the mental videotape and look at it all over again. I could see the place with amazing detail but I couldn't recognize whatever it was I was looking for. Finally, about ten o'clock that night, I called Bootsey and told him I wanted to check the place one more time before he started his demolition project. We agreed to meet at the warehouse the next morning at 9:00 A.M.

I went to the office early. I was plowing through the pile of paperwork that had built up over the past several days and was about half way through my third cup of coffee when I took a call from Detective Paul Harris with the Denver Police Department. We visited for over fifteen minutes. Denver had made a lot of progress with the investigation, more than we had in Montana.

After the call I drove over to Myra's warehouse. Bootsey was sitting on the front steps waiting for me, taking in the sun. It was another beautiful day, not a cloud in the sky.

"Bootsey!" I exclaimed as I stepped out of the patrol car. "When did you last see Fletcher?" I leaned on the railing next to the steps while Bootsey put on his introspective, thoughtful look.

"Sunday after the party. We had breakfast. I know I was in no shape to have breakfast that Saturday."

I counted back with my fingers. "June 28th," I said out loud, mostly to myself. "What did you two talk about?"

"Mostly nothing," came Bootsey's reply. "It was kind of awkward. You know how it is when you get together with guys to say goodbye, you mostly make small talk, tell one another to keep in touch but you both know you're never going to see one another again."

"Yeah, I know what you mean but think this through very carefully. Near as I can figure, you were the last person to see Fletcher. Maybe he said some little thing that will lead us to him."

Bootsey paused for a moment and then said, "I can see

us together that morning. We were in the Carmichaels restaurant. Fletcher always stayed at Carmichaels. I said something to him about what he was going to do next and Fletcher told me 'I'm hanging it up, Boots. I'm retiring and heading south, and I'll be doing that just as soon as I check out of the motel and pick up my fishing gear over at the lab.' I took him fishing on Rock Creek and up at the lake a few times. He really enjoyed it."

"That's all?" I asked.

"That's all," answered Bootsey quietly.

"Well, I was hoping for something more. Denver PD called me this morning. They located the other two people who used to work for Star Western. Neither one reports having seen Fletcher since before he made the trip up here to close the deal with Flying Horse. Both got e-mails from Fletcher on Saturday saying that the deal had closed and their checks were in the mail. They both got some type of bonus and the checks arrived, as promised, the following Tuesday."

"Glad to know he was fair with the hired help," came Bootsey's sardonic reply.

"There's more," I said. "Denver PD looked into Star Western's finances. The money from Flying Horse was wired to Star Western's account in Denver. On Saturday after the deal closed Fletcher paid all of the company's outstanding bills, including the payroll taxes. The balance was then wired to an account in the Cayman Islands."

"Now that's genius for you!" exclaimed Bootsey.

"Genius?"

"The guy pulls the perfect swindle and he's smart enough to pay all the taxes. No FBI or IRS on his tail, just a county sheriff from Montana and a couple of cops from Denver who'll tire of the case in about two more days."

Now it was my turn to pause. Bootsey had a point. If you want to hide from the law, you don't want to be on the FBI's radar screen. But I wasn't going to admit that to Bootsey. Instead, I said, "I was thinking of it another way, Bootsey. Maybe Fletcher...ah hell, your theory makes more sense than mine. Let me in, I've got work to do."

"The door's open, Pete. I am going to run over to the bank and have coffee with Charlie at the ambulance garage. I'll be back in an hour or so."

Inside, I panned the warehouse once more, then closed my eyes and tried to visualize it. Something was signaling me but I couldn't recognize it. I started a methodical search of the building, first going through the offices and then the assay room. There I carefully examined the containers holding the various chemicals used in the assay process, including opening up the can labeled "Litharge." The can was about 15 inches across and ten inches deep. The lid was held in place by a series of metal tabs which folded down around the side of the can. Each tab had a hole punched in it approximately three-eighths of an inch across, big enough for the blade of a medium-sized screwdriver, which I used to bend the tabs outward until the lid came loose. Inside I found a brilliant yellow powder about the texture of sifted flour. If nothing else, I now knew what lead oxide looked like.

As I looked around the assay room, I saw another empty litharge can being used as a container for various laboratory tools. I remembered Bootsey saying that all the empty litharge containers had been thrown away. Here was one that had not been discarded.

I carefully removed the tools—a couple pair of tongs, a ruler, hammer, two screwdrivers, and a bunch of sample envelopes—and sure enough, there was a ring of yellow powder around the bottom edge of the can. There was more than enough for a sample and I carefully poured the powder into an evidence envelope. Satisfied with my work I started to put the can back when I saw it, a small artifact that I immediately recognized. It put a whole new spin on the case. After bagging and labeling specimen number two, I went next door to the assayer's office, found a soft drink in the refrigerator, and sat down to think through my discovery.

My contemplative mood was short-lived. I heard a door close and then Bootsey's voice proclaim, "Holy shit! Pete, Pete, over here!"

I ran out of the assayer's office into the larger warehouse and saw Bootsey at the far end of the building, waving at me frantically and yelling, "Pete, he's here!"

I rushed toward Bootsey. Once he saw I was coming he disappeared behind the farthest rack of core storage shelves. I was in hot pursuit, yelling, "Who's here?" When I entered the aisle between the last storage rack and the outer wall, I saw Bootsey standing next to Aaron Fletcher's pickup truck.

Instantly, I knew what had been sticking in my craw. When you looked across the main room of the warehouse from near the front door, a small piece of the truck's cab was barely visible between the stacks of core boxes. I had seen it a hundred times but it had never registered with me.

"He's not in the truck, Pete!" Bootsey said loudly. "But his suitcase and computer are in there and there's some boxes in the back, files I'll bet."

"Didn't you tell me that he was going to pick up some fishing equipment?" I asked.

"Yeah…"

"Where did he keep it?"

"Over there." Bootsey pointed toward the little concrete block storage room where Galt's Auto Repair used to keep their oxygen and acetylene tanks.

"Careful, Boots, let me handle it. We have to treat it as a crime scene." Using my night stick as a lever, I lifted the metal cross bar used to lock the metal door and pulled it open.

There, lying on the floor, his jacket used for a pillow, was the decaying body of Aaron Fletcher.

For the second time I heard Bootsey, typically a man for whom profanity is an exception, exclaim "Holy shit!"

"Boots, get out of here now," I ordered. "Call the office and tell Johnny Titan what we've got and to get down here right away with the evidence kit. Then call Fred Early. He should be at the funeral home."

Fred, Johnny, and I did a full workup on the body at the warehouse. There was nothing in the storage room except Fletcher's body, his fishing equipment, a backpack, and a pair of hiking boots. Apparently, once he realized he was locked in the room, he tried to cut a hole in the concrete block wall using pieces of the fishing reel and pole, but he never got very far. Near as I could tell, he finally lay down and waited for someone to rescue him, or to die.

After we'd finished our work, I stood by the door just surveying the scene one last time before we sent the body over to the mortuary. Bootsey saw something in my face.

"Pete, you look puzzled," he said.

"I am. Why would Fletcher keep his fishing gear here?"

"Easy," answered Bootsey quickly. "He came up from Denver on the plane. Why would he want to carry that stuff back and forth when he flew? He had the warehouse rented, why not use it?"

"Why not leave it in the office?" I asked.

"Look at that rod and reel. It's top of the line. Leave that where someone might see it through the window and there's a good chance it goes bye-bye."

I couldn't dispute Bootsey's logic. The warehouse was off by itself down by the railroad tracks and could easily be broken into if someone was inclined.

The post-mortem confirmed that Fletcher had died of thirst. I talked to Boots and Myra and both said that nobody had been in the building for at least ten days after Fletcher went in to retrieve his fishing pole.

Johnny and I tested the hinged locking bar to see if it could close and lock the door without human intervention. It could. The door wasn't balanced so when opened it would slowly swing shut on its own. It was heavy and hit the door frame with a decent force. About one in five times when this happened, the locking cross bar would jar loose and fall into place. The only fingerprints we found on the door or cross bar were Fletcher's.

County Coroner Fred Early ruled it an accidental death. It was determined that when Fletcher went into the room to get his fishing equipment, the door closed and locked behind him, trapping him without food or water until he died.

Bootsey was maudlin. His last hope, a need for some type of justice after being swindled out of his mine, had vanished with the discovery of Fletcher's body. About a week later, the analysis of the evidence I had found in the assay lab arrived in the mail from the State Crime Lab. Bootsey was right. The litharge had been charged with silver to bogus the assays. The other sample was exactly what I thought it was as well. Then Deputy Titan and I made a house call.

"Good evening, Myra. You know Johnny Titan, I believe."

"That you, Pete?" I could hear Bootsey's voice coming from the nether reaches of the house.

"Yep," I answered loudly.

"C'mon in. Myra, show some manners. Invite Pete in for some pie. It's apple tonight, Pete, and couldn't be better."

Myra swung the door open but said nothing, a taciturn look on her face. As I stepped across the threshold, Bootsey was there to meet me. "How'd you know I'd be here, Pete?"

"I didn't, Boots," I replied, looking at him and then back toward Myra. "Johnny and I came down to talk to Myra to clean up a couple of final details about Fletcher."

"What's to clean up?" replied Bootsey with a hint of confusion beginning to spread across his face. "Fletcher salted the litharge, scammed the money, put himself in his own jail cell and died. End of story. End of my mine."

"Maybe not, Boots."

"What in heaven's name are you driving at?" Bootsey replied.

"I didn't want to do this in front of you, Bootsey, but you're here." I paused for a few seconds during which time Myra backed away from the door. "Lots of people got hurt by the scam. You lost your dream of seeing another mine operating here in Rodgersburg, and only God knows how much in royalty payments. The town lost a chance for some good jobs. Boscomb lost his company and a lot of money, and Fletcher lost his life."

"Well, he deserved that, Pete," Bootsey replied quickly.

"Maybe so, maybe not. But one person made out like a bandit."

Bootsey's eyes narrowed and his brow furrowed, and his upper lip began to twitch.

"Your sister," I said.

"Yeah, so what?" answered Bootsey, but I sensed some excitement in his voice. "She told me from the get go that she was only taking cash up front, no stock, no royalties, just cash. She told me to do the same thing, only I wasn't smart enough to listen to her."

"Nobody can fault Myra's business sense," I said. "What I want to know is why she salted the litharge."

"That's crazy, Pete, and you know it," answered Bootsey, but his voice was tentative.

"No, I don't know it and, fact is, I have evidence to prove it."

The last statement finally prompted Myra to talk. "Sheriff Pete, I just don't know what's gotten into your head."

"Myra," I answered. "You're a trained assayer and certainly know how assaying works. You own the building where the assay lab was located and had access to the premises twenty-four hours a day. More importantly, you provided janitorial services for the lab, so you had a plausible reason for being there after hours."

Myra's eyes flashed in anger. "I don't know what's come over you, Sheriff Pete," she said, her voice echoing the ire in her face. "Sylvester's right, you're acting plumb crazy. Of course I was around the lab, I've been the janitress for over a year. But, I don't know nothing about salted assays except for what Sylvester told me, God as my witness."

"I want to believe you, Myra." I looked her straight in the eye and I watched her blink in rapid fashion. She knows I am on to her. Time to put the hammer down. "And then there's a little matter of this," I said as I held up a little diamond stud earring. "I found this in the old litharge can where the assayers stored their hand tools. It matches the earring you reported missing last summer when you thought you lost it at the Elks Fourth of July barbecue."

Myra didn't respond but Bootsey's eyes got big and he said, "Let me see that, Pete." After fumbling it for a second or two in his meaty hands, Boots turned to Myra. "That's one of those earrings I gave you at Christmas, a few years back."

Myra dismissed Bootsey's comment with a wave. "I am always losing earrings and you're always giving them to me. I think earrings are all you've given me the past few years. I must have lost it when I was cleaning up the work bench in the lab. It just fell into that tool can."

"I don't think so, Myra. Judging from the dust and grit on those tools, that's not something you've been cleaning. More importantly, there was a bit of litharge residue left in the bottom of the can. I had it analyzed and guess what...silver dust had been mixed in with the litharge in an amount equal to twenty ounces per ton." I paused and stepped close to Myra. "I've got more, Myra. Fact is, the County Attorney thinks we've got more than enough for an indictment."

Myra looked away and said nothing, but I could see that my words had registered with Bootsey. He was getting anxious.

"Myra," I continued, "we can do this the hard way or the easy way. Either way, it's getting done."

Myra looked at me and then at Bootsey. "I did it for you, Sylvester."

"You did what?" injected Bootsey cautiously.

"Rigged the assays. When that Fletcher fellow came sniffing around looking for properties to lease, I saw a chance to help you. All these years, you've been talking about making a big score in the mining business. I believed you. So did Pal and Art. That's why they were always game for tying up with you in your grand plans." With that, Myra sat down on the end of her sofa and shook her head several times before continuing. "I am no geologist but I figured that if there was any real ore on those claims of yours, Sylvester, the guys running the Galena Queen would have found it long ago. I also thought that if I could goose the assays enough to make them look good, Fletcher would give you a lot better lease on renewal or pay you a pretty piece for the claims. That's all I thought would happen.

"Fletcher took the bait—hook, line, and sinker—got excited and wanted my land too. By then I got scared, but I was in too deep so I tried to push him away by asking an outrageous price but even that didn't dissuade him. So I had to sell him the land, and the rest is history."

"And Bootsey got nothing," I added.

"That wasn't part of the plan," she said. "I thought Sylvester wanted to make money from his mining claims. I didn't realize until just recently, and foolishly now that I see it, that all Sylvester wanted, was to be a part of a mine—like an owner. He wanted a mine, not the money."

"You got that right, Sis." Bootsey's voice was quivering

and I expected an explosion. "A mine, a place where guys get jobs, where we get good things out of the earth. The money? Myra, good God, I'm eighty-one. What do I need money for except to piss it across the bar with Gil?"

Bootsey turned away from his sister. Myra dropped her eyes to the floor. Neither could bear to look at the other.

"I've got to take you in, Myra," I said quietly. "At a minimum, you're going to have to give the money back to Boscomb. He provided it to Fletcher to buy your property."

"I know," answered Myra. She almost seemed relieved. "You know what the real wrong in this thing is?"

"No, what?" I replied.

"The joke's on me."

"How's that?" asked Bootsey.

"Remember those three holes that Fletcher drilled on my property? I figured they'd be worthless and Fletcher would go away. But, he finds a vein with thirty-two feet of true width averaging fifty-two ounces of silver per ton, thirty-four percent lead, six percent zinc, and some copper. I never juiced those assays. They're real."

POSTSCRIPT

Myra pled guilty to one count of fraud in State District Court. Judge Pollard sentenced her to ten years on probation and required that she perform twenty hours of community service each week. She now divides her time as a volunteer at the Rhyolite County Library and Rodgersburg Hospital Auxiliary.

Flying Horse Minerals petitioned the court and asked that Myra be required to pay restitution for the money it lost in the transaction with Star Western Exploration. The judge rejected their request and justified his decision by observing she never defrauded Flying Horse, only Star Western.

The attorneys for Flying Horse are now pursuing recovery of the funds from the bank in the Cayman Islands where Fletcher deposited the cash. The case is moving very slowly. I suspect they will prevail eventually, but by then, everything the bankruptcy estate recovers will end up being paid to the lawyers.

Bootsey got his land back. He had a "development clause" in his contract with Star Western which required that it put a mine into commercial production by a date certain or the company was obligated to pay him more money. The development clause was binding on Flying Horse as well. Bootsey explained to me that he insisted on the clause because he didn't want Fletcher acquiring the property and then sitting on it, and not moving quickly to develop a mine. When Flying Horse couldn't pay the extra fare called for by the development clause, they returned the mining claims to Bootsey. Flying Horse or, more accurately, its bankruptcy estate still owns Myra's land. One of these days it'll be sold, but probably not to a mining company. A land developer likely will come in and subdivide it.

Myra didn't get to keep the money she scammed from Fletcher. Judge Pollard gave her a choice. She could pay a stiff fine or donate the $1.4 million she earned from Star Western to one or more court-approved charities. Myra chose the charitable option and gave the money to the Rodgers Foundation, which funds the operation and maintenance of Tower Park. She has become somewhat of a town celebrity as much for her guile in running the fraudulent scheme as for her court-induced generosity.

Bootsey is back being Bootsey, contacting mining companies, seeing if he can interest someone in leasing his property, and developing a mine. Each time I see him he offers the same observation, "There just aren't guys like Fletcher around anymore, Pete. Guys willing to take a chance and get things done."

Hope springs eternal.

NOTES

CHAPTER ONE

1. See the works of John D. MacDonald, biographer of Travis McGee. There are twenty-one books in the series, which were written between 1964 and 1984. The McGee series is immediately identifiable because each title contains the name of a color, such as "The Deep Blue Goodbye," "A Tan and Sandy Silence," "The Lonely Silver Rain," etc.
2. See the works of Rex Stout, biographer to Nero Wolfe. Stout wrote forty-seven books and thirty-nine novellas describing Wolfe cases beginning in 1934 and ending, posthumously, in 1985.
3. See the works of James Crumley, biographer to both C.W. Sughrue and Milo Milodragovich. There are eight books in the series written between 1984 and 2006.
4. John S. Fitzpatrick and John D. Watson. *Sherlock Holmes: The Montana Chronicles* (Helena, MT: Riverbend Publishing Inc., 2008).

CHAPTER TWO

1. Aurelius, Marcus, *Meditations* (Roslyn, NY: Walter J. Black, Inc, 1945),, p. 126.
2. Ibid., p. 93.
3. The Book of Sirach, 25:8, The New American Bible, (Nashville, TN: Catholic Bible Press, 1969).,
4. J.F.C. Fuller, *The Conduct of War* (New Brunswick, NJ: Rutgers University Press, 1961), p. 51.
5. Lou Holtz, Lou, *Winning Every Day* (New York: Harper, 1981), p. 181.

CHAPTER THREE

1. 1985. Niccolo Machiavelli; trans. Harvey C. Mansfield, *The Prince* (University of Chicago Press, 1985).

CHAPTER FOUR

1. From the musical *Showboat*. Music by Jerome Kern, lyrics by Oscar Hammerstein II. Opened on Broadway at the Ziegfeld Theater on December 27, 1927.
2. From the musical *Phantom of the Opera*. Music by Andrew Lloyd Webber, lyrics by Charles Hart. Opened on London's West End

at Her Majesty's Theater on October 9, 1988. The Broadway production opened at the Majestic Theater on January 26, 1988.

CHAPTER SIX

1. 1989. H.A. Dorfman and Karl Kuehl, *The Mental Game of Baseball* (South Bend, IN: Diamond Communications Inc., 1989).

CHAPTER EIGHT

1. Guest, Edgar. *Sermons We See.* http://sofinesjoyfulmoments.com/quotes/sermon.htm.
2. From the musical *Paint Your Wagon.* Music by Fredrick Loewe, lyrics by Alan J. Lerner. Opened on Broadway at the Shubert Theater on November 12, 1951.
3. From the musical, *South Pacific.* Music by Richard Rodgers, lyrics by Oscar Hammerstein II. Opened on Broadway at the Majestic Theater on April 7, 1949.
4. From the musical, *Cabaret.* Music by John Kander, lyrics by Fred Ebb. Opened on Broadway at the Broadhurst Theater on November 20, 1966.
5. Originally produced under the title of *Con Te Partio* by Polydor Records. Music by Francesco Sartori, lyrics by Lucio Quarantotto and Frank Peterson. First sung by Andrea Bocelli at the San Remu (Italy) Festival in 1995. Rereleased under the title of *Time To Say Goodbye* as a duet featuring Andrea Bocelli and Sarah Brightman as the theme song of a light heavyweight boxing match between Henry Maske and Virgil Hill on November 23, 1996.

ABOUT THE AUTHOR

John Fitzpatrick is a native of Anaconda, Montana. For the past thirty years he has worked as a lobbyist for the metal mining, telecommunications, and utility industries. He resides in Helena, Montana, with his wife, Connie. They are the parents of two sons, now adults with families of their own.

He is the author of *Sherlock Holmes: The Montana Chronicles*, published by Riverbend Publishing.

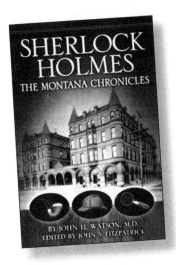

ALSO BY

JOHN S. FITZPATRICK

Sherlock Holmes:
The Montana Chronicles

Here are the long-lost records of four intriguing mysteries solved by the famous English detective Sherlock Holmes when he traveled to Montana in the late 1880s. Accompanied by his loyal friend Dr. John H. Watson, Holmes used his inimitable eye for clues, his great deductive reasoning, and some clever subterfuge to crack cases ranging from murder to mistaken identity. The stories are filled with accurate details of life in early-day Montana.

"The stories are ingenious and engagingly told. Great fun to read." – The District Messenger, THE NEWSLETTER OF THE SHERLOCK HOLMES SOCIETY OF LONDON

"Highly recommended...a 'must' for every dedicated Baker Street Irregular!" – MIDWEST BOOK REVIEW

ISBN 978-1-931832-96-0
$12.95

RIVERBEND
PUBLISHING

www.riverbendpublishing.com